"Finely gradated bifacia... irregularity which would indicate that this specimen was originally a projectile point, broken and subsequently reworked to function alternatively as a hafted knife..."

Warren McIntyre made a note in his field book, then returned to the archaeological dig. His tanned shoulders glistened with sweat and his dark hair was held back by a ragged cotton bandanna. On this windswept prairie hill he looked like a part of the empty landscape all around him, as much at home as the pair of eagles soaring overhead and the coyote watching from a wary distance.

Warren's own people had roamed these hills and plains for twenty thousand years, long before the wild land had been settled and tamed by ranchers. Being an archaeologist, finding and documenting the secrets of his ancestors before they were lost forever, mattered more to him than anything in the world.

At least, his job used to be the most important thing in Warren's life. But that was before rancher's daughter Libby Lyndon came along and turned his world upside down....

MEN at WORK
MARGOT DALTON
MAGIC AND MOONBEAMS

Harlequin Books

TORONTO • NEW YORK • LONDON
AMSTERDAM • PARIS • SYDNEY • HAMBURG
STOCKHOLM • ATHENS • TOKYO • MILAN
MADRID • WARSAW • BUDAPEST • AUCKLAND

HARLEQUIN BOOKS
225 Duncan Mill Road, Don Mills,
Ontario, Canada M3B 3K9

ISBN 0-373-81027-X

MAGIC AND MOONBEAMS

Copyright © 1990 by Margot Dalton

Printed in U.S.A.

Dear Reader,

I was delighted to learn that *Magic and Moonbeams* was being reissued as part of the MEN AT WORK series. This book has always been especially close to my heart, because it's set in the place where I grew up.

I was raised in western Canada on a family ranch more than a century old, where my great-grandmother traded sacks of flour and sugar to passing Blackfoot tribes for buffalo robes and buckskin moccasins. As a child I roamed the prairie in search of exquisitely carved stone arrowheads that fired my imagination making me wonder and daydream about the long-ago people who made such beautiful objects.

Warren McIntyre, the hero of *Magic and Moonbeams*, is a descendant of the Plains Indians and shares this fascination of mine. In fact, he's made archaeology his life's work and devotes himself to excavating the history of his vanished ancestors.

I've now written more than thirty books, but Warren remains one of my favorite heroes of all time. I'm so happy that a whole new group of readers will be able to enjoy him, too!

Sincerely,

Margot Dalton

CHAPTER ONE

THE JUNE MORNING was fair and glorious, a symphony of blue and gold, fragrant with the scent of wildflowers. Open prairie rolled off on all sides to a limitless horizon, misty in the far distance and swirling with thin wisps of low cloud that glowed like mother-of-pearl against the deep sapphire of the sky. The only sounds were occasional trills of bird song from nests hidden in the tall grass, the lowing of distant cattle and the gentle whispering rustle of the morning breeze.

High in the soaring arch of prairie sky, so far up that the rich blue faded to ivory, a hawk circled and swooped, rising and falling on the warm air currents, scanning the vast open plain for signs of life and movement. Insects hummed busily in the early sunlight and scampered here and there, busy with their own small pursuits. In a shallow golden valley a rattlesnake, curled on a flat rock to bask in the warmth, gradually uncoiled its sinuous mottled length, flowed from the sun-warmed surface and slipped noiselessly away into the brush, vanishing at the barely discernible sound of an approaching horse.

The gentle drumming of hoofbeats grew louder and a rapid swish of movement in the prairie grass became audible. Soon a horse and rider topped a small rise and slowed to a walk, moving quietly down through the valley starred with masses of wild roses. The delicate pink flowers were in full bloom on this late spring day, and their heady scent filled the whole world with sweetness.

The young woman on the horse reined in, pausing to sniff the exquisite fragrance, her eyes closed in bliss and her face turned up to the sun. Her tall, slender body tensed and swayed lightly to the skittish dancing movements of the horse as she enjoyed the caressing warmth and the beauty of the day.

Her face was lovely, a fine oval shape tanned golden-brown by the prairie sun with high cheekbones and a wide, sweetly curving mouth. She had dark red hair with coppery highlights, pulled back loosely into a thick braid that hung down the back of her faded denim shirt. Escaping the braid, a few sunny tendrils curled around her face, lifting and stirring in the morning breeze. Her eyes, when she opened them and glanced down at the colt, were an odd, disturbingly beautiful color, a changeable shade of green that could vary—depending on her mood and the lighting—all the way from gray to hazel.

She smiled at the tense, twitching ears of the young sorrel horse and reached to pat his neck. "Calm down, boy," she murmured in a soft, husky voice. "I told you there's nothing to it. Nothing to be scared of. Just relax, okay?"

The horse turned his head, alert to the sound of her voice, and sidestepped nervously. The woman sat him easily, as if their bodies were welded together, and smiled at her mount's skittishness. With the smile, the austere beauty of her face was transformed into a glow of warmth as exquisite and appealing as the lovely wildflowers that surrounded her.

A coyote topped the rise they had just traversed and paused on the rim, staring down at them with intent, cautious interest. Catching the scent and movement, the colt nickered and leaped into a pivot while the woman gripped with her knees and grasped a portion of mane to keep her balance.

She was riding bareback because the colt was young, just barely a two-year-old, and not yet accustomed to the weight of a saddle. In fact, she had just begun training him and was not yet even using a bridle and bit on the horse, just a loose hackamore with a single rein and a *bosal*— a braided lump of rawhide under the horse's chin that controlled his movements by exerting a gentle pressure on the sensitive nerves in the jaw.

Curiosity satisfied, the coyote turned silently and drifted away, his long tail flowing on the breeze, while the woman soothed and calmed her mount. Then, using her knees, she urged him gently up out of the little flower-filled valley and toward a barbed wire fence that crossed the prairie a quarter of a mile away. She gazed around her as she rode, alert to everything, checking on the condition of the grass, the amount of water in the natural sloughs still brimming with the spring melt, and the scattered groups of cattle that they encountered.

The big colt, meanwhile, continued to look for things to be alarmed about, dancing skittishly at every movement or shadow while the woman stroked him and talked to him constantly, trying to reassure and accustom him to her voice and the feel of her hands.

"You know what you're like?" she said to the sorrel colt who pricked his ears nervously and jerked his head against the rein. "You're just like my sister," she went on. "You really are. Always looking for a chance to make a fuss. Real little troublemakers, both of you."

She grinned fondly and squinted at the fence in the distance, looking automatically for a gate, still thinking about Peggy.

She and Peggy were identical twins, and at twenty-four Libby looked so much like her sister that people still sometimes had difficulty telling them apart. Libby had been motherless, but she'd lost her mother so early that she had few memories of her. And with a twin sister to play with and her father's wise, solid, enduring love, Libby had had a wonderful childhood, growing up free and unfettered on these spacious, wild stretches of land.

She and Peggy had depended a lot on each other, Libby mused, absently stroking the colt's warm, burnished neck. They'd been practically inseparable when they were little. But times changed and people developed differently....

Libby, who had always been the quiet and private one of the twins, much more inclined to be obedient and follow the rules, had surprised everyone by taking the unconventional road. After a few experimental relationships, entered into mainly to satisfy her curiosity and learn what all the fuss was about, she expressed no further interest in the young men who crowded around seeking her attention. She wasn't ready to marry anyone, she said calmly. She was determined to get an education and pursue a career and she didn't feel any desire for a husband or babies, not for a long time.

"Who ever would have thought," she said aloud to her mount, "that it would have turned out this way? Who'd have suspected that Peg, the wild thing, would be rinsing out diapers, while *I'd* be free and independent with my own office and my own apartment and a whole world to explore."

Suddenly, overjoyed by the beauty of the morning and the rich promise of the future, Libby nudged the horse into a canter, then into a full gallop, bending low over his neck and gripping tightly with her knees, skimming across the prairie with her long plait of hair streaming behind her. The colt had a smooth, swinging gait, effortless and swift, and she laughed aloud in delight, finally pulling him up as they neared the gate in the barbed wire fence. Her cheeks were pink, her eyes shining like stars as she slid from the horse's back and looped the rein over her arm.

Elated and excited by his run, the colt danced and heaved. She paused to speak to him in low, reassuring tones, stroking his quivering neck until he calmed and dropped his head. Then she unlatched the gate, led him through and bent to pick up the post and refasten the gate.

Suddenly everything seemed to happen at once.

A dainty horned lark, crouched on her nest beside the gate, flew up in alarm as the horse danced too near her place of concealment. Started by the eruption of movement just under his nose, the colt reared and pulled back abruptly, flailing sharp hooves in the air. Libby jerked on the rein, the horse twisted to one side, and the clip that held the rope beneath the nose strap gave way, leaving the hackamore rein dangling uselessly in Libby's hand.

The colt shook his head in surprise, then, realizing he was free, trotted a few experimental steps and eyed the woman warily over his shoulder, his sides still heaving and lathered.

"Good boy," she said gently, stepping toward him and extending a quiet hand. "Good boy. Don't you go anywhere. Just stand there, and be nice, and I'll—"

Overhead, a diving hawk screamed in fury as its quarry escaped in the tall grass. The colt flung his head up, alarmed at the sound, galloped away several yards and looked back once more at the woman who was following him. Then, as if making a decision, he dropped his head and set off toward the rising sun, running easily, his hooves flashing in the light, his coppery hide gleaming.

Libby stood by the gate, slumped in dejection, while

she watched her mount vanish in the distance. She was irritated but not worried, knowing all too well that the colt would head directly for the ranch buildings and be resting indolently in the shade of the big barn, casually stealing hay and flicking his tail at flies when Libby finally struggled home.

"Damn!" she muttered. "Just like Peggy, all right—anything to drive me crazy."

She finished closing the gate and grinned ruefully as she shaded her eyes and stared in the direction of her fleeing horse, already fading into a tiny speck on the horizon.

"Well, *you're* certainly gone for good, aren't you?" she murmured aloud, as if the horse were still somewhere nearby, listening. "And now it's a four-mile walk just to get home."

Resolutely she dusted her hands on her jeans, tucked her shirt in, tightened the laces on her sneakers and set off in the same direction that the colt had taken, walking across the prairie with an easy, hip-swinging stride that carried her rapidly into the glow of the rising sun.

BEFORE MUCH TIME HAD PASSED Libby had completely forgotten her frustration over the loss of her horse and her concern about all the work that was waiting for her at home. The June morning was too beautiful to be spoiled for long by anything. She gave herself up to enjoyment of the day, of the rich solitude and the springtime fragrance that surrounded her. Soon she lost track of the time and was surprised when a familiar landmark reared up on the horizon to the south.

It was a high bench of land rising away from a valley that followed the course of a natural creek, and it interrupted the level expanse of prairie with startling suddenness. On the flattened summit of the bench a few gnarled chokecherry trees were clearly visible, shining rich green in the morning light. Libby paused, trailing the coiled loop of the hackamore rein, and looked wistfully at the land formation.

It can't be more than a mile out of my way, she thought. And I haven't seen the Stones for such a long time....

Sternly she reminded herself of all the chores she still had to do, already delayed by hours because of the colt's misbehavior. But she continued to waver, gazing with longing at the high sweep of land.

All at once she made her decision, altered her course and walked swiftly in the direction of the solitary grove of trees, her face alight with anticipation.

She and Peggy had discovered and named the Singing Stones when they were little girls, riding on the prairie on their very first ponies. The plateau had been their private place, one of the bonds that held them together, and for many years they never told another living person about the secret of the Stones. They had come here often when they were little to play and pretend and shiver at the magic feeling within the rough stone circles.

But Peggy had lost interest in the Stones as she grew up and gradually stopped coming, preferring the more tangible pleasures of boys and dates and clothes. Libby, though, had never really outgrown the fascination, deep excitement and wonder bordering on fear that always gripped her when she visited the ancient rock formation.

She climbed the steep incline on the shaded western slope, working her way up toward the summit where the sun spilled down across the swaying grasses. As she topped the final rise and stood at last on the level surface of the lofty bench, all the old feelings came flooding over her, leaving her breathless and limp with pleasure.

At first glance there was little to see on the sunny plateau. But, to someone who knew what was there, the rarity and wonder of this place was soon apparent. The top of the benchlike formation was a rectangular space, about half an acre in size, and almost completely covered with intricate circles of prairie stone, patterned with many colored lichen and half buried in the native sod. The circles formed a design, painstakingly wrought by ancient hands somewhere back in the misty predawn of human occupation here on the Great Plains.

Long ago, as little girls, Peggy and Libby had found and explored this place, becoming intimately familiar with the features of the design. There was a huge outer circle spanning the whole perimeter of the plateau and enclosing another series of rings and piles of rock that shaped a large human form, with circles for the head, torso, hands and feet, and long connecting lines of stones for the limbs. But the most magical thing of all, the thing that always made Libby catch her breath and filled her with a strange, inexplicable joy, was the massive central stone. This big monolith, about six feet high, with a smooth-cut face, was angled toward the south, at the center of the rough human shape. On it were hundreds of intricate pictures and signs, carefully worked into the surface of the stone and highlighted with splashes of lichen. Delicate figures, animals, stars and sun, human hands and hieroglyphic figures told ancient stories of bravery and tribulation, of sorrow and triumph.

Libby could never look at this prehistoric art gallery without feeling a surge of wonder and awe, almost a sense of reverence. She was sure that the stone circles, called "medicine wheels" in the archaeology books she consulted, were once a place of worship for ancient

mads. The depth of their simple, passionate faith still seemed to cast a spell over the lofty plateau.

She stood in front of the patterned wall of stone, facing it with the rising sun at her right hand and the prairie wind sighing from the west, and waited in tense silence. Gradually the sound of the wind changed, deepened and grew silvery and diffuse and then became delicate and rhythmic, like faraway music.

Libby sighed in bliss and stood with her eyes closed, swaying lightly to the distant, throbbing sound, lost in reverie.

She had learned this secret long ago, the fact that if you stood in just this position and were quiet and still, the stones would sing to you. As a child, she had simply accepted this miracle, but now that she was older she sometimes wondered just what caused the music. Was it the shape of the land formation itself or the way the wind whispered in the high grass or something in the positioning of the central stone...?

But deep down, in spite of her maturity and her years of study, she still believed that the Singing Stones were just pure magic.

The whispering, bell-like tones of the silvery music rippled and cascaded on the prairie breeze. Libby forgot her runaway horse and the chores waiting at home, forgot everything but the joy and mystery of this place, and the depth of her happiness.

Eyes still closed and lips parted, she smiled dreamily in the sunlight, letting herself sink deeper and deeper into a world of fantasy. Time slipped away, and centuries and ages became meaningless. She felt at one with the universe, lost in some ancient ritual, carried so far beyond herself that she could feel the warm glow of campfires and hear distant drumbeats and the worshipers chanting before the massive picture stone, giving thanks for a successful hunt, praying for protection through the bitter cold of winter....

A small rustling sound nearby drew her reluctantly from her dream. She opened her eyes, turned to her right and caught her breath sharply, staring in confusion and wide-eyed amazement. A tall Indian brave stood there in the rising sun just beyond the outer circle of stone, watching her quietly.

Libby continued to gaze in wonder, her eyes dazzled by the glow of the sunlight surrounding his entire form in a nimbus of golden light. She could just discern his general outline, the contours of his face and his long, muscular body. He was tall and well proportioned, wearing nothing but leggings and moccasins, his bare upper torso darkened and gleaming in the morning light. A headband was wrapped around his forehead, holding back his thick dark hair, cropped off just above the nape of his neck. His face was strong and silent, with high, blunt cheekbones, shining dark eyes and a wide mouth set in straight, firm lines.

Libby continued to gaze at him in silence, knowing that he was a creation of her imagination. She had conjured up many strange things here at the Singing Stones, but none of her fantasies had ever seemed so absolutely real as this tall, quiet Indian brave who stood watching her across a span of countless ages.

He began to move toward her. Libby caught her breath in sudden terror. He seemed so *real*. She could even see the ripple of muscles in his big arms, the sunlight gleaming on his broad shoulders, the startled glow in his dark eyes.

Slowly the man moved forward until he was almost close enough to touch. The reality of his presence—of those blunt cheekbones and piercing dark eyes—was so intense that she was nearly overwhelmed. He opened his mouth to speak, and Libby swayed on her feet, close to fainting.

A strong hand closed on her arm and a voice sounded, the words indistinguishable at first. Libby shuddered in horror and closed her eyes, summoning all her reserves of strength to keep from losing control.

"Hey," the man was saying, "is something the matter? Are you all right?"

Libby opened her eyes and stared into the dark, handsome face so close to hers. She blinked in confusion and forced herself to meet his gaze.

Now that he was so near, blocking the rays of light that had surrounded and half obscured him, she could see him more clearly and knew that she had been mistaken. He wasn't wearing leggings and moccasins, but khaki jeans and leather hiking boots. And the headband wasn't beaded deerskin; it was a faded calico bandanna, knotted casually around his forehead to keep perspiration from running into his eyes.

She laughed awkwardly at herself and drew away, still trembling and rubbing her arm.

"Are you all right?" he repeated, looking at her in concern.

"Yes," she murmured, her voice low and shaky. "Yes, I'm…I'm fine. You just startled me, that's all. I'm sorry."

"Nothing to be sorry for. I doubt that you were expecting anybody to sneak up on you here on a windy hilltop in the middle of nowhere."

He looked at her in growing curiosity, at her slender, shapely body, her beautiful green eyes and glowing, tanned skin and her rich plait of red hair.

Libby avoided his eyes, still feeling awkward and ill at

ease. She turned aside and bent to pick up the coiled hackamore rein that she had dropped on the ground at her feet,
while the man stood in silence, watching her.

"Where did you come from?" he asked finally. "How
did you get here and why?"

Gradually she began to pull herself together and
achieve a measure of calm. She looked up at him, stunned
once more by the sheer masculine presence of him, of his
brilliant dark eyes and strong, finely molded features. His
mouth was wide, but the lower lip was full, giving him
an appealing, sensual look that was at odds somehow with
the rugged planes of his face....

"I should be the one asking that," Libby said with an
effort at dignity. "After all, you're the one who's trespassing."

"Am I now?" he grinned, and his dark eyes danced.

"Yes," Libby said calmly. "You are. My family owns
all this land—" she waved her hand at the spreading
plains, flowing to the horizon in all directions "—just
about as far as you can see."

He said nothing, still looking down at her with warm
interest.

"So," Libby said, feeling uncomfortable again under
his steady gaze, "what *are* you doing here?"

"Mapping," he said briefly.

"Mapping?" she repeated blankly. "What's that?"

"You know." He waved his hand at the space around
them. "Making charts, diagrams, doing a couple of initial
pits to establish a control statement...."

"Of this place? Of the stones?"

"The big designs and patterns shaped from the placing
of individual rocks, like this huge human form that's visible from the air, make what's called a medicine wheel.
And this type of rock carving—" he indicated the big

central stone, touching the patterned surface with a reverent brown hand "—this is what's known as a petroglyph. And it's a fabulous one."

"But..." Libby hesitated, searching for words, fighting down a rising sense of panic. "But...how can you do that? Who gave you permission?"

He looked at her calmly. "We don't need permission."

"Of course you do!" Libby forgot her nervousness and stared at him, her green eyes darkening with indignation. "This is private land! It's been in my father's family for over a hundred years, and you can't do things here without our permission."

"I'm afraid that's where you're wrong," the man said easily. "I'm an archaeological consultant to the government agency that has authority to enter any property with or without the owner's permission in the interests of authenticating and preserving rare prehistoric sites."

"Then I'd like...I'd like to see your credentials, please," Libby said stiffly.

"Certainly. As a matter of fact, they're in the mail. I sent out a complete statement of intent on government letterhead, along with a proposed schedule and a profile of my own credentials and those of my crew before I organized the initial survey. I'm surprised my letter hasn't arrived yet."

Libby was silent, remembering that she had neglected for several days to run into town and pick up the mail.

"Of course," he added, "we do like to talk to the owner in advance, too, just as a courtesy, and I obtained your family's telephone number, but I've never been able to find anyone home. I stopped in at the ranch house yesterday before I drove out here, but there was nobody there then, either."

"I'm...I'm there by myself right now," Libby said.

"It's a lot of work to...I'm not in the house very much except later at night."

His eyes began to sparkle again, and his mouth twitched upward in amusement. "All by yourself, are you?" he asked solemnly. "Am I to assume that you're Graham Lyndon, the rancher who owns this property?"

"Of course not," she said with dignity. "Graham Lyndon is my father. Everyone calls him Gray," she added.

"I see. And what's your name?"

"Elizabeth Lyndon."

He smiled gently. "And does everyone call you Elizabeth?"

"No. Everyone calls me Libby."

"Libby," he repeated in pleasure, looking with frank admiration at her tall body and her lovely, flushed face. "Libby. That's nice."

"Look," she began tensely, feeling awkward again under the intensity of his gaze, "I'd really like to know what—"

"My name," he interrupted her calmly, "is Warren McIntyre."

He extended his hand, and Libby shook it, thrilling unexpectedly to the firmness of his grip and the warmth of the callused brown fingers that enclosed hers.

"McIntyre," she repeated. "That doesn't sound like an—" She caught herself and bit her lip in confusion.

"Like a what?" he asked, watching her face with interest.

"Nothing," she said. "It was just a silly thought."

He arched a dark eyebrow and gave her a questioning look.

"When you first...when I first saw you," she explained reluctantly, "over there in the sunlight, I thought you were...you looked like an Indian brave. A sort of time traveler, you know? It gave me a real start. I thought you should have a name like Painted Skies or Soaring Eagle or something.''

He grinned. "Well, I guess there's some validity in your first impression. My grandfather was a Scottish homesteader who had a Mohawk wife. Some of my grandmother's sturdy genes have obviously been passed down to me.''

Libby relented and smiled briefly, warmed in spite of herself by his engaging humor and sincerity.

"No wonder," he went on cheerfully, "that you looked like you'd seen a ghost when you turned and saw me. I was afraid you were going to faint.''

"So was I," she confessed.

They went on gazing at each other until Libby finally turned aside, disturbed by the warmth spreading through her and the strange pounding of her heart.

"This place," she asked, forcing her voice to remain casual, "how did you happen to find out about it?''

"Aerial surveys," he said briefly. "The oil companies scout by plane for possible oil-bearing formations, and they're required to turn copies of all their photographs over to us for routine examination. We found the stone circles on one of them.''

"And then...?''

"Then," Warren said, "we do microscopic studies of the photos, chart the location, look it up on the property maps and contact the owner before doing a preliminary exploration.''

"Except in this case," Libby said dryly, "you sort of omitted that last step.''

"I tried," he protested. "I really did. But this Graham Lyndon—Gray, your father—he seems to be a very elusive character.''

"He's not in the country right now," Libby said. "He's off on vacation in Europe for three months—the first holiday he's had in years. He and his wife left a few weeks ago."

"Your father's wife," Warren repeated, grinning again. "Is that a quaintly formal way of referring to your mother?"

Libby glanced up at him, startled, and then shook her head. "I see what you mean. No, my mother died when I was three years old. My father just remarried a few years ago."

"I see. So do you have a wicked stepmother?"

Libby thought of her stepmother, Joanna, as she had last seen her disappearing into the passenger lounge at the airport terminal hand in hand with Gray. Her dark curly hair had been standing on end like a child's, her deep blue eyes sparkling with joyous excitement. Libby smiled fondly at the memory and turned to Warren. "Not at all," she said. "I love Jo. She's one of the nicest people I've ever known."

He was gazing at her, clearly startled by the radiant beauty of her face when she smiled, and it took him a moment to collect himself. "And you...and you're telling me that you're at the ranch alone, then?" he said finally. "You're looking after that whole big place all by yourself?"

She nodded. "It's not so bad. There's not as much work in the summer, now that the branding's done and the stock's all turned out to pasture. I just have to do the chores, check the fences regularly and see that things are—"

She paused, confused by his direct, admiring gaze. "Besides," she went on after a moment, "I'm not all by myself, not all the time. My stepbrother, Keith, is home sometimes to help, although he's spending a lot of time on the rodeo circuit this summer. And then there's Mac Burman, my neighbor…''

"That's the old fellow down the road?" Warren asked with a sudden flash of white teeth against his tanned face. "Tall and gangly, plays the violin?"

Libby looked at him in surprise.

"You know my Uncle Mac?"

"He's your uncle?"

"No, not really—but I've called him that ever since I was a little girl. We're pretty close."

"Well, I stopped in at your Uncle Mac's place yesterday to ask directions to your place. He was sitting out on the back steps in a cowboy hat, playing 'Amazing Grace.' Astonishing, the skill of the man. I sat right down on the bottom step and he gave me a little concert."

Libby chuckled, picturing the scene, and her eyes glowed with affection. "Mac," she said, "is a darling."

Once again he seemed disconcerted by her smile, and he gazed at her in thoughtful silence for a moment before gathering himself together.

"Right," he said briskly. "And he told me how to get to your place, so I drove over there, but nobody was home. A most impressive ranching operation, by the way. I can't imagine you looking after it all by yourself."

Libby raised her chin a little. "Why? Because I'm so young? Or a woman? Or both?"

He grinned, with that same engaging flash of white teeth, and shook his head. "Oh, no. You're not getting me drawn into one of *those* discussions. No way. I have no doubt at all that you're absolutely the most capable rancher in the district. Even though," he added solemnly, averting his gaze and looking out over her head, "at the moment, you *do* seem to have misplaced your horse."

Libby looked down in dismay at the empty hackamore rein in her hand and then back up at him. He met her glance, his face still carefully expressionless, but his dark eyes were dancing.

"It's...it's a colt I'm training," she said defensively. "He's just young, and he's really nervous and skittish. He shied at something when I was closing a gate and broke away from me."

"So you have to walk home?"

Libby nodded, refusing to be drawn in by the laughter in those brilliant dark eyes.

"Well, I've got my Jeep right down at the base of the cliff. I'll give you a ride the rest of the way."

"No, thank you," Libby said politely. "It's only a couple of miles and I'm enjoying the walk."

"But I can—"

"Really," she said with sudden firmness, looking up at him, "I'd rather walk. It's such a beautiful day."

He hesitated, watching her face, and she turned away to look at the monolith beside them with its strange vivid markings.

"What happens next?" she asked. "To my Stones, I mean?"

"*Your* stones?" he repeated.

Libby waved her hand at the high, decorated rock face, encircled by its careful pattern of stones. "I've always loved this place," she said. "Ever since I was a little girl. It seems..." She hesitated, and then, seeing the seriousness of his expression as he gazed down at her, she went on. "It seems sort of...magical, you know?" she said cautiously, glancing up at him. "As if anything could happen here, inside the inner circle, and the rules of time and physics don't really apply somehow...."

She broke off, disturbed by the intensity in his dark eyes. There was a brief, awkward silence.

"So," she said at last, her voice brisk and businesslike, "what happens now? What will you be doing here exactly?"

"First, as I said, a preliminary mapping." Warren squinted briefly at the sun, measuring its angle, and then turned back to her. "Just to determine the general configurations of the patterns. Then we'll dig a control pit to chart the sediments that are deposited here and see if we can get a tentative dating. After that we'll collate all our data and determine whether the site should be expanded and developed."

"Expanded?" Libby asked in sudden alarm. "Developed? What exactly do you mean by that?"

"Don't worry," he told her gently, seeing her expression. "All that sort of thing will probably be—"

"Warren!" a voice called suddenly just below the crest of the plateau. "Hey, Warren, where do you want the transit?"

Libby turned away, startled, and watched as a girl mounted the plateau and stood looking at them in surprise.

Libby estimated the girl to be four or five years younger than herself, blond and attractive with a ripely curving figure in tight denim cutoffs and a clinging pink T-shirt. Her wheat-gold hair was carefully tied back in a long French braid that accentuated the prettiness of her tanned features. She looked in childlike amazement at the two people standing near the big rock, and her blue eyes grew suddenly cool.

"I was just wondering," she said to Warren, ignoring Libby altogether, "what you wanted me to do with the transit. Do you want it up here right away, or are you going to use it at the base of the cliff first?"

Warren waved his hand. "Just leave it. I'll be right down." Then, sensing some inexplicable tension, he said, "Sandy Hall, this is Elizabeth Lyndon. Everyone calls her Libby," he added, smiling and looking directly into Libby's eyes, though he was addressing the other girl.

"Hi, Sandy," Libby said casually. "Sorry to interrupt your work. I was just leaving. Nice to meet you."

The blond girl watched in silence as Libby turned and walked across the cliff face, stepping carefully over the outer circle of stones.

"Libby!" Warren called, looking at her slender, departing figure.

"Yes?" She hesitated and glanced back at him, her eyes very green in the morning light.

"Are you sure you don't want a ride home? It's no problem."

"I'm absolutely positive," Libby said calmly. "I've taken you away from your job long enough already."

"Would you like me to stop by later on and show you the charts and preliminary test results on the site?"

"Well, I suppose so," Libby said casually. "I'd be interested in seeing them if I'm home."

She saw the girl's blue eyes flash a warning behind Warren's muscular, tanned shoulder. Without another word Libby turned, ran lightly down the cliff face and set off in an easterly direction across the prairie toward the ranch house, her long legs carrying her swiftly away from the Singing Stones and the disturbingly attractive man who stood high up within them, watching her vanish into the sun.

CHAPTER TWO

A FULL MOON spilled light across the high expanse of land, tipping each spear of grass with silvery radiance and blackening the mysterious shadows beyond the hilltop. Thin wisps of cloud drifted over the face of the moon, wrapping it sinuously in trailing shreds of lace while the distant, ghostly music swelled and ebbed among the stones.

Libby stood near the painted monolith, her dress of soft buckskin cool against her skin. She gazed with breathless, throbbing excitement at the deep shadows beyond the outer stones, waiting. A movement flickered in the silvered grasses, and the music rippled as a man's form appeared, took shape, glowed like finely worked marble in the moonlight.

He stood there, tall and still, watching her silently, his naked chest and shoulders gleaming palely in the shining mist. He wore only a leather loincloth and a casual knot of eagle feathers that dangled from his beaded headband. She stared at him, breathless and afraid, but knowing that she wanted him, yearned for him desperately, more than anything in all the world. She ran to him across the moonlit grass, her moccasined feet barely touching the ground, and he swept her into his embrace.

Nothing had ever felt so exquisite as the strength and warmth of those muscular arms enfolding her body and the passion of his searching lips, searing fire in the chilly

moonlight. His hands moved over her body slowly—
slowly touching her throat, her breasts, her hips and
thighs, while she shuddered with ecstasy....

A cow down in the corral lowed a soft warning to her
calf. A bull far out on the prairie bellowed urgently in
reply. The early-morning chorus of bird calls spilled from
the tall poplar trees surrounding the ranch house, and sunlight fell across the braided rug in her bedroom in a long
golden rectangle.

Libby stirred reluctantly, lying still in her narrow white
bed with her eyes closed, trying to sink back into her
dream and recapture the delicious feeling of the man's
arms around her, of his lips on hers and his brown hands
caressing her body.

Suddenly she was fully aware, and she felt a quick, hot
stirring of embarrassment. She pushed aside the memory
of the dream, opened her eyes and lay with her hands
behind her head, staring at the ceiling and thinking.

Her mind worked in orderly fashion, outlining the routine chores and other things that needed to be done, running over the whole ranch and the outlying pastures,
thinking about the livestock that was her responsibility for
this long summer by herself. But woven like a dull, recurrent thread through the efficient pattern of her thoughts
was an underlying uneasiness, a sense that something was
wrong.

She remembered the handsome young archaeologist on
the hilltop and forced herself to look beyond his obvious
physical attractiveness to the reason for his presence there
on her father's land. Frowning, she tried to remember
what he had said about researching the site, and the possibility of "expansion and development," whatever that
meant.

There was still a dreamlike sense of unreality about the

whole experience, probably because of the way the man himself had seemed at first to be a creature of fantasy. But Libby suspected that his intentions regarding her family's property and the threat he presented were all too real.

Expansion and development, she thought again. I wonder what it means. Does he mean crews of government people coming onto our land, putting up some kind of building or shelter around the stones, or what? I wish—

Abruptly she shook her head and stepped onto the floor, peeling off her long-sleeved cotton nightgown and standing naked in the square of sunlight that lay across her soft old rug. Her body was lovely, sleek and tanned, with high, firm breasts and long, slender legs, her muscles flat and taut from long days of active physical work. She stretched and flexed with the utter lack of self-consciousness that arises from a life of absolute privacy and then padded, still naked, along the upstairs hallway to the bathroom.

Her face was still thoughtful and intent when she returned to her room, dressed rapidly in clean, faded jeans and shirt, brushed and replaited her long red hair and ran downstairs to the kitchen to make her breakfast.

Her hands worked automatically while her mind continued to tug and worry at the problem of the archaeological team and the possible consequences of their activity. For the first time since Gray and Jo had left for Europe she felt a bit lonely, just a little fearful of her isolation and of the heavy responsibility on her shoulders. She felt, too, an urgent need for someone to talk with and decided finally to drive down and visit Mac after she finished the morning chores.

As soon as she thought of her neighbor with his shining bald head and his sweet, gentle blue eyes, she felt better. She finished her coffee and filled a bowl with scraps and pellets for the dogs and another with slices of bread soft-

ened in milk for the motherless litter of kittens down in
the barn. By the time she went out into the morning sunlight to feed the household pets, the worry lines had
smoothed from her face and she was humming softly to
herself.

HOURS LATER, with chores done and the livestock
checked and accounted for, Libby climbed into her little
yellow Jeep and drove across the rutted prairie trail in the
direction of the neighboring ranch. The wind whipped
through the open cab, tugging at the tendrils of red hair
that escaped her braid, while a tall plume of dust followed
her and marked her progress. She drove into Mac's ranch
yard and parked by the corrals, looking around for the
familiar, tall, gangling figure of her neighbor and friend.

Mac Burman was in his fifties now and had been a part
of Libby's life since before her memory began. In fact,
the Burmans and the Lyndons had lived side by side in
the vast isolation of these Alberta prairies for over a century, helping each other generously when needed,
staunchly keeping their ranches going against all obstacles
and overcoming together the many trials and terrors of
weather and natural disasters.

Mac, though, was the last of the Burmans. He had been
an only son and he had never married. Libby's father said
that Mac had been in love once with a girl from a distant
ranch, but she had jilted him and he had been too shy to
search for another love, so after the death of his parents,
he'd lived his life all alone.

Libby knew the girl Mac had once loved. She was now
grown into a grandmother, placid and immensely fat. It
was difficult for Libby to imagine any of these people
young and passionate, and though Mac's lost love had
probably been pretty once, it was Libby's firm opinion

that she could never have been deserving of someone as wonderful as Mac, who was probably far better off without her....

Just as she framed this thought, Mac himself appeared around the corner of the chophouse, carrying a pail. Libby swung herself out of the cab of the Jeep and ran to hug him.

"Uncle Mac," she said, burrowing happily against his plaid shirtfront, sniffing the familiar, clean scent of hay and sunshine, of soap and oil paints, that had always, since her earliest memories, been uniquely his own.

"Well, now," he said calmly, setting his pail down to return her hug and then holding her at arm's length while he examined her. "What's all this?"

Libby pretended to be hurt. "Can't I even be glad to see you?"

"Not *that* glad. Not my little Elizabeth. She's always been the standoffish one, watching and thinking, but not hugging or saying much."

Libby grinned. "That was just because Peggy was always around, being dramatic and emotional. She was so good at it that I just let her do it all."

He nodded in agreement and returned her smile. Libby walked beside him to the corrals, warmed and comforted by his quiet presence.

Malcolm Burman was tall and spare, with a gleaming bald head and vivid blue eyes in a weathered face and a shy smile of ineffable sweetness. Because he never had much to say for himself, people who didn't know him well tended to underestimate him, but Libby made no such mistake. She knew that Mac was wonderful. For one thing, he was an accomplished musician, capable of wringing tones of heartbreaking beauty from his old violin. And he was an artist, painting graceful depictions of prairie scenes that sold with amazing swiftness from the elegant gallery in Calgary that carried his work.

But most of all Mac was wise and loving, with a gentle, generous soul that endeared him to family and friends. He glanced sidelong at Libby once more, his eyes thoughtful as he looked down at her bright hair.

"What do you hear from the honeymooners?" he asked, pausing by the entrance to a long, weathered shed.

Libby smiled. "They called a couple of days ago from Paris. Dad sounds so wonderful…more relaxed than he's been in years. He really needed a holiday. And Jo was just on cloud nine. She was talking so fast about all they'd seen that she kept getting mixed up and having to start over, and Dad kept laughing in the background."

Mac chuckled fondly. Jo, Gray Lyndon's new wife, was also Mac's own beloved niece, who had brought her son out to live with Mac after a tragedy in her own life and had met and married Gray as a result. Jo's happiness, Libby knew, was a source of deep joy to Mac.

"And how about you?" he asked, looking searchingly at Libby. "Can you manage? You're not feeling lonely up there or overworked or anything?"

Libby shook her head. "Not a bit. I *told* all of you that I can handle this with no problem at all. I'm really enjoying it. After all," she added, "I've spent four years studying at college and another two years in the city, working in an office. A summer on the ranch is exactly what I want right now."

Mac nodded, still looking at her intently.

"Let's go see the pigs," Libby said brightly. "How's Hiram?"

"Hiram," Mac said, opening the door of the shed and holding it wide for Libby to precede him, "is just as bossy as ever."

She laughed and blinked in the musty dimness of the shed, looking around at Mac's latest batch of busy, burrowing, squealing little pigs.

Mac's pigs were a source of never-ending amusement to the neighboring ranchers. Five years earlier when his niece, Jo, had arrived at Mac's ranch hoping to use her skills as an accountant to save Mac from bankruptcy, she had decided to his horror that weanling pigs were the key to financial survival. And she had been right—the pigs had saved Mac from losing his ranch. But to an established cattleman, a pig was an object of derision, and raising them was just not an acceptable occupation.

With his gentle, wayward nature, though, Mac had grown to like his pigs, continuing to raise them even though his cattle were showing a profit once again and he no longer really needed the income from the pigs.

Libby studied the tall, heavy, spotted hog in the middle of the shed, far larger than any of the others busily butting and tending the tiny pink newcomers, shooing them energetically back and forth between the water troughs and the sleeping areas. For some reason Mac adored this particular pig and would never allow him to be sold.

"Why do you call him Hiram?" Libby asked suddenly, still looking at the big hog. One ear drooped over his eye, giving him a rakish, devil-may-care look that contrasted oddly with his fussy, responsible nature.

"He always reminds me of Hiram Wickstead, the postmaster in town long before you were born. Knew everybody's business, Hiram did, and thought it was his personal responsibility to keep everybody in line all the time. Plumb wore himself out just being so bossy."

Libby chuckled and then watched, smiling, as Hiram became aware of Mac's presence and catapulted across the shed to rub against the long blue-jeaned legs. Mac scratched behind the droopy ear, while Hiram extended his head, grunting softly, his little eyes closed in bliss.

"Stupid pig," Mac said gruffly. "Git! Git along now. You've got work to do. That little black pig's going to climb right into the water trough if you're not quick."

As if he could understand every word, Hiram turned his head, saw the errant piglet and bustled across the straw, rear end swaying briskly, curled tail switching, to give him a stern nip.

Libby and Mac laughed and went back out into the sunlight and across the yard to Mac's clean little bunga-low. Inside the bright kitchen Libby moved about as if she were at home, getting down the cookie tin and ar-ranging mugs and sugar bowl on the table while Mac washed his hands and brewed a pot of coffee. When, fi-nally, they sat in the sunlight companionably sipping their coffee, she ventured at last to bring up the topic that was worrying her.

"I was out riding yesterday morning," she said casu-ally, "in the West Five and I ran across an archaeological team up at the stone circles."

Mac nodded. "The young fellow stopped in a couple of days ago to ask for directions. I tried to call and warn you, but I couldn't catch you in the house."

"I've been really busy," Libby said absently, arranging cookie crumbs in a neat little pile on the napkin by her coffee mug.

"Nice young fellow," Mac said. "Good-looking, too," he added, and watched with sudden alertness as a delicate flush mounted on Libby's tanned cheeks.

"I suppose so," she said casually. "I didn't really no-tice."

"Seemed like a real smart young fellow," Mac said with equal casualness.

Libby thought of the letter she had picked up the previous afternoon in town, with its neat technical composition and its impressive array of scholastic credits and professional achievements. "I suppose so," she said again.

Her head was lowered, her long dark lashes sweeping in a shadowy fan across her warm cheeks. Mac, still watching her, allowed one corner of his mouth to tug upward in a glimmer of a smile, but instantly composed himself when she glanced over at him.

"I've been...kind of worried about it," she said. "Ever since I saw them up there."

"Why?"

"Well...he said something about mapping the site, you know, and then he just hinted at the possibility of some kind of development...."

Mac nodded thoughtfully, stirring another spoonful of sugar into his coffee. "Gray wouldn't like that," he said, voicing what both of them were thinking.

Libby met his eyes, her face miserable. "He'd *hate* it, Mac. You know how he hates having strangers on his land. He doesn't even like the gas wells on the property, and they're no problem at all, really.... I don't know how he'd deal with an archaeological site that might take years to be finished and cause all kinds of difficulties with stock and fences and—"

"Can't you just ask them to do their business somewhere else? It's your land, after all."

Libby shook her head. "It's the stones, Mac. They're really a rare thing, I guess, especially the big picture rock in the middle. Warren...the archaeologist, I mean...he called it a petroglyph, and the whole big design of stones is a medicine wheel apparently," she added as an afterthought. "I just don't know what to do, Mac. I feel as if

I should be dealing better with this somehow, but I don't know how to go about it, and I don't want to bother Dad about anything when this is the first holiday he's had in years, and he and Jo are so happy...."

Mac stared into the distance, his bald head shining in the sunlight, his blue eyes thoughtful. "I wonder..." he began slowly.

"What?" Libby asked, reaching down absently to fondle the silky ears of Mrs. Brown, Mac's old collie-cross dog. Mrs. Brown's feathery tail thumped softly on the kitchen linoleum while Mac remained deep in thought. "What, Mac?" Libby prompted him.

"I was just trying to remember. Seems to me that years ago when I was a boy there was talk of another set of stone circles like that and a picture rock that was even bigger somewhere around here. Too bad you couldn't find it for them and get them out of your hair."

Libby stared at him in surprise. "Mac...how can that be? Why haven't I ever heard about it?"

"Oh, this was years ago. Before my time even. It was sort of a legend among the old homesteaders back when I was just a boy."

"But..." Libby frowned, thinking. "If it was on somebody's land in the district, Mac, we'd all know about it, wouldn't we? Everybody knows every square yard of their own property."

"Not in the community pasture," Mac said quietly.

Libby's eyes widened. "You think it could be somewhere in there?"

Mac nodded, and they both fell silent for a moment, thinking about the huge tract of land. Community pastures on the prairies were large allotments of government land, often too rough and isolated to be practical for private ownership. Groups of ranchers formed a cooperative and leased the crown land from the government, running their cattle on it communally, thus giving each of them access to more grazing land than any one of them could hold individually.

The community pasture adjoining the Lyndon and Burman ranches was over two hundred square miles of rugged coulees, ravines, windswept sand dunes and grasslands, and there were places in the vast, rough expanse that had never been explored by anybody.

Mac grinned. "What you should do, Lib, you should tell them they're not allowed on your property and then let them know there's an even better site out in the community pasture. That'd keep them busy for a year or two, hunting for some little stone circles in *that* chunk of land."

Libby smiled and then shook her head. "It wouldn't work, Mac. My stones are right there under their noses, and I can't keep them out. Warren—the archaeologist—he said in his letter that the government has the right to explore prehistoric sites wherever they want, with or without permission. They can even expropriate the land if they want to."

"Expropriate it!" Mac stared at her with all the horror of the true landowner threatened by a loss of property.

Libby nodded miserably and then looked thoughtful again. "I wish I knew more about that other site in the community pasture. What do you remember about it, Mac? Did anybody ever...?"

He gave her a sharp warning glance. "I don't remember anything about it. I'm sorry I mentioned it. And don't you go getting any silly ideas, Elizabeth Lyndon. I *know* you. And I'm telling you right now that it's too wild and dangerous for you to be wandering around in that kind of country by yourself."

"Oh, come on, Mac. I've ridden hundreds of miles in the community pasture ever since I was a little girl."

"Just around the edges," Mac said. "You've never been into the center. Nobody has, not in your lifetime. And you're not going to. Now, promise me you won't get silly and—"

Libby was saved from answering by the sound of a vehicle approaching and stopping abruptly. She and Mac exchanged a glance and then got up together, followed by the dog, and went out into the yard.

A dusty green Land Rover was parked by the corral with a figure behind it, standing on the lowest corral rail and studying the little pigs as they squealed and played in the sunny pen opening off their feed shed.

When Libby and Mac drew nearer, they could see that the person expressing such interest in Mac's pigs was small and slender, wearing faded green khaki pants and shirt, hiking boots and a limp safari hat. Mac and Libby exchanged another eloquent glance.

"I believe this just might be another of your archaeologist friends," Mac muttered from the corner of his mouth.

"Dr. Livingstone, I presume," Libby whispered, and giggled.

But they both sobered and started in surprise as their visitor turned and climbed briskly down from the fence. The person in the safari outfit was a woman, possibly in her early fifties, with masses of thick graying hair tucked beneath her hat, fine aquiline features and lovely gray eyes set in dark lashes.

She was a truly beautiful woman, Libby thought, with the kind of loveliness that came not from artifice or effort, but from centuries of good breeding and a lifetime of mental and physical activity, coupled with many hours of healthy outdoor labor. Her fine-boned face was tanned, with warm laugh lines extending from the corners of her eyes and mouth, and her expression was vivid with humor and interest.

"Hello there. Lovely pigs," she said by way of greeting in a pleasant husky voice. "I'm particularly taken with the nursemaid."

"His name is Hiram," Libby said. "He likes to look after the little ones."

"So I see." The woman smiled, her eyes crinkling warmly, and extended her hand. "My name is Alexandra Coleman."

"I'm Elizabeth Lyndon," Libby said, shaking the proffered hand, "and this is Malcolm Burman."

Shyly Mac shook hands as well, but seemed completely incapable of speech. He gazed at the small, brisk woman as if she were some rare, exotic creature suddenly come to earth here in his yard.

"I'm a developmental consultant for the government agency dealing with prehistoric sites," the woman explained. "I was told to ask for directions here to a site that's currently under investigation in the area."

"Warren McIntyre called you?" Libby asked with a growing sense of impending doom.

"Yes. He radioed in this morning and said he had something I should look at. You've met Warren?"

Libby nodded. "The site he's working at is on my family's property."

Alexandra Coleman looked momentarily confused. "Then you don't...you mustn't live *here*. Warren said this was the neighbor's place."

"Yes. This is Mac's place," Libby said, indicating Mac, who still stood beside her in tense, awkward silence.

"I see," the woman said politely, giving Mac another

brief, cursory glance and then turning back to Libby. "So you live on the adjoining ranch where the petroglyph site is located?" Libby nodded, and Alexandra gave her a shrewd glance. "And you're not very happy about it, are you?"

Libby looked at her in surprise and then shook her head. "No," she said briefly. "Not very."

"The past belongs to the people, my dear," the little woman said quietly. "History is no respecter of property. It's our right and privilege, all of us, to have access to our national heritage."

"I suppose so," Libby said reluctantly. "It's just…it's hard, you know, when the heritage site happens to be smack in the middle of a working ranch. It's…kind of awkward."

The gray eyes rested on her a moment longer, intelligent and penetrating. Alexandra Coleman placed a gentle hand on her arm, gave it a little squeeze and climbed nimbly into her Land Rover. "Perhaps," she said, resting her elbow on the sill of the open window, "you could give me some directions?"

"I'm just on my way home," Libby said. "If you follow me, I'll take you along the trail and show you where to turn off. The back road from here will take you right to the site."

Libby got into her own Jeep, waved to Mac and pulled away from the corrals with the other woman close behind her. When they left the yard, Mac was still standing there alone in the dusty sunshine and gazing after the departing vehicles with a strange expression of stunned, painful wonder.

A SOFT SPRING RAIN began late in the evening after all the chores were done and Libby had bathed, changed into

old jogging pants and a faded college sweatshirt and prepared to relax for a few hours before going to bed. She
stood on the front veranda of the spacious, luxurious Lyndon ranch house, gazing out at the mists of rain that
slanted across the rolling, darkened pastures and shim-
mered in the leaves of the poplar trees around the house.
The fragrance of sage and flowers and damp earth was
delicious, and she drew in deep breaths, smiling with pleasure.

Then she closed the door, put some music on the stereo,
built a fire in the huge hearth and curled up with a book.
Libby had always loved the rain. She gave herself up to
enjoyment of the evening, putting all the nagging concerns about the archaeological team out of her mind and
feeling instead a warm surge of deep, singing contentment.

She heard a vehicle coming up the long, winding approach road and looked up, wondering idly who it might
be. The neighboring ranching families, many of whom,
like Mac, had been on their land for generations, all knew
that she was alone here for the summer. By some kind of
unspoken arrangement somebody stopped in to see her
almost every day just to make sure that she was all right
and not in need of any help.

But when she put her book down and crossed the deep
carpet to peer out behind the drapes, she saw that the
vehicle was one she didn't recognize—a late-model black
Jeep pulling up to park under the trees near the veranda.
Suddenly her mouth went dry.

Warren McIntyre got out of the Jeep, strode with a
lithe, rapid step along the flagstone walk and came running up the veranda steps. From where Libby stood, peep-
ing out between the drapes, he was clearly visible in the
glow of the big yard light. He wore clean blue jeans and

a soft corduroy shirt of rich golden-brown that set off his dark complexion and his fine, sculpted features. Raindrops sparkled like bright prisms in his thick black hair and glimmered on the plastic tube he carried in one lean brown hand.

Reluctantly Libby moved across the room to answer the bell and stood hesitantly in the doorway, looking out at him. He smiled down at her, his face creasing warmly, his eyes lighting with pleasure. Much to her annoyance her heart began to thud in her chest and a flush mounted her cheeks, making her grateful for the dimness of the living room.

"Hello, Libby," he said.

"Hello, Mr. McIntyre...Warren," she rejoined automatically.

"You said that I could drop by and give you some information on what we're doing at the site...."

"Yes...yes, I remember. Would you please come in," Libby said, summoning her composure and stepping aside to let him pass.

He paused in the entryway looking around with approval at the warmth and comfort of the big country living room with its warm braided rugs, hardwood floors, oil paintings and crackling fire.

"This is nice," he said. Then he added with a teasing grin, "Romantic, too. Were you expecting somebody?"

Wordlessly Libby indicated her old jogging pants with patches on both knees, her heavy woolen socks and faded, shapeless sweatshirt. Warren laughed and she responded with a rueful answering grin.

"Okay," he said, "maybe not. But you're still beautiful, Libby Lyndon, even in your sweats. You look better in that outfit than most women would in a lace-trimmed negligee."

"I'm not much for lace-trimmed negligees," Libby said cheerfully. "They scare the horses."

He chuckled again and followed her across the room to a chair she indicated near the fire.

Libby hesitated. "Would you like some coffee or anything?"

"No thanks. We just ate back at camp."

She pictured him having a cozy late-evening meal inside a lighted tent with the voluptuous blond girl while the rain fell softly outside. For some reason she found the image vaguely annoying.

"You must have all the comforts of home, I guess," she said, curling up in the opposite chair and keeping her voice casual. "I didn't notice your camp when I was there."

"We pitched the tents behind that grove of birch trees at the base of the hill, sheltered from the wind."

"Tents?" she said lightly. "How big is your camp?"

"Just two tents. One for Sandy and one for Tim and me. I guess," he added, "you didn't meet Tim, did you? The kids were busy unpacking equipment."

She felt a ridiculous surge of relief and quelled it sternly. Nevertheless, she couldn't resist pursuing the topic just a little further. "Both your crew members are there already, are they? You mentioned in your letter that there were two of them."

He nodded. "The kids are undergraduates getting field credits for working with me this summer. I think they'll both be pretty good." He grinned. "Except," he added, "that I anticipate some emotional problems."

"Oh? How?"

"Poor Tim," he said, still smiling, the strong planes of his face gleaming in the firelight, "is already so much in love with Sandy that he can't tell a scalpel from a shovel.

And she doesn't even seem to know he's alive. I don't know why," he added thoughtfully. "Tim's a really nice kid."

Because she's crazy about *you*, you idiot, that's why, Libby told him silently, and wondered if he could really be that ingenuous....

"But I didn't come here to bore you with camp gossip," he was saying. "I thought you might be interested in what I'm doing, just in the initial stages." He waved the plastic tube at her and smiled. "Well, that's not entirely true," he confessed. "It's *partly* true, but mostly I really just wanted an excuse to see you again."

Libby smiled back, thrilling to the warmth and the sincere admiration in his dark, flashing eyes. But she kept her voice light and teasing. "Oh, come on. All this flattery is just to get on my good side so I won't throw you off my land."

"As we've told you, Libby, you *can't* throw us off your land. But," he added cheerfully, "I certainly wouldn't mind getting on your good side just the same."

"Then leave on your own," she said bluntly. "Find another site to work at and you'll be my very favorite archaeologist."

He regarded her steadily, his dark face thoughtful. "You really mean it, don't you? You're upset about the idea of any development up there."

She nodded and cast him an appealing glance.

"I just feel...so responsible, you know? My father's away, and I know that if he comes home and finds some kind of full-blown operation there in one of our busiest, most valuable pastures, he's going to be so..." Libby paused. "I really wish," she said in a low voice, "that you were working somewhere else, that's all."

Warren hesitated and then changed the subject. "I can't

believe you have all this responsibility,'' he said, watching her carefully. "I mean, you can't be more than, what? Twenty-two or so? And you're looking after this whole big ranching operation by yourself. It's amazing.''

"I'm twenty-four actually," Libby said with dignity. "And I've *always* lived and worked here, ever since I was born. It's not so amazing that I know how to look after things.''

"Is this your lifetime goal?" he asked with interest. "I mean, are you going to be a lady rancher? Is that your ambition?''

Libby smiled. "Hardly. As a matter of fact, I have my degree in social work, and I've been working in the field for two years. I'm taking a promotional position that's being vacated by retirement early in September, and I haven't had a holiday since I started work, so I decided to take the summer off, spend some time out here and let my parents have their holiday at the same time.''

"Why social work?" he asked.

She glanced up quickly and saw that he was genuinely interested, so she answered him. "Because," she said quietly, "I thought it would be good for me.''

"In what way?''

"I've always been a really quiet, private person. Left to myself, I'd probably just stay out here forever, far away from people and involvement, riding and walking on the prairie and reading and daydreaming. And I know that's not entirely healthy. So I decided," Libby concluded simply, "to take up a kind of work that would force me to be involved with people, just in the interests of character development.''

He gazed at her and shook his head in wonder. "You're an amazing person, you know that, Libby? Just amazing. The first time I saw you, the other morning, standing in the circle of stones with the wind in your hair, I thought you were just—'' Warren broke off and studied her bent head, shining rudely in the firelight. ''Where did you get your degree?'' he asked, his voice casual once again.

She smiled. ''The same place you did. In fact, I was a freshman the year you did your final graduate studies.''

Warren stared at her, his dark eyes puzzled.

''Your professional résumé,'' Libby said with another teasing smile. ''The one you sent in the mail, remember? I know everything about you.''

He grinned back, delighting in her sparkle. ''Not *everything*, I hope. Say, did you by any chance have old Walrus for freshman English?''

Libby choked and giggled. ''Didn't everyone? He spent three months trying to teach us the Middle English pronunciation of the *Canterbury Tales*.''

Warren threw his head back, laughing, and began a stirring and surprisingly authentic Middle English rendition of the Nun's Priest's Tale. Libby chimed in, giggling as her tongue stumbled on the archaic pronunciations that had been so dear to the heart of old Walrus, the freshman English instructor.

After a moment they stopped, still laughing helplessly, and smiled warmly at each other. Their eyes met and held for a long moment until finally Libby sobered and looked away, staring in confusion at the soft, leaping flames on the hearth.

Warren studied her delicate profile, his face troubled. ''Libby,'' he began gently after a long, awkward silence, ''it's not all up to me, you know. I'm just a technical adviser. It's my job to map and document the site and make recommendations to Alex. She's the one who arrives at the final decision about development.''

''Alex? That's Alexandra Coleman?''

"Yes, it is. I gather you've met her, as well."

Libby nodded. "When you talk about 'development,'" she began slowly, "what exactly do you mean?"

He shifted awkwardly in his chair and looked into the crackling glow of the fire. "It could mean a lot of things, depending on the nature of the site. Anything from a published archaeological profile to an interpretive center for tourists."

"An *interpretive center!* What does *that* mean?"

"Well, it'd be a sort of field museum. There'd be a building with exhibits and guides—a whole complex."

Libby stared at him in horror. "But this is…it's *private land!*"

"Not if it contains a national heritage treasure, Libby. Then it's public domain."

"Oh, my God," Libby said wearily, gazing into the fire with an expression of brooding unhappiness.

Warren sat looking at her in silent compassion. "Look," he said finally, indicating the plastic tube on his lap, full of the careful charts and diagrams that she had, as yet, expressed no interest in seeing. "I'm really sorry about all this. But we have to—"

"What if I told you there's another site nearby?" Libby asked abruptly. "A similar one but even better, and one that's on public land?"

He looked at her with quick interest. "Nothing like that has ever shown up on other aerial surveys."

"It's in…I think it's in a very rough tract of land. Possibly overgrown with brush and not visible from the air."

"And you know where to find it?" he asked eagerly. "Would you take me there?"

She shook her head. "Not…not just yet. First, I want your assurance that if I were to show you another, better site, you'd be likely to change your mind about developing the one on our land.''

Warren was silent for a moment, his dark face thoughtful and intent. Finally he looked up at Libby, meeting her eyes directly.

"Let me put it this way," he said slowly. "We're certainly going to go ahead with a major archaeological study of this site on your land, just because it's so rare and valuable. But as far as tourist availability and public access, which I suspect would be your major concern...?"

He shot Libby a quick questioning glance, his dark eyebrows rising, and she nodded soberly. "Well," Warren went on, "there's only funding available for one site of that magnitude and, of course, if there were another similar one on public land, then I think we could be fairly certain that the alternate site would receive the bulk of that kind of development."

"Good," Libby said briskly. "That's all I wanted to know." She looked at her watch. "I'm sorry to be rude, Warren, but I have to be up before five, so I'd better..."

"Right. I have to be up early, too." He got to his feet, moved to the door and then lingered, looking down at her searchingly. "Libby," he began softly, "I hope we don't find ourselves in conflict, you and I, over this archaeological site. Because I find, more and more, that I want to get to know you a lot better. I'd really like us to be... friends.''

"So would I," Libby said simply. She looked up at him, and he reached out a lean brown hand, cupping her cheek and gazing thoughtfully into her eyes, while her face grew warm and her heart pounded.

They stood for a long time locked in silence, green eyes meeting dark brown in charged silence. Finally Warren dropped his hand. "Good night, Libby," he whispered. "See you soon."

She murmured something in reply and stood on the veranda, watching as he ran down the steps and strode along the path to his Jeep. Then she closed the door slowly and leaned against it, her eyes distant and intent, her face still burning from the touch of his hand.

CHAPTER THREE

"PARDON ME, SIR," the secretary said politely, reaching for the telephone. "I'll be with you in just a moment."

She was tall and willowy, with gray wings sweeping upward in her dark, carefully styled hair, and delicate, perfect makeup that must have taken hours, Mac thought, to apply. In fact, she was the kind of woman who most frightened him. He lingered awkwardly near the reception desk, examining a wall of plants nearby with deep concentration to hide his nervousness.

Mac wore his standard dress-up clothes—a fine gray wool suit in a western cut, highly polished riding boots and a small string tie. He carried a pearl-gray Stetson, his bald head glowing under the discreet, recessed lighting.

The secretary looked up at him with a courteous, inquiring glance, and he steeled himself to speak to her. "I'd like...I believe that Alexandra Coleman works on this floor."

"Yes," the woman said, nodding her elegant head. "Dr. Coleman's office is just down the hall that way." She indicated the hallway with a graceful, manicured hand. "Second door to your left."

Mac was briefly nonplussed by the "Dr.," and then adjusted to this new information. She was, after all, clearly a very clever lady, Alexandra Coleman. It wasn't so surprising that she was also well educated, especially considering the nature of her position....

He realized that the receptionist was looking at him curiously, and gathered himself together. "Thank you, ma'am," he said shyly, and smiled at her.

All at once she no longer noticed the old-fashioned rancher's clothes, the shining bald head or the gaunt nervousness of the man at her desk. She saw only the immense sweetness in his blue eyes and the gentleness of his expression and was surprised to find herself returning his smile with unusual warmth. He turned and strode down the hall toward Dr. Coleman's office, while the elegant, dark-haired young woman watched his tall departing figure with a thoughtful, bemused look.

Mac hesitated in front of a plain golden oak door, set with a brass nameplate reading, Dr. A. E. Coleman, Developmental Consultant. For a moment his courage almost failed him and he felt an urgent longing to flee out of the building, back down the crowded city street to his truck and out onto the broad, peaceful prairie that he loved.

But a great deal was at stake here, and Mac knew it, so he forced himself to knock gently on the door.

There was no answer. He knocked again, experiencing a sharp flood of emotion that was half relief and half disappointment. Finally he tried the door, found it unlocked and eased it open to step inside the empty office.

He would have known without being told that it was Alexandra Coleman's office. Mac had only seen the woman for a few moments...hadn't, in fact, really exchanged a single word with her, but he had memorized everything about her. He recognized her in the sweep of glass behind the desk, the masses of plants, the rough earth tone ceramics and Indian artifacts in glass display cases, the ranks of books and papers, the casual raincoat and hat tossed over an oak clothes tree behind the door.

The room was full of her, and Mac felt a keen pleasure just looking around it.

Suddenly he caught his breath and gazed in stunned amazement at the side wall. On it hung a small, delicate watercolor, an exquisite rendering of a prairie scene with a pair of waterfowl against a pastel sunrise, circling a melting slough in search of a nesting place.

Mac had painted the scene just over a year earlier.

He edged cautiously across the room to look at it more closely, feeling a ridiculous upsurge of joy, almost as if he had come across his own long-lost child. He formed a deep attachment for all the pictures he painted and always regretted having to part with them, but the gallery owner was so persuasive and Mac never ceased to be astounded by the ridiculous amount of money that city people seemed to be willing to spend for his little daubs of paint.

He stood very still, his eyes riveted to the small canvas, picturing Alexandra Coleman walking into the gallery, seeing the painting, wandering away and coming back to it, finally opening her handbag with those brisk, decisive movements and taking out her checkbook, walking back out into the street with his painting under her arm....

At the thought, Mac felt a surge of warmth that made him feel, just for a moment, a little light-headed, almost dizzy with happiness.

Suddenly he tensed, hearing the door swing open behind him. Alexandra Coleman entered the office, stopping abruptly when she saw him there and looking at him with startled silence. She wore a suit of soft, dusty blue suede with a darker blue blouse that set off her gray hair and fine features. She looked, Mac thought, adorably feminine, and entirely lovely.

"Dr. Coleman," he said shyly, extending his hand. "We met a few days ago. My name is Malcolm Burman."

She continued to look at him in surprise, her gray eyes wide and perplexed, searching her memory. All at once she smiled, and her white teeth gleamed against the tan of her cheeks. "Ah, yes," she said in her warm, husky voice, shaking his hand briskly. "I remember. You're the man with the pigs."

If Mac, who owned nineteen square miles of some of the richest ranching country in the world and a herd of over two hundred fine Hereford cows, objected to being referred to in this manner, he gave no sign of it. He just nodded politely and gave her one of his gentle, luminous smiles. "That's me," he said.

"Please sit down, Mr. Burman," Alexandra said, passing him with a delicate, tantalizing aura of some spicy fragrance and seating herself behind her broad desk. "What can I do for you?"

Mac sank awkwardly into the comfortable leather chair opposite the desk and sat tensely forward, turning the brim of his hat in his long, callused fingers. "I wanted," he said finally, "to talk to you about...about these stones on the Lyndon property."

She glanced over at him alertly, her fine eyes wide with interest. "Yes? What about them?"

"You see," he began awkwardly, "it's just that...it's..." He was silent a moment, searching for words, while the woman across the desk waited patiently.

"Yes, Mr. Burman?" she said again, prompting him gently.

"It's just that...you see, Libby's really worried about it," he said. "She's so unhappy about the whole thing. She was down to see me again yesterday, and she just doesn't know what to do."

"Libby?" Alexandra frowned, and then her face cleared. "Ah, yes. That's the Lyndon girl, isn't it? The beautiful redhead who was at your place the other day when I stopped in to ask directions?"

"Yes, that's her."

Dr. Coleman toyed with a ceramic paperweight on her desk, her face troubled. "I could tell that she was… concerned. And one can hardly blame her. It must be distressing, after all, to have your privacy disrupted by a lot of people who just appear from nowhere and tell you that they have every right to do as they please with your own property."

She looked up, and Mac met her gaze in silence. "But," she went on, "the fact is, we *do* have that right, Mr. Burman. And, in the interests of authenticating and documenting a valuable prehistoric site and making it available to the public, we will certainly exercise our rights."

"Her family is away, you see," Mac began, looking at the slender woman opposite him with desperate appeal, "and she has all the responsibility for the property, and she doesn't know what to do. Would it be possible for you to just wait till next summer maybe? Just postpone all this for a while until…"

The consultant shook her head. "I'm afraid not. We're scheduled to go ahead with a project in the area this year. The funds and personnel are in place, and I can hardly see the project being scrapped at this point."

"Dr. Coleman, let's be honest with each other," Mac said with a sudden crispness in his voice that caused her to look up at him in mild surprise. "Let's not talk government or ifs or perhaps or projections—or anything. Let's just talk facts."

"Certainly, Mr. Burman." She folded her hands on her desk and gave him a steady, level glance, waiting. Despite his concern over Libby's situation, and his own nervousness, Mac was nevertheless deeply interested by the fact that those slender brown hands wore only one ring, a large ornate sapphire on the right hand, and none at all on the left....

"What exactly is going to happen out there, ma'am? What will you be doing?"

"That all depends on the results of the dating survey and Warren's preliminary—"

"Please, Dr. Coleman," Mac interrupted. "I've already gone out and talked to Warren—just yesterday. *He* says that what happens all depends on you."

"Very well. I think," she said, looking directly at Mac, "that this site is going to prove to be the oldest petro-glyphic collection in North America and quite probably the most valuable yet discovered. It will take me some time to make a final decision, but I'm fairly certain, in view of what I consider to be this site's potential, that I will likely be recommending the development of some type of year-round interpretive center or field museum, accessible to large numbers of tourists, with an all-weather road and a small resident staff."

Mac sagged in his chair, looking down at the hat brim between his fingers as the silence in the room grew and lengthened. "Well," he said at last, "you've certainly given me a straight answer, anyway. Thank you, Dr. Coleman." He got heavily to his feet, turned toward the door and then paused. "That's kind of a pretty picture," he said casually, indicating the framed prairie scene on the wall.

"Isn't it?" she said, her face softening. "I just love it. I found it in a little gallery downtown about six months ago."

Mac turned back, his heart flooding with pleasure at the glow on her austere features as she gazed at the painting.

"I wish," she mused, "that I could find out who the artist was. I'd give anything to get in contact with the person who painted it, but the gallery owner refuses to give out his name."

"Why?" Mac asked, his voice suddenly hoarse.

"I don't know. I suppose it's someone who values their privacy or—"

"Not that," Mac said, clearing his throat. "I mean, why would you want to find the artist?"

"I'd like to commission a whole set of them. It's a small scene, you see, and obviously a springtime one. I'd love to have one of each season and hang them together in a group."

Mac looked at the wall, visualizing the grouping as she described it, feeling an artist's keen delight at the mental image. "That *would* be nice," he said. "Real nice." He ducked his head shyly and reached for the doorknob. "Well, goodbye, Dr. Coleman. Thanks for your time."

She nodded politely, and his last glimpse of her was a flash of dusty blue and a gleam of silver where the sun shone on her crown of graying hair. He swallowed hard, trudged down the hall and waited quietly for the elevator to carry him down to the bustling lobby.

Out on the street he breathed the warm spring air deeply, fitted his hat carefully on his head and started off toward the parking lot, thinking about the other paintings she wanted, musing over possible settings for each of the individual seasons.

WHILE MAC WAS PAYING his visit to Alexandra Coleman, Libby was making her own small assault on what she was beginning, more and more, to perceive as the enemy.

She finished her morning chores and then dressed with unusual care, putting on clean jeans and a snug yellow

T-shirt that she knew looked wonderful with her ruddy hair and her tan. Finally she selected one of the brood mares, a dainty, quick-moving little bay that needed exercising, saddled her and set off to check fences in the direction of the stone circles.

The sun shone warm and rich on the waving grass, bright green tipped with gold, and the day was so calm and pleasant that she almost forgot the real purpose for her ride. Libby relaxed in the saddle, lulled by the easy, rhythmic movements of the horse's gait, the rich smell of sage and sun-warmed leather and the soft, caressing breeze on her face. But when she neared the stretch of land containing the bluff with the stone circles, her happiness turned abruptly to tension.

She veered off course, set the little bay into a canter and started across the prairie in the direction of the high land formation. This time, approaching it from the east, the first thing she saw was their campsite, with the two gray dome tents and a clothesline strung between a couple of birch trees nearby, holding an assortment of jeans, T-shirts and sleeping bags hung out for a morning airing.

Once again she was assailed by the landowner's sense of outrage at the casual presumption of these trespassers, accompanied by a deep fear of the terrible power they had to do whatever they wished with her property.

As she neared the camp, she could make out two people working at the base of the cliff. She reined her mare down to a trot and approached more cautiously, soon realizing that the workers were the girl, Sandy, and a tall, sturdy, blond young man who must be the love-struck Tim. They wore shorts and T-shirts, and they were occupied in shoveling masses of soil onto a big screen, sifting it and picking out small objects from the mesh surface.

There was no sign of Warren McIntyre.

Libby trotted up beside the two of them and reined in. The little mare, excited by her run, danced nervously to one side while Libby sat her easily, swaying in the saddle, her hands low on the reins. The two young people looked up at her, their faces, after an initial shock of surprise, registering vastly different expressions. Tim's youthful, open face showed frank, warm admiration while Sandy's pretty features froze at once into a look of suspicion and dislike.

"Hello, Sandy," Libby said with a smile. "And this must be Tim. My name is Libby Lyndon," she added for his benefit, since Sandy didn't seem about to make introductions.

"You're the lady who owns the ranch," he said, setting aside his shovel and continuing to regard her with approval.

"Not really," Libby said. "My father owns the ranch. I'm just looking after it for the summer."

"Warren told me," Tim said while Sandy watched them in cold silence. "He's really impressed by you," the young man added cheerfully. "I can see why."

The blond girl's eyes flashed blue fire. She turned aside deliberately to pick items from the screen and line them up along the wooden frame. Libby saw how the girl's hand trembled, and felt a stirring of sympathy.

"What are you doing there, Sandy?" she asked. "What exactly are you looking for in all that dirt?"

"Whatever we can find," Sandy said stiffly. "This is from the control pit up on the hilltop. We sift it for any artifacts there might be and then label and catalog them."

Libby dismounted with an easy, fluid motion, looped the rein over her arm and looked with interest at the vast array of small bones and chipped stone tools spread on a nearby table.

"And you've found all this stuff?" she asked in surprise. "Up there on that barren hilltop?"

Sandy nodded curtly.

Libby picked up a thin bone fragment, not much more than a sliver, and examined it. "What's the point in studying something this tiny?" she asked with genuine curiosity, ignoring the coldness of the girl's reaction. "What can you learn from these little bones?"

Sandy hesitated, torn between her dislike of Libby and her desire to talk about something that clearly meant a lot to her. Finally her professionalism won out and she said, "You can learn all kinds of things from little bones. We assume that these are animals they were eating, so we can find out what kind of diet these people had, what cooking methods they were using, what tools they used and even how prosperous they were as a society. For instance, look at this particular piece...."

She went on, warming to her subject, while Libby listened in fascination and Tim returned to his methodical task, shoveling soil onto a big screen. Before long, flattered by Libby's attention and her eager questions, Sandy began to relax a little, even smiled cautiously. Libby returned the smile.

"You're obviously an expert, Sandy," she said. "I'm really impressed. I had no idea that these little things could tell such a story."

Sandy shook her head. "I'm not an expert," she said. "Far from it. I'm just a student, and there's so much to learn. Warren, now, he can pick up something like this—" she indicated a little scrap of rock, sharpened on one side to a keen knife edge "—and he can talk to you for an hour about it, telling you how it was made and how it was used and where the rock came from and how old it's likely to be—"

She broke off awkwardly, flushing and biting her lip. Libby looked at her with compassion, seeing all too well how even the mention of Warren's name caused the girl pain. And, at the same time, she noticed how Tim, across the screen, had grown very silent while Sandy spoke about the senior archaeologist. Tim's broad shoulders were tense, his young face bleak and unhappy.

Lots of undercurrents here, Libby thought. All kinds of problems...

She forced herself to keep her voice light, glancing around as if in idle interest. "Speaking of Warren," she said casually, "where is he, anyhow?"

"Up on the cliff," Tim said, jerking his head toward the ledge that reared above them. "He's charting the pet-roglyph."

"Oh, I see." Libby hesitated, once again uncomfortably aware of all the powerful tides of emotion that surged around them. "Well, do you think he'd mind very much if I interrupted him for a minute? I'd like to ask him something."

Tim turned and grinned at her. "I think," he said with a warm, significant smile, "that he'd be *really* happy to see you."

Sandy tensed beside the screen, gripping a stone awl rigidly in her hand and staring down at the coarse mesh surface.

"Sandy," Libby said gently, waiting for the girl to look up.

"Yes?" Sandy murmured almost inaudibly.

"This must be awfully hard for you," Libby said.

"Why?" Sandy jerked her head up and stared at Libby, her jaw squared, her blue eyes flashing dangerously. "Why should anything be hard for *me*?"

"Well, because living conditions are pretty rugged out

here,'' Libby said in that same gentle tone, indicating the two tents and the makeshift clothesline. ''And I'm sure you must crave a deep hot bath and a hair wash every now and then. Why don't you come over to the ranch house one of these days and spend the night? I'd like the company, and I'll bet you'd love to have the bathroom all to yourself for a couple of hours.''

The blond girl stared at her, her eyes widening in surprise, her wary expression softening while Libby looked back with a quiet smile. ''Thanks,'' Sandy said at last, dropping her eyes and letting little piles of silt fall aimlessly through her fingers onto the face of the screen. ''That's…that's really nice of you.''

''Well,'' Libby said, ''don't just say that and then forget about it. I really want you to come. Maybe,'' she added, ''I can drive out one evening after you finish work and pick you up.''

Sandy smiled awkwardly at her again, and Libby was struck once more by the girl's attractiveness.

No wonder Tim has that look in his eyes when he watches her, Libby thought. And she's really nice, too. She's just been cool to me because she's so jealous.…

Libby turned aside, marveling in passing at the endless complications and problems that people created in their lives in the name of love.

Not for me, she thought resolutely. I can get along very well without all *that* misery.…

She flashed a last smile at the two young people, tossed her rein over a low branch nearby and began to climb the steep cliff face while they stood down at the base by the screen, watching her in silence.

The wind tugged at her hair and sang in her ears as she climbed, and her soul lifted joyously, filled with a rich cascade of music and breathless anticipation. This was all familiar to her, the same feeling that she always experienced as she climbed toward the stone circles.

But, as she ascended into the glowing sun, she wondered if some of her exultation now was also because Warren McIntyre was on the high crest of land, waiting for her inside the ancient circle of stone.

She topped the ridge of waving grass and hesitated, pausing to adjust her eyes to the midday light that washed over the flat, elevated expanse. Warren stood in front of the painted, patterned monolith at the center of the formation with his back to her, not yet aware of her presence. Libby shaded her eyes with her hand and studied his lean, muscular body, wondering what it was about him that made her feel so strange, so trembly and excited and warm.

He turned, caught sight of her and smiled in delight, his cheeks creasing, his dark eyes flashing a welcome. Then he tucked his clipboard under his arm and came rapidly across the grassy surface toward her while she waited silently. He wore a white T-shirt that accentuated the darkness of his hair and eyes and the rich tan of his muscular forearms. Faded jeans hugged his lean hips, and his feet were light and comfortable in a pair of fitted deerskin moccasins that laced snugly around his ankles.

Once again Libby had the disturbing impression of a virile young Indian brave, his step lithe and sinuous, his movements silent and powerful. She remembered her dream of a few nights earlier and the vivid intensity with which she had experienced his hands on her, his passionate hungry kiss, his lean, powerful body pressing against hers....

Once more she blushed at her own thoughts, but her face was already delicately warm from the exertion of the climb, and she hoped that he wouldn't notice her discomfort. She forced her voice to remain cool and detached as she greeted him.

"So," he said, taking her arm happily and drawing her toward the massive picture rock, "to what do I owe this pleasure?"

"I was out riding, checking fences," Libby said, dismayed by the way her heart raced just at the feeling of his hand on her bare arm. "And I thought I'd stop by and see how you're doing."

He looked down at her, dark eyes thoughtful, straight black hair falling across his tanned forehead above the calico headband.

"So," he said finally, "is it a neighborly call or a scouting foray into enemy territory?"

Libby laughed awkwardly. "Maybe a little of each," she confessed.

"Well, whatever your motivation, Libby, it's good to see you. *Really* good," he added significantly, his eyes wandering over her shining hair, her sunny yellow shirt and the curving, slender body beneath it.

"What are you doing up here this morning?" Libby asked, falling into step beside him and moving into the circles of stone.

"Diagrams," he said briefly. "Here, let me show you."

He drew out his clipboard, held it up and flipped out a few pages. The papers were covered with careful, beautifully detailed scale replicas of the face of the picture rock. Warren was occupied with reproducing the hundreds of figures carved into the stone, rendering them in neat black outline on the pages.

Libby stared at his work in awe, moving closer to peer at the face of the rock and then back again to study the sketches. "That's amazing," she breathed. "Just amazing."

"What is, Libby?"

"The way you bring it to life. I mean," she went on earnestly, looking up at him, her eyes very green in the noonday sunlight, "I've been coming here ever since I can remember and looking at this rock. And except for a few of the obvious things, like the sun up there and the hands and these little arrows, I could never really see anything in it but a lot of lines and squiggles."

He grinned. "That's why I went to school for seven years, Libby. To get my eye trained to interpret these things."

She nodded thoughtfully, returning to her study of the diagrams and the rock face. "This is wonderful. Now that it's delineated on paper I can see so much more—the little horses, and the other animals, and the people... What's this?"

"I'm not sure. I think it represents the moon in various phases."

"Oh," Libby murmured again, oblivious to everything, even the warm admiration in Warren's eyes as he watched her. "And this? It's repeated quite a few times."

"I'm assuming that's a pronghorn antelope. See the belly markings, and the little characteristic jut of horn?"

"I see," she said with rising excitement. "And it's all tied together, right? Here's a flight of arrows, and here's the little half moon, and here's the group of men...so this means that they went hunting on a certain day...?"

"Not necessarily. I mean, that's what people have always assumed, but I'm not so sure that I buy it."

"Why not?"

"Well, think about it," Warren said. "Look at this rock. It's not easy to create lasting images on a surface like this. If you tried it, like I have, you'd learn that very quickly. And this is obviously a special place, right? I mean, it's the highest point of land for miles around, and the rocks have been laid out with great care.''

He was warming to his subject, his dark eyes shining with enthusiasm, his mobile face animated as he explained his theory to her. Libby smiled, moved in spite of herself by the man's overwhelming physical appeal.

"And," she said softly, "it feels like pure magic when you stand here inside the central circle. It feels like a special, wonderful, enchanted place.''

"Yes," he said, smiling down at her. "It feels like magic. Although I can't very well put that in any of my reports. But there's still no doubt at all that this was a place of very special significance and importance to whoever used it. And something like a little story about the day's hunt—don't you think that's kind of petty to be inscribed here?''

Libby stared at the big stone face with its colorful splashes of lichen, reaching out a thoughtful fingertip to touch one of the tiny symbols. "You're right," she said finally. "It would be sacrilege to put something ordinary and everyday up there. It would be like…like graffiti in a cathedral.''

"Exactly," he said, delighted by her understanding. "So, what do you think it is?''

"I don't know," Warren said. "I've studied a lot of these petroglyph sites, though never anything as fabulous as this one. But I tend to think it has some kind of religious significance, that these stone circles were places of worship—''

"That's what I've always felt!" Libby interrupted him in excitement. "Ever since I was a little girl, this felt awesome and sacred to me up here, like a kind of church. And maybe the pictures," she went on, frowning at them in concentration, "maybe they're like a kind of Bible, do you think? Symbols of stories, like our Old Testament, that interpret scriptural laws to people—''

She broke off, startled by the intensity of his gaze. He was staring down at her, his dark eyes burning with an emotion so tangible that she trembled to look at him.

''So,'' she said with forced casualness, turning back to the patterned rock face, ''you think these figures are all symbolic? That they're allegorical and tell some kind of story?''

''Yes. That's what I think.''

''Could I see the biggest diagram again, please, Warren?''

He handed her the sheet he had been working on when she came up the hill. ''It's not finished,'' he said. ''I was just trying to put together a composite from all the little areas I've mapped in detail. But it'll take a long time to have the whole picture.''

Libby studied the mass of tiny figures and symbols, troubled by some nagging thought or impression just below the surface of her consciousness that she couldn't seem to catch. It had something to do with these little pictures, and with something Warren had said....

But the fleeting thought was too elusive to capture. Maybe later when she was alone and far away from his disturbing presence she could isolate the idea and give it some substance. Just now, while he was so near, she could hardly remember her own name....

She looked up at him. ''I suppose,'' she said slowly, ''that there's no doubt at all now about the importance of the site.''

He returned her look steadily. ''None at all.''

''So what happens next?''

''I don't really know yet. What happens next will depend on a lot of things, Libby.''

She stared up at him, troubled and angered by the feeling that facts were being kept from her, that everybody else knew more about what was going on than she did. Even Mac had seemed troubled and evasive the last time she spoke with him, as if even *he* was keeping some private information from her.

"Mainly, though, it all depends on what you say in your report," Libby pointed out.

"Libby," he said, still in that same grave, quiet voice, "nothing in my report is likely to discourage a major study and development of this site. Not unless I file a false report, and I'm not going to do that. Not even for your sake, or my own."

"Not even for your own sake?" she asked, puzzled. "How would it be in *your* best interests to file a false report?"

"Because," he said, "I'm afraid of how you're going to react to all this. Believe it or not, I understand how you feel, and I genuinely hate doing anything to upset you. But that's still not enough to make me file a false report. To me, professionalism takes precedence over everything else, and it always will. I couldn't call myself a scientist if I were to behave otherwise."

Libby nodded. "I understand. That's pretty clear, I guess. Unless…"

"Unless what?"

"Unless there really were another site, as I said the other day, that could distract all you government people from this one on our land."

"Libby, I wish you'd tell me more about this other site."

"Never mind," she said hastily. "Forget it. I'd better be getting home. I have a lot to do this afternoon. The vet's coming out to vaccinate the yearlings, and I have to—''

"Libby," he interrupted her.

"Yes?"

"Libby, can I come by tonight and see you later in the evening?"

"I don't think... I really don't think that's a good idea, Warren. I have to get to bed early tonight because I'm going to be...doing something tomorrow. I mean, I have to get up really early."

He nodded, his dark eyes unfathomable, and walked with her to the edge of the cliff. All the way down Libby could feel those dark eyes burning into her back. She shivered in the warmth of the noonday sun.

At least she hadn't been lying to him, she thought as she gathered up her reins, mounted the skittish little bay and exchanged a few words with Tim and Sandy before reining around and heading back toward the ranch. She *was* going to be getting up early, and she was going to be very busy tomorrow.

Libby was heading out, at first light of dawn, into the wilds of the community pasture to hunt for Mac's fabled petroglyph site.

And she was going alone.

CHAPTER FOUR

THE NEXT MORNING Libby drove through the damp, chill hush that shrouded the prairie just before dawn, casting an occasional worried glance out the truck window at a wide, swirling band of cloud along the horizon.

At this time of year rain was more likely on the prairie than at any other season, increasing the chances of her having an accident or of her horse slipping and maiming itself. And she hated the idea of being stranded in a place as isolated as the community pasture, especially when she was all alone and nobody knew where she'd gone.

But, just as she began to feel really concerned, the pale morning sun slipped above the smudge of cloud, unfurling a carpet of glittering light across the dewy, waving grass. Libby's spirits lifted and she rolled the window down, breathing deep of the fresh scent of damp earth and sage, enjoying the wild, joyous chorus of bird song that rose from the carpet of grass spreading all around her.

The broad expanse of land was utterly still, except for the birds. There were no people anywhere, no other vehicles on the narrow dirt trail winding off toward the edge of the earth. Occasionally she passed little groups of sleeping cattle, placid, humped shapes in the misty light of dawn. In the lightening sky to the east a lone golden eagle circled on wide, silent wings, scanning the ground with needle-sharp eyes, watching for the tiny movements of small scurrying rodents in the tall grass.

Libby's eyes followed the eagle for a moment. She smiled, thinking how much she loved this wild, open land, how painfully she missed it when she was working in the city. In her job she dealt all the time with the pain and suffering that resulted from social interactions, and it was such a blessed relief to be away from people altogether, free and solitary on these wide plains where she had grown up....

Libby cast a glance back at the horse trailer rolling smoothly along behind the big ranch truck where her favorite horse rode quietly, his head down, munching hay in his manger as he traveled. She pulled up by a gate in a stout four-wire fence, got out to open it and stood gazing off at the limitless sweep of land that constituted the community pasture.

She was about twenty miles from her own home and ten miles from the nearest neighbor. The pasture that she now entered was a rough, irregular tract of land, approximately two hundred square miles in area, spanning deep coulees and ravines and bisected by a winding, swift-running creek fed by underground springs that carried water through the pasture even in the driest years.

But despite the rich grazing and the constant water supply, this land had never been homesteaded, mostly because the sandy soil was so prone to wind erosion. The surface was brutally rough, impassable in many places to any type of vehicle, with deep, sheer ditches gouged out by the wind, and high sand dunes that reared up toward the sky, stark and gleaming in the prairie sun.

Libby had always loved the community pasture, responding on some deep level to the wildness and mystery of the place. Since earliest childhood she had looked forward to their visits here, to the times when she and Gray and Peggy would trail their cattle in for the summer and then ride back in the fall along with the other ranchers to gather the herds, then separate their own cattle and take them home, riding slowly behind the grazing cattle through the rugged valleys in golden autumn sunlight.

But this wasn't autumn. It was early summer, and it wasn't a cheerful community gathering at the pasture. In fact, it was the first time that Libby had ever been out here all alone, without family or neighbors, and she shivered suddenly at the feeling of barren isolation. The world seemed so vast and silent, the horizon so far away, the rough tract of brush-covered prairie so closed and forbidding in the early-morning chill.

With quick resolution she hurried back into her truck, pulled it through and fastened the gate behind her and then drove into a clump of scrub poplar near the fence so that her truck and trailer would be concealed while she was riding.

Not that anybody ever passed this way for months on end, but she still dreaded the possibility, however remote, of being seen and having to explain to some curious rancher just what she was doing.

Still moving rapidly, Libby unloaded her big bay gelding, patted him cheerfully and threw on her saddle and tack. After a moment's thought and another worried glance at the wide scarf of pearl-gray that shrouded the horizon, she tied a long yellow slicker behind her saddle and tucked her lunch and a thermos into a waterproof pouch in one of the saddlebags.

Finally she swung gracefully up into the saddle, settled herself and wheeled the bay gently to the north, starting off at an easy rocking canter toward the distant place where the gilded prairie grass rolled up into a dull silver sky.

As she rode, Libby scanned the horizon constantly,

squinting at distant landforms, at gullies and hills and ravines, looking for high plateaus similar to the bare hilltop
on her family's land where the Singing Stones were located.

The task was difficult here in the community pasture
because it wasn't at all a flat, uniform tract of land like
much of the surrounding prairie. Here deep coulees fell
away at her horse's feet with startling suddenness, dense
brush and clumps of stunted trees dotted the landscape
and sandy hills sculpted by the wind thrust sharply upward from the surface of the prairie.

Knowing the treachery of this terrain, Libby rode cautiously, watching for badger holes and other depressions
in the light soil, frowning at the irregular sweep of land
around her. After about a mile she urged the bay up a
steep, grassy bluff, pausing on the summit to search
among the gnarled sagebrush for stone circles and then
reining in to scan the surrounding countryside.

From this high place she could see the land that spread
for miles around in rugged emptiness, an expanse of deep
coulees and high, barren cliffs, any one of which might
be hiding the secret she was looking for.

Libby sat her horse silently, gazing at the isolated land,
feeling a growing misery and hopelessness. She bit her
lip and frowned, trying to remember Mac's exact words,
wishing she had pressed him for more details about the
location of the fabled petroglyph site. But she knew that
it would have been dangerous to do so. Mac was perceptive, and if he even suspected that she intended to come
out here looking, he'd do something to stop her, like calling her father or telling Warren McIntyre....

The wind rose and began to whine and howl through
the tall grass, swirling around the big horse's white-
stockinged, dancing legs and touching Libby's face and

hair with icy fingers. A few drops of rain spattered on the pommel of her saddle and glistened in the bay's dark mane.

Libby shivered with sudden cold and a growing, nameless fear. Reaching behind her hastily, she untied the saddle strings and shook out her long waterproof coat. She slipped it on, grateful for its enclosing warmth, and arranged the full divided skirt so that it fell neatly on either side of the saddle, covering her blue-jeaned legs and boots.

Then she pulled her battered old gray Stetson lower over her eyes, rode slowly down the hill and headed her horse relentlessly north toward the distant horizon.

BY LATE AFTERNOON the rain had settled into a steady drizzle, carried on a snarling wind that shivered and moaned through the groves of stunted trees. Libby rode slowly, weary and chilled to the bone, uncertain of directions under the lowering sky.

In her long day of riding she had seen so many hills and valleys, so many gnarled trees and massive boulders and bends in the creek that she had lost all sense of orientation. Familiar landmarks no longer served as guides, and she was forced to give the horse his head, trusting him to find his way back to the entry road where she had parked the truck.

Libby slumped over the saddle horn, rocking unconsciously to the gentle canter of the big horse's long, easy gait, fighting off a growing sense of miserable hopelessness. Back home in the sunny ranch house her plan had seemed so easy. She would simply ride the community pasture, methodically search out all the highest points of land, climb them one by one until she discovered the stone formations and then take Warren McIntyre there in triumph.

Libby frowned at the gray sky above her, thinking about her fears and concerns. The worst thing, she thought, was that she wasn't even certain those fears were justified. Nobody—not Warren, or Alexandra Coleman, not even Mac—would come right out and tell her what was happening. Nevertheless, she sensed instinctively that there was going to be a problem, had sensed it ever since her first conversation with Warren McIntyre up on that sunny, barren hilltop among the Singing Stones.

Libby moved restlessly in her saddle, thinking about tourists and interpretive centers, about similar government facilities she had seen, with their cafeterias and film theaters, their washrooms and picnic tables and hiking trails. She shuddered and leaned to pat the horse's damp neck absently, as if in search of a little warmth and comfort.

Gray would be so upset with trails and roads winding across his land, and hundreds of tourists wandering around with their Bermuda shorts and expensive cameras, climbing through fences, getting lost, scaring the cattle....

"Oh, God," Libby muttered aloud in helpless misery.

Her big horse pricked his ears in sympathy and slowed to a gentle trot, rocking easily through the rainy afternoon light.

Libby understood, of course, that there was no simple solution to this problem that had dropped so suddenly into the peaceful solitude of her summer. Even if she found the other site, there was no assurance that the government would then abandon their plans for the Lyndon property. In fact, Warren had already indicated that a major study would still go ahead on the Stones, probably for years.

But if there was even a remote chance that the most threatening part of the plan, the massive tourist facilities and public access, could be moved to another site, leaving the Singing Stones just to the archaeologists and scientists, then it was worth any effort. And Warren had certainly hinted that if another site were found, that would likely be the case.

Libby smiled grimly. Through her job associations, she knew a lot about the strange subterranean workings of government, enough to know that the only real certainty was uncertainty in all things. But she was alone in this situation, with a crushing responsibility to do whatever she could to protect her family's property.

And all that she could do, the only thing she could think of, was to find the other site.

She had no doubt at all that the ancient stones existed somewhere in the pasture. The early settlers here on this rugged land had been practical, no-nonsense people, and local folklore was never wrong about things like the rumored stone circles. The problem was simply that finding them wasn't going to be nearly as easy as she had first thought.

For one thing, there were high points of land everywhere, and treacherously changing landscapes that seemed to alter as you looked at them. Every hill looked like a possible site for a stone grouping, but there were hundreds of them that had to be scaled and searched. On this rugged terrain it would be a formidable task for dozens of people on horseback, let alone one solitary woman.

There was plenty of evidence of early human occupation in this tract of land that must have been, in past centuries, incredibly rich in game and water. But apart from a few isolated groups of stone teepee rings, just like those scattered everywhere on the prairie, Libby had found nothing faintly resembling what she sought.

She reined the big bay to a walk, patted his neck and

smiled down at him, talking aloud to his alert, twitching ears just to keep her spirits up.

"Well, Scout, do you have any idea where we are? Does any of this look familiar to you? I hope it does," Libby murmured, "because I'm completely lost. I don't know if we're going north, south or straight up."

The tall gelding tossed his head and clanked the bit against his teeth as if trying to reassure her, and Libby smiled bleakly once more.

"Okay, old friend," she said. "Just so long as *one* of us is confident. I'd hate to waste a whole day and then get lost besides."

She spurred the tired horse back to a gentle canter and settled wearily into the easy, swinging rhythm, thinking about Warren McIntyre. Often, when she was tired, the memory of him seemed to creep unbidden into her mind these days, slipping through her thoughts and daydreams like a haunting strain of soft music.

She saw his tanned, intent face wavering against the misty horizon, heard his deep, masculine voice laughing on the wind, felt the cool strength of his lean hands in the rough caress of rain on her cheeks. All at once her body began to ache and yearn with a deep, inexplicable longing, and she roused herself in the saddle, troubled by her own thoughts.

The bay horse quickened his pace. Libby looked ahead and saw gratefully that he had found his way back to the fence and the poplar grove where she had parked the truck. Stiff with fatigue, she slid down, removed the saddle and blanket from the horse's steaming back and gave him a quick rubdown, wrapping him snugly in a heavy body blanket before she loaded him into the warmth and comfort of his portable stall.

She drove the twenty miles back to the ranch house

over rutted prairie trails that were slick and muddy from the rain, maneuvering the big truck and trailer expertly to avoid potholes and washouts. When she arrived, she unloaded her horse, fed and watered him, hugged him briefly and turned him into the small hay meadow near the barn.

Then she hurried through her evening chores, ate a couple of peanut butter sandwiches standing up at the kitchen counter and at long last trudged upstairs to immerse herself blissfully in a deep, steaming bubble bath.

THE BIG RANCH HOUSE bulked large and square against the blackened rainy sky, a few lights glowing dimly behind closed drapes. Warren McIntyre parked his Jeep under the trees and sat with his hands resting on the wheel, gazing up at those lighted windows, thinking about the woman who lived here.

She was such a remarkable, unusual woman, Elizabeth Lyndon, he thought. At first glance she seemed younger than she really was, as shy and beautiful as one of the delicate, lovely flowers that bloomed in rare seclusion on this wild sweep of prairie. But like those same flowers, there was a subtle hidden toughness to her that belied her appearance, that demanded a man's respect and admiration.

And he couldn't deny that there was a purely feminine appeal, as well, a rich womanly sweetness and allure that was all the more devastating because it was largely unconscious.

She doesn't even know how desirable she really is, he thought. And, God help me, I don't know how much longer I'm going to be able to keep my hands off her....

He shifted awkwardly on the hard seat of the Jeep. Then, with sudden decision, he unfolded himself from the small cab, took out a big leather folder and walked with his lithe, springing stride up the walk to the covered veranda.

Libby answered the bell after several minutes and stood looking up at him with big, startled eyes.

Warren gazed back at her, almost overwhelmed by her appearance. Her long red hair wasn't tightly plaited as usual, but gathered loosely in a knot on top of her head, with little fiery tendrils escaping to curl damply around her face. She wore a short white terry-cloth robe belted snugly around her trim waist, and her long, bare legs were beautifully shapely, still warm and pink from her hot bath.

Her wonderful, changeable eyes looked smoky-gray in the dim light of the entrance foyer, smoldering in their dark lashes, and her tanned, delicate face was flushed with embarrassment.

"I'm...I'm sorry," she murmured in a distracted voice. "I thought you must be Alice from the next ranch. She said she might be— Please, come in and I'll just run and change my..."

Warren stared down at her intently, fighting a crazy, overwhelming urge to gather her into his arms, slip the skimpy white robe aside and kiss those beautiful naked shoulders, crush his lips against her sweetly curving mouth.

Finally, seeing how she shifted nervously on her bare feet, he gathered himself in hand, swallowed hard and stepped inside, closing the door gently behind him.

"Sorry," he muttered huskily. "I shouldn't be keeping you standing out here in the cold."

"That's all right," she said in confusion, hesitating beneath the hall light that set her hair afire and cast rich, alluring shadows on her face. "I was just...having a bath," she added unnecessarily. "If you'd like to...to go in and sit down by the fire, I'll throw some clothes on and be back right away.''

Don't go, he wanted to say. Come and sit by the fire with me, sweetheart. Let me slip that robe off. Please, let me look at your beautiful body and touch your skin and try to tell you all the things I'm feeling....

But she was already gone, running lightly up the stairs and disappearing from the upper landing while he gazed after her, his dark eyes sober and intent.

Warren wandered into the big living room, settled himself by the fire and waited. When she returned after a few minutes, wearing her customary blue jeans and plaid shirt, her hair neatly pulled back and braided, there was no trace of the beautiful, shy, half-naked woman who had answered the door. Now she was all business, composed and alert, casting him a cool, wary glance before she seated herself in one of the padded leather armchairs.

"So," she said casually, reaching for a big pillow and holding it on her lap, toying with its fringed edges, "how was your day?"

"Not great," he said. "I couldn't do any digging or mapping because of the rain, so I spent the day in my tent, analyzing core samples."

She nodded absently, avoiding his gaze, her downcast eyelashes forming dark, sweeping shadows on her delicate, high cheekbones.

"How about you?" he asked finally. "How was *your* day?"

"So-so," she said briefly, casting the pillow aside and getting up restlessly to poke the fire.

Warren watched her slender back, the firm curve of her hip in the soft denim as she bent toward the hearth, and his mouth went suddenly dry. "What did you do?" he asked. "Were you out working, even in that rain?"

"I was riding," she said without turning around. "All day."

He nodded. "Libby…" he began, and hesitated.

She looked over her shoulder, casting him a cool, questioning glance.

"Libby, we really have to talk about this," he said, indicating the big leather folder on the floor beside his chair. "About the site, I mean, and what's going to happen there."

"Nothing's going to happen," she said abruptly, coming back to sit opposite him, her eyes level and challenging.

Warren tensed, returning her gaze in silence for a moment. "What do you mean?" he asked at last.

"Just what I said. It's not going to happen, Warren. I just won't allow it, that's all. I'm going to find some way to stop you, no matter what I have to do."

Warren watched her calm, lovely face, stunned by her words. "You can't stop me, Libby," he said finally. "You already know we have every right to—"

"I know all about your rights!" Libby burst out. "Everybody's told me about your rights! You, Alexandra Coleman—even Mac keeps telling me you have every right to do what you're doing. But what about *our* rights, Warren? Who's concerned with protecting our rights?"

"I am," he said quietly. "Whether you believe it or not, I'm very concerned about your family, and particularly about how you, personally, feel in all this. But I don't really see what can be done to change things."

"You can just quit," Libby said stubbornly. "You can tell them whatever you want to…that the site isn't worth developing, and you're going to look somewhere else. All you'd have to do is write one line, and all this horror would just end."

"Libby...I can't do that. You know I can't."

She stared at him, her face dimly illuminated by the flickering glow from the birch logs on the hearth.

"Warren," she began in low, earnest tones, "my great-great-grandfather, Adam Lyndon, homesteaded this land over a hundred years ago. My family has held on to this property through drought, prairie fires, grasshopper plagues, and the Depression, through hoof-and-mouth disease, blizzards and crushing debts—just because it's our home and we love it."

"Nobody's going to take the land away from you, Libby."

"But you might as well be! Nobody will come right out and tell me, but I'm not stupid, you know, Warren. I have a pretty good idea what's going to happen out there. You plan to put in roads, cross our land, crowd us with tourists and destroy our privacy. And I'm telling you, Warren, that it's terrible. It's just completely intolerable."

"And what about the public? What about their right to our shared history and heritage? Libby," he went on, leaning forward earnestly, his dark eyes blazing with conviction, "I haven't got the final results back from the carbon dating, but I'd guess that this particular site dates back almost ten thousand years. That's incredibly ancient by New World standards. And the petroglyph is one of the finest that's ever been discovered on this continent, and the least disturbed. It will take years to study it properly, and it will change all our perceptions of Paleo-Indian religion. It's like another Rosetta Stone, Libby. Should we abandon all this just so the privacy of the Lyndon family can remain undisturbed?"

She stared at him, her eyes strained and enormous, her face white. But before she could answer the phone rang, and Warren watched in silence as she went into the hall to answer it.

"Really?" he heard her ask breathlessly. "Oh, Rob...I don't know what to say. It's so— How much? Oh, *wonderful!* Tell her I'll be in to see her as soon as I can. Thanks, Rob. I'll call them. They're in Italy now. Okay, I'll tell Mac, too. Goodbye, Rob. Tell Peg I love her."

Libby hung up and came back into the living room, her face alight with happiness, her eyes shining like emerald stars in her tanned face, all conflict forgotten for the moment.

"That was my brother-in-law," she said shyly to Warren. "My twin sister, Peggy, just had a baby about an hour ago at the hospital in Calgary. A boy, almost nine pounds."

He smiled down at her, delighting in her obvious pleasure at the news, loving the way her face glowed and softened as she spoke about the baby.

"Your twin?" he asked, still smiling. "Are you identical?"

"Absolutely," she said solemnly.

"My God," he groaned in mock horror. *"Two* of you! Just the thought is enough to make me weak at the knees."

Libby stared at him, startled, and then her eyes began to dance with merriment. She threw her head back and joined in his laughter, her face still flushed with joy and relief over the word of her small nephew's safe arrival.

After a moment Warren's laughter subsided and he gazed down at her intently, reaching out a lean brown hand to grip her arm and draw her gently close to him.

"Libby..." he murmured huskily.

She sobered and met his eyes, moving into his arms with a kind of dreamy reluctance.

He gathered her close, thrilling at the warmth and slender, rounded firmness of her body melting into his like a soft, vivid flame. Her long red hair smelled of rain and sunshine, and her skin was still warm and delicately scented from her bath. His arms tightened around her as he bent his dark head to kiss her glowing hair.

"Libby..." he murmured huskily. "Oh, girl, you're just so..."

She lifted her face, her green eyes looking into his with a sober, unfathomable expression. He kissed her lips, gently at first and then with rising passion, intoxicated by the rich sweetness of that soft, curving mouth that had haunted his mind ever since he'd first seen her.

Her lips parted and he pressed forward, crushing her mouth with his own while his hands began to wander over her beautiful body. Slowly he stroked her long, slender back, her curving waist and firm, rounded hips, stunned by her warm, womanly perfection. Gradually, controlling his urgency with a firm effort of will, he brought his hand up between their straining bodies to cup her breast. She wore no bra beneath her old plaid shirt, and his hand burned at the ample fullness lying heavy against his palm, and the small, firm nipple thrusting beneath the soft fabric.

He moaned soundlessly, lost in desire, still crushing her mouth against his. At last she pulled away from his kiss and shrugged his hand aside, turning her head to bury her face against his shoulder. But she remained in his embrace, her slender, curving body trembling with emotion.

Warren didn't press his advantage. Instead, he held her quietly, patting her back and stroking her hair with tenderness. While she stood unmoving within the strong circle of his arms, he looked over her head at the flickering shadows of firelight on the rich paneled walls of the living room, his dark, sculpted features withdrawn and somber.

He knew he was taking advantage of her at this moment, and he didn't much like himself for it. The woman in his arms wasn't there out of any desire for him. In fact, given her choice she would probably have preferred that he didn't even exist, because he meant nothing but trouble to her. She had been drawn to him just now only out of loneliness, and fear of the future, and a desire to share with someone her joy over the news of her sister's baby....

When she drew away and turned aside to sink down into her chair again, he made no move to stop her. Instead, he sat opposite her, gazing intently at her delicate profile as she stared into the leaping blue and orange flames in the deep hearth.

"Libby," he began gently, "I'm sorry if I was out of line. I think I've made it pretty clear how attractive you are to me, but God knows I don't want to push it. I'm doing enough pushing in your life these days without complicating matters."

She looked directly at him then, and he was stabbed by the depths of emotion in her eyes, the sorrow and confusion and tragic helplessness.

"Oh, Libby..." he whispered, shaken and dismayed. "Libby, please believe me when I say that I—"

"I think," she began in a low, trembling voice, "that you'd better leave now, Warren."

"Won't you just let me—"

"Please, Warren," she said, her voice a little stronger. "Please, just go now, and I'll talk to you again. Please."

"When?" he asked, getting to his feet and picking up his leather folder. He stood in front of her, the firelight flickering on his high, tanned cheekbones and glimmering in his dark eyes. "When will I see you again, Libby?"

"Later in the week," she said, looking away from him. "Some evening when I've caught up on my work. I want…I want to pick Sandy up and bring her over here for the night, just to give her a break from camping."

He looked startled at this, but said nothing.

"And," Libby said, half to herself, "I want to look at that big stone again. I want to look at the pictures on it."

"Why?" he asked. "Why do you want to look at the petroglyph?"

Her cheeks flushed lightly and she shrugged, avoiding his eyes. "No special reason, I guess," she said, trying to keep her voice light. "Except, that if it's going to ruin our lives, I should at least take the trouble to be familiar with it, don't you think?"

He stared at her intently, struck by something in her tone, and in her expression.

But she still refused to meet his eyes. Instead, she got up, walked beside him to the door and said good-night with forced cheerfulness, keeping a careful distance between them.

Warren started his Jeep, stared for a moment at the golden squares of flickering light that were the living room windows, then turned around in a soft spray of mud and gravel and started slowly down the long approach road leading away from the ranch house.

As he drove, peering out into the rain-washed blackness through the rhythmic sweep of the windshield wipers, he battled a whole array of emotions. His powerful male body still pounded and throbbed painfully with desire at the memory of her slender beauty in his arms, the feeling of her soft, heavy breast against his hand. He remembered the wild thrill of her momentary yielding, and the aching disappointment of her withdrawal from him.

But he was deeply troubled by something in her face,

some undertone in her quiet voice when she said she wanted to look at the petroglyph.

Elizabeth Lyndon, Warren thought with a frown of concern on his dark face, had something on her mind. And he realized he was afraid to know what it might be.

CHAPTER FIVE

MALCOLM BURMAN GOT UP from the hard wooden chair beside his kitchen table and stretched briefly, tall and spare in clean faded blue jeans and a soft red plaid shirt. He walked across the small, quiet, brightly lit room, paintbrush in hand, to draw the curtain aside and peer out the window into the darkness.

Mrs. Brown, his old collie dog, who lay on a battered sheepskin jacket near the door, opened one eye and watched him, her feathery tail thumping softly on the floor in silent adoration.

"Still raining," Mac reported to her without turning around. "I hope that ugly spotted hog has those new little fellers all bedded down and dry."

Mrs. Brown yawned hugely in reply, her muzzle opening to reveal the cavernous depths of her pink, black-spotted mouth. Then she closed her eyes, rested her chin on her paws and went back to sleep.

Mac turned from the window, watching the drowsy old dog with a smile and thinking about the new batch of little pigs. He liked the mental picture of them, all cozy and cuddled in warm beds of straw, bedding down with happy little squeals and grunts of pleasure while the rain lashed and pounded on the weathered roof of their snug old shelter.

Briefly Mac considered taking the flashlight and going over to the shed just to look at them and have a little philosophical chat with Hiram, his favorite pig. But the cold, snarling rain, driven on a chilly east wind, discouraged the thought.

Instead he moved over to his small refrigerator, took out a bottle of white wine and poured a drink into a daintily stemmed crystal wineglass that stood on the counter by the sink. Then, carrying the goblet carefully, he returned to the table and seated himself, dipped his paintbrush in a jar of murky water and rolled it thoughtfully into a block of powdered umber.

He frowned at the square of watercolor paper tacked to a small easel on the table and began to apply the warm, earthen color to a patch of melting snow near a shining expanse of water misted with thin blue ice. His gentle, weathered face was thoughtful and serene as he worked, his finely shaped bald head shining in the glow of the overhead light. The only sound in the snug room was the rhythmic swish of Mac's brush, the gentle snuffling noises of Mrs. Brown's contented sleep and the pattering of the night rain against the windows.

Mac was so absorbed in his work that he was badly startled when the outside door suddenly flew open, admitting a gust of cold night air and a tall young man in a wet denim jacket.

"Keith!" Mac exclaimed, jumping a little. "I didn't know you were here. I didn't hear your truck."

"Sorry if I scared you, Mac. I left my truck down in the Quonset," the young man explained briefly. "I just got back from Montana, stopped in to see Lib for a minute and then came right down here. I have to leave before six tomorrow morning."

"Well, get out of those wet things before you catch pneumonia."

Mac watched fondly as Keith shrugged out of his

jacket, tossed it onto a hook by the door and dropped a heavy, damp rucksack beside Mrs. Brown, who opened her eyes indignantly, struggled to her feet with a weary, martyred air and sidled indignantly into the living room.

The broad-shouldered, muscular young man in the warm kitchen bore little resemblance, Mac thought, to the thin, rebellious boy who had arrived on this doorstep with his mother five years earlier at a bad time in all of their lives. Now, at twenty, Keith McLean was living a life he loved, attending college in the winter and spending his summers on the rodeo circuit, traveling from Texas to Alaska while his mother Jo, who was also Libby's step-mother and Mac's favorite niece, tried hard not to worry too much about him.

Keith had moved with his mother to the Lyndon ranch when she married Gray Lyndon. But he had been careful to leave a number of his possessions behind him at his Uncle Mac's place and, over the years, had established himself in the comfortable position of having two homes, dividing his time between them to suit his own pleasure and convenience.

Mac watched as Keith picked up a towel hanging at the end of the counter, scrubbed it vigorously through his dark, springing curls and then headed for the refrigerator. The boy balanced a tall, heavy glass mug of milk in one hand, drinking it in great gulps as he built a gargantuan sandwich with his free hand. Masses of cold cuts, sliced tomato, mayonnaise and pickle soon littered the counter.

Mac eyed the welter of food with a gentle, ironic smile. "Do you need a little help with that, son?"

"No problem, Mac." Keith stuffed the corner of the sandwich into his mouth, tore it off and chewed hugely. "I'll clean this all up later," he said between bites. "I'm just starving, Mac. Haven't eaten for three hundred miles.''

Like most rodeo cowboys, Keith tended to reckon elapsed time in distance rather than hours, because he was constantly on the move.

He finished the sandwich and began immediately to construct another, while Mac looked on with undisguised affection.

"Well, how did you do?" Mac asked finally, leaning back in his chair and stretching the muscles in his long back.

"Pretty good. Third in the bareback and day money in the bull riding. I drew Widowmaker this afternoon," Keith added with his mouth full. "He spins real hard to the right. Hardly anybody ever rides him."

"So I've heard," Mac said dryly. "Your mother still hates it when you ride bulls, you know," he added, squinting thoughtfully at his painting.

"Yeah, I know," Keith agreed cheerfully. "But she's a lot better than she used to be. Gray keeps her from getting too crazy. Besides," he added with obvious satisfaction, bending to peer into the refrigerator again, "she's in France or Italy or someplace right now."

"Venice," Mac said with a dreamy, faraway smile as he picked up his paintbrush again.

"Whatever," Keith said, lifting out the remains of a deep-dish apple pie and examining it with warm approval. The boy turned, pie in hand, and glanced at Mac's painting, frowning with sudden interest. "Hey, Mac, that's the slough in the upper pasture," he announced.

"It is indeed," Mac agreed serenely.

"Didn't you paint a picture of that slough last year? I remember going out with you to take pictures of it."

"I did," Mac said. "I sold it."

"So how come you're doing it again? I thought you never painted the same thing twice."

"That was a spring scene," Mac said calmly. "This is a winter thaw." He bent forward, his face concentrated, adding a wispy edge of shining turquoise to a ragged patch of ice at the edge of the water.

Keith glanced at the older man with sudden suspicion, disturbed by something strange in Mac's voice, a different look in those vivid blue eyes. He began to say something, thought better of it and returned his attention to the pie, taking a carton of ice cream from the freezer and adding a mammoth scoop to his dessert.

"How's Peggy?" Mac asked, tracing a delicate reflection of blue sky in a melting silver pool.

"Just great, I guess. Still in the hospital. Lib says she's going into Calgary tomorrow to see her and the baby."

Mac smiled in pleasure, and Keith paused, flapping his free hand, rendered momentarily speechless by a massive forkful of pie and ice cream. When he was capable of coherence, he continued.

"Rob says the kid looks just like you, Mac. Bald and handsome."

Mac chuckled and went on working quietly while Keith stared at the little watercolor, still curious.

"How come—?" he began.

"How's Libby feeling today?" Mac asked to forestall further questioning about his painting.

"She's acting kind of weird," Keith said. "I can't figure out how come."

"She's worried," Mac said calmly, wetting his big brush and feathering a subtle pearl-gray wash across the horizon.

"Yeah?" Keith asked. "What about?"

"About the archaeological team in the West Five. Didn't she say anything to you?"

Keith frowned, his fork halfway to his mouth. "She just said they were looking at the stone circles up there and that there might be some kind of government study or something."

"There's likely going to be a lot more than that," Mac said. "And I'm sure Libby knows it."

"More? What do you mean, Mac?"

"I talked to the lady who—" Mac hesitated, his weathered cheeks reddening a little while Keith stared at him in surprise.

Mac took a hasty sip of wine and continued, his voice deliberately brisk. "I talked to the developmental consultant for the project. They're planning a year-round tourist interpretive center up there with a resident staff. And I think the young archaeologist who's working at the site has more or less told Libby what's going to happen."

Keith was staring, his boyish face aghast, his blue eyes dark with anger. "They can't do that! Gray isn't even *home!*"

"They can do whatever they like," Mac said mildly. "They're the government."

"God," Keith said as he moved around the little kitchen, cleaning up the mess made by his late-night snack. "No wonder Lib was upset."

Mac was silent, staring at his painting and trying to decide if a small antelope near the edge of the slough would make it too cluttered.

"Well, they can't do it," Keith said darkly. "When I get back from these next rodeos, I'll talk to Libby. We'll damn sure think of some way to stop them."

Mac glanced sharply at his hotheaded young nephew. "Now, Keith, don't you go and—"

"Don't worry, Mac," the boy said, putting away the damp dishcloth and smiling grimly. "Don't you worry a bit. I have to get some sleep," he added. "It's a long drive tomorrow."

Keith strode from the kitchen and clattered down the basement stairs to his room while Mac sat in troubled silence, his gentle, kindly face full of concern. Finally he shook his head and went back to work, his thoughts returning, as they always did these days, to Alexandra Coleman. Smiling, Mac pictured her tanned, alert features, her fine gray eyes and the way the warm laugh lines rayed out from them, creasing whenever she was amused.

Alexandra Coleman would like an antelope in the painting, Mac decided. She'd look at it with pleasure every morning, a little touch of wilderness and mystery on the wall where she worked, trapped in that gray, bustling city....

Still smiling, he selected a fine-bristled sketching brush and began to outline the dainty form of the antelope with quick, skillful strokes.

While Mac worked, the image of her lingered hauntingly in his mind, every detail of her face and form etched indelibly on his artist's memory.

He loved everything about her.

Apart from the neighbors that he had always known, Mac had had few encounters with women during his shy and secluded life. They always made him feel awkward and tongue-tied, anxious to be away and on his own where he could be comfortable again.

But Alexandra Coleman was somehow different. Though he felt shy in her presence, he also felt strangely at ease, as if he could tell her anything and she would understand. He had only had two brief conversations with her, once in her office and once over at the archaeological site when he went to talk with Warren. But there had been something in her face, in the alertness of her warm gray eyes and the gentle intelligence of her smile that told Mac she was a kindred spirit....

And she lived alone. He knew that because he had asked Warren casually one day while he was visiting the archaeological site. Warren said that her husband, an Alberta oil man, had been killed many years ago in an accident at a drilling rig, and Alex had never remarried.

Suddenly, thinking of her solitude and his own, Mac was engulfed by a wave of terrible loneliness, a desolate, shattering surge of longing that swept through him and left him chilled and empty.

He looked at his painting in growing dissatisfaction. The work was going well, and it made him feel closer to her somehow to be doing this thing for her, although she would never know who the artist was.

But it wasn't enough. He had to think of something else, something that would satisfy this deep, insistent urge to express himself to her without the terrifying necessity of revealing his identity. Some way to make Alexandra Coleman understand how he felt about her, and what kind of man he was....

Mac worked on in thoughtful silence, detailing the graceful antelope that stood drinking from the shining slough. Impulsively he added another antelope, a larger, stronger one that stood just behind, head up, sniffing the wind, protecting the beautiful little doe at the water's edge.

Lost in his dreams, drowning in loneliness and deeply, painfully in love for the first time in his shy and private existence, Mac sketched quietly while the rain murmured against the blackened windowpanes and the chill prairie wind sobbed and whispered around the eaves of his snug little house.

SUMMER SUNLIGHT SPILLED through the wide hospital windows, lighting Peggy Simmons's red hair so that it blossomed like a rich flame against the stark white pillows.

Libby sat in a hard chair beside the bed, smiling at her twin sister. When they were girls, she and Peggy had always worn their hair long, and during their adolescence, Peggy's had been a wild, fiery mane held back, usually, by a vivid, dramatic headband. Now, though, as befitted Peggy's dignified new status as young wife and mother, she had her hair cropped sensibly short so that it curled aggressively all around her beautiful face.

In the crook of her arm, Robert Lyndon Simmons lay in a warm, blanket-wrapped bundle, frowning fiercely and gnawing with silent intensity on his fist. Libby leaned forward, gazing in wondering pleasure at the indignant little red face, the tiny wrinkled hand and almost invisible gingery fluff on his rounded head.

"See? Red hair," Peggy said with satisfaction, lifting back the blanket. "I always knew our genes would be dominant."

Libby thought suddenly of Warren McIntyre and his Mohawk grandmother, and her tanned cheeks grew warm.

Peggy shot a quick, alert glance at her sister, who carefully avoided the changeable green eyes that were identical to her own and reached out a shy hand to touch the baby.

"Just look at his *hands*, Peg," she breathed. "Aren't they just the most beautiful hands you've ever seen?"

"The hands of an artist or musician," Peggy agreed placidly. "Although Rob says they're made for keyboard-

ing. And *I* say,'' she added with a grin, ''that one computer freak in the family is enough. Here, Lib, do you
want to hold him?''

Reverently, Libby cradled the warm little body of her
nephew, lifting him into her arms and burying her face
against him, breathing in his milky, powdery fragrance.
''He's so sweet,'' she murmured, entranced. ''He's just
so sweet.''

Libby, who had so recently been delighting in her freedom and the breadth of her horizons, now felt a sharp stab
of yearning as she gazed down at the drowsy baby against
her breast, and a sudden, deep envy of her sister's domestic happiness and contentment.

Peggy glanced at her twin again in thoughtful silence,
then turned aside, fingering the glossy leaves on the single
long-stemmed white rose in a bud vase on her nightstand.
''So,'' she said casually, ''what's up?''

Libby looked over at her, still cuddling and rocking the
baby in her arms. ''Pardon?''

''Come on, Libby. You never were any good at keeping
things from me, and you haven't changed that much, you
know. You're still as honest and transparent as you were
when we were in kindergarten. And you've got something
on your mind.''

''I told you, Peg. I'm worried about this archaeological
team on our land. I'm afraid they're going to—''

''And I told you to forget it,'' Peggy said comfortably.
''No matter what they've told you, I still don't believe
they can go ahead and do anything major without Dad's
permission as the landowner. And they're sure never going to get *that*,'' she added with a grin.

Libby nodded uncertainly, reaching down with a gentle,
tanned hand to adjust the blanket around Robert Simmons's fat little chin.

"Besides," Peggy went on cheerfully, looking at her red-faced baby with frank adoration, "Rob says the government always takes ten years to do *anything*, so you don't have to be brooding about it every minute, Lib. Nothing's going to happen this year."

"I guess you're right," Libby said, gazing back at her sister with troubled eyes, "Warren—he's the archaeologist who's doing the research—says that…"

But Peggy wasn't interested in scientific analysis. Her concerns were much more practical, feminine and immediate. Seeing Libby's momentary faltering, she pounced instantly. "Warren! Finally we're getting to what's *really* on your mind. Just who is this Warren, pray tell?"

"I told you," Libby said, irritated by the warm, telltale flush that crept over her cheeks again. "Warren McIntyre. He's the archaeologist who's working on our—"

"You've got the hots for him," Peggy said.

Libby stared at her sister, aghast. "I do *not*," she protested. "I never said a *word* about—"

"You didn't have to," Peggy said placidly. "You can't hide something like that from me, kid. I can tell just by the look in your eyes."

"That's ridiculous," Libby said stiffly, looking down at her tiny nephew and smoothing his blanket with shaking fingers.

"Wow," Peggy remarked, gazing at her sister in awe, completely unruffled by her furious reaction. "This guy must be some incredibly gorgeous hunk if he can even make the Lofty Lady Libby melt into a puddle."

"Now look here!" Libby began in outrage. "I don't know what makes you think *you're* so damn—"

"Forget it," Peggy said serenely with an infuriating little smile. "Forget I ever said anything. As far as we're concerned, this...*Warren*—'' she lingered over the name, grinning significantly at Libby, who glared back at her, green eyes flashing ''—this guy is just some boring little fat pink scientist type with a bald head, right? And speaking of guys who look like that, I think my son is getting hungry.''

Libby handed the squirming baby over to her sister, still fuming. ''You *always* do this,'' she said through tight lips. ''Nobody else in the world can make me so mad that I'd just like to—''

''You love me. You can't help it,'' Peggy said serenely. ''We're identical twins. We're two halves of the same person.''

''Don't remind me,'' Libby muttered, and then relented and smiled faintly as Peggy opened her nightgown, baring a creamy breast to her tiny Robert, who immediately fastened himself in position and began to nurse lustily.

Peggy gazed down at her son, patting his small, heaving back with dreamy tenderness. Libby watched the two of them, smiling mistily, her anger evaporating in another wave of love and strange, troubled yearning.

ALEXANDRA COLEMAN SHIFTED restlessly on the soft leather seat in the expensive little restaurant, tuning out the words of her luncheon companion and turning to gaze wistfully through the leaded glass windows at the June sunshine.

Jason McKellar, opposite her, sipped his liqueur and glanced over at her with sudden suspicion. ''Alex?'' he asked. ''You *do* think Wednesday would be good, don't you?''

''Pardon?'' Alex turned back, smiling apologetically. ''Sorry, Jason. I was...I guess my mind was wandering a little.''

"I was discussing tickets for the symphony," he said patiently, "and I wondered if Wednesday would be good for you."

"Oh." Alex hesitated, and then nodded abruptly. "Sure. Why not? Wednesday's fine, I guess. I'm doing some fieldwork on Warren's new site during the day, but I should still be home in time to wash the dust away and get the gravel out of my shoes."

Jason drained his liqueur glass and set it down, catching the waiter's eye to signal for a refill.

"I don't see why in your position that you still insist on doing your own fieldwork. Surely you could hire staff who would—"

"Certainly I could," Alex interrupted him, aware that her tone was rebellious, and not really caring. "I *like* doing my own fieldwork, Jason. In fact, these days it's probably the only thing that makes my job bearable," she added, half to herself.

He frowned thoughtfully, and Alex stole a critical glance at him.

Jason McKellar looked just like what he was, a successful stockbroker in his fifties with a well-tended head of abundant silver hair and a vast and tasteful wardrobe.

In short, Alex thought, still rebellious, he was a marvelous catch for a lady of a certain age.

And there was no doubt that she could catch him if she wanted to. During the months that they had been dating, Jason had made no secret of his attraction to her. But there were things about him that irritated Alex so much—irrational things, she knew, like the fact that his tie was so perfectly coordinated, with one stripe precisely matching the navy worsted of his suit, and the other carefully synchronized with the oyster of his crisp dress shirt, all highlighted by tasteful burgundy.

I don't care what anybody says, Alex thought. There's something just a little creepy about a man who chooses his ties that carefully....

Instantly, knowing she was being unfair, she suppressed this mutinous thought and forced herself to smile at him.

"I saw a tie in a shop window on my way over here today, Jason," she said cheerfully. "I think I'm going to buy it for you, and you'll have to wear it all the time to please me."

He smiled, showing fine white teeth, clearly pleased that she wanted to buy him a gift. "What's it like?" he asked.

"It's fluorescent pink," Alex said. "With little yellow happy faces. I loved it."

His dark eyes widened in alarm. "But, Alex," he began nervously, "don't you think that might be a little...?"

"It's a *joke*, Jason," Alex said wearily. "Just a joke. Believe me, I would never, never buy you a fluorescent pink tie."

He watched, puzzled and uncertain, as she edged her way out of the padded booth, gathered up her handbag and briefcase and paused to smile at him. "Well, I'm off," she announced. "No, don't come with me. Stay and finish your drink. I have to run."

He was still gazing after her with a perplexed expression as she walked briskly out of the restaurant, her dainty, elegant figure and shining crown of silver hair drawing warm, admiring glances from men half her age.

Still feeling mildly rebellious, Alex lingered deliberately on the way back to her office, gazing into shop windows and lifting her face to the warm June sunlight. As she walked she struggled with the feelings of restless discontent that haunted her so often these days, wondering just what it was that she wanted, what was missing from her life.

After all, she had a varied, interesting job, a nice apartment and a loyal group of friends. The only thing she lacked, really, was a man in her life, except for Jason—Alex made a wry little face—and the absence of a man had never been anything to cause her a great deal of concern.

But what, then, explained this gnawing emptiness, this strange, restless yearning that came creeping over her at times and made her feel so troubled and dissatisfied?

Maybe I just need a holiday, she thought, entering her building and crossing the marble-floored lobby. Maybe I should take a long summer trip this year, go to Europe or London or something....

She rode up to her floor, greeted the receptionist with absentminded affection and unlocked the door of her office. Inside the room Alex glanced automatically at the painting on the wall, feeling comforted as she always did by the wild sweep of land, the subtle colors and the sense of space and freedom.

Then, still a little detached and mildly resentful, she attacked the pile of mail that had arrived over the noon hour.

Halfway through the mountain of government bulletins, graduate theses, new archaeological publications, economic guidelines and anxious, hopeful applications for employment, Alex paused and turned to gaze once more at the little watercolor on her wall.

Her tanned face was sober and intent, her gray eyes troubled. She toyed absently with the dark green paisley scarf around her neck, lost in thought.

She was just so tired of her life. She was tired of developing new sites, tired of dealing with endless, senseless government bureaucracy, tired of running like a hamster on a wheel.

I want to quit, she thought, startling herself. I want to retire and buy a little house in the country and have a couple of big dogs and spend my time doing research and writing a book on Paleo-Indian sites in the New World.

Alex tensed her hands into fists, shocked and frightened by the sudden, disturbing clarity of her thoughts. This dream had been living quietly for a long time at the back of her mind, but she had always avoided bringing it out into the light of day and examining it, terrified at the thought of such an upheaval in her life.

But maybe she couldn't avoid the issue any longer. Maybe it was time to be giving some thought to the future, now that she was past fifty and the years had begun to slip away with such alarming speed.

Alex sighed deeply, swiveling her chair to gaze in unhappy silence at two gulls quarreling on the dirty windowsill over a scrap of someone's abandoned hot dog.

Then she wheeled her chair back into position, squared her slender shoulders and returned to her mail. Near the bottom of the pile she came across a personal letter addressed in an unfamiliar hand. This was a rarity in Alex's official mail, and she examined the creamy white envelope with interest, trying to guess who it might be from. There was no return address, just a city postmark and her name in a fine, strong masculine hand with a beautiful, flowing line.

Alex opened the envelope, began to read and then stopped in alarm. What she held in her hands was an anonymous letter, a ''you don't know who I am but there are some things I wanted to tell you'' kind of missive. Alex returned to the letter, annoyed at first, then puzzled, and finally just a little frightened.

She couldn't understand the motivation of the letter writer. He wasn't lodging a political protest over the government's handling of heritage sites. He wasn't airing some private grudge. He wasn't even expressing an unhealthy or lecherous interest in Alex, although she'd thought at first that was the intention.

Her unknown correspondent seemed, strangely enough, to have only one purpose—to entertain her. And he had an uncanny understanding of how to go about it.

Dear Alexandra,

I often think of you in that high-rise office building and wonder how you stand it. I think you'd much rather be out in the open with the wind on your face, hiking over the prairie. I thought of you especially the other day when I found a curlew's nest by the edge of the creek, hidden among the bulrushes.

Curlew nests are very hard to find, but I think they're worth the patience. The eggs are so delicately made and such a subtle color, and they seem like a hidden treasure down there in the bulrushes warmed by the sun, with a hundred red-winged blackbirds on duty singing overhead to protect them from intruders.

Speaking of treasures and other beautiful things, last night I watched the sunset and wondered if you could see it, too, or if your view is blocked by buildings all around you. It was one of those sunsets that start with a wash of pale green and then deepen to turquoise, then shade to violet, with a little flurry of pink-tinted clouds like feathers skimming just above the horizon. The stars came out so gradually that I was hardly aware of them until the sky was blazing. And it was so quiet that I was certain that if I could just listen hard enough, I'd hear the stars singing.

Have you ever had that feeling that something as beautiful as the stars must make music, but we just aren't able to hear it?

Tonight, though, the sky was a brilliant, livid red, and that means tomorrow will be a fair, hot day. I'm glad of that, because I plan to go out sketching wild roses, and I want the light to be good. I wish you could come with me. The roses are so beautiful this time of year. But at least I'll be thinking about you, so in a way you will be there, too, among the blossoms.

With sincere best wishes from,
A Friend

Alex sighed in bliss, picturing the sunsets, the bird's nest, the masses of wild roses, the stars singing quietly in the darkened sky. Then, suddenly coming back to reality with a crashing thud, she sat up straight and stared at the letter in her hands.

Who had written it, and why? Who did she know who could write such a letter?

Certainly not Jason, she thought with mild scorn. The man who had written this letter had a gentle, artistic style and the soul of a poet. That was no description of Jason McKellar.

And certainly not one of her co-workers. Like her, they all dwelt in this multistoried office complex, scurrying home each night to their own private cubbyholes in the multistoried city. This man who wrote of curlew nests and sunsets was someone who spent his days out in the open, with a wide sky above him and a thousand miles of prairie all around him.

Probably, Alex decided, it was one of her students. She taught a class in New World Antiquities at the university, and she always enjoyed the keen, irreverent, questioning minds of her eager students. This was just the kind of thing one of them might do, too, some shy and imaginative young man who had developed a painful crush on her and had no other way of expressing himself.

It was the only logical explanation, yet it left Alex feeling vaguely unsatisfied. Something about it didn't ring true. There was a tone to the letter that seemed more mature than a college student. For instance, although her correspondent clearly admired Alex deeply and had observed her with meticulous care, he was so quaintly old-fashioned and respectful, denying himself the luxury of familiarity even when he was protected under a cloak of anonymity. There wasn't a sentence, not a single word in this letter that was in any way suggestive, even overly personal.

All he wanted to do was tell her about the beautiful things he saw around him, because he seemed to understand that she had a hunger for that kind of beauty.

Alex shook her head, grinning at herself in mild derision. She knew that she was kidding herself. Her mystery letter writer had to be a college boy, some moonstruck youth with a bad case of calf love. Someone she'd taught over the winter semester, probably spending his summer out in the open as a surveyor's assistant or something, and dreaming about the elegant older woman who was so confidently unattainable.

But, though she knew that her wishes were completely irrational, Alex still didn't *want* her unknown admirer to be a callow youth. She wanted him to be her own age, the soul mate that she longed for, somebody to walk with and talk with and feel comfortable with, a man to confide in and share her hopes and fears with, to sit cozily by the fireside with as winter spread a deep, cold blanket of white across the sleeping prairie....

"Well, you fool," Alex said aloud, almost awed by her own stupidity. "I guess it's true," she muttered, getting up restlessly and crossing the room to gaze at her tanned face in the little gilt mirror near her coatrack. "I guess there's really no fool like an old fool, is there?"

But she didn't feel old. She felt trembly and warm and rich with anticipation as she held her letter full of sunshine and wild roses.

She felt about nineteen years old.

Avoiding the cool gray eyes that stared back at her from the mirror, Alex tucked the letter carefully away in her large leather handbag and patted the bag gently a couple of times before she hung it in its place on the coatrack.

Then, with a light, springing step, she walked back to her desk, settled herself into her chair with a brief, far-away smile and returned briskly to her work.

...

CHAPTER SIX

LIBBY SAT CROSS-LEGGED about halfway up the sun-
bleached stack of golden hay bales, resting on one flat
rank of bales and leaning back against the higher one. She
shifted a little, bothered by the rustling coarseness of the
hay tickling her back through the thin fabric of her denim
shirt and shook her head restlessly in the warm afternoon
sun that gilded her hair with a flaming halo and made her
eyes sparkle bright green.

She felt no pleasure in the peace of the day and the
molten gold of the afternoon sunshine. A worried frown
creased her forehead and she squinted against the bright
light and gazed up at Mac, a few feet above her, who was
tossing baled hay down into the box of his truck.

He tensed his wide shoulders to grasp a bale from over
his head, balanced it against his knee and dropped it
neatly into the waiting truck. Then, feeling Libby's eyes
upon him, he looked down at her and smiled, tipping his
tractor cap back on his bald head.

"'All June I bound the rose in sheaves,'" he quoted,
still grinning cheerfully at Libby. "'Now, rose by rose I
strip the leaves and strew them where my love may
pass.'"

Libby chuckled, and her face cleared briefly. "You've
been reading Browning again," she said.

Mac nodded serenely. "I love reading Browning's poetry in the springtime. He makes me glad to be alive."

Libby smiled fondly at her neighbor and friend, and her face clouded again. "Mac," she began slowly, plucking at the rough stems of hay in the bale beside her, "you should have told me, you know. You should have told me as soon as you found out."

Mac tossed a final bale onto his load and folded himself down near Libby, his vivid blue eyes full of concern.

"Lib, I thought you *did* know. You've talked with Warren a couple of times, and I was certain he'd told you."

"Not in so many words," she said, biting her lip and staring blindly down at her hands. "He kept talking about studies and possibilities and future considerations—you know?"

She glanced up at Mac, who nodded soberly.

"I knew they were going to be doing a big study of the site," Libby went on, her voice low and strained, "but I thought that tourist interpretive centers and all that kind of thing would be years away—if ever. I thought I didn't have to be terribly concerned because Dad would be home before anything happened, and he'd deal with them, and everything would get straightened out somehow. I really had no idea…"

Mac reached out a big hand and patted her shoulder awkwardly.

"Mac…" Libby glanced up at him, her eyes bleak with pain and suddenly more gray than green. "Mac, let's go over there to the site. Okay?"

He hesitated, looking down at her in alarm. "Right now?"

Libby nodded. "This is the first time I've felt that I really know what's going on, that I'm not being kept in the dark like a little kid. I want to go over there and…and make him tell me exactly. I want to know when they're starting and what they're going to be doing, so I can decide what to do about it.''

"Libby, girl, there's nothing you can do about it. This is the government. They have all the power in the world.''

"But—'' she began in despair ''—but if they're going to start right away, maybe I should call Dad, shouldn't I? I can't have him come home from his holiday and find…and find…''

Her voice broke. Mac patted her shoulder awkwardly once more, gazing at the distant horizon, his eyes full of sadness.

"It seems such a shame to spoil their holiday,'' he murmured, "for something inevitable.''

Libby's face set all at once into stern, determined lines as cold and lovely as carved marble. "Maybe,'' she said slowly, "it's not all *that* inevitable, Mac.''

Her neighbor looked at her, his cheerful, weathered face troubled. "Libby,'' he said, "please don't do anything foolish. Promise me you won't. I don't want you and Keith getting into—''

"Keith!'' she interrupted in surprise. "What's Keith got to do with it?''

"He feels the same way you do about this tourist facility. He says he's going to do something about it, and you and I both know the boy well enough that the thought is just a little scary.''

Libby absorbed this information in silence, looking so thoughtful that Mac was alarmed all over again. "Now look here, Elizabeth…'' he began in his sternest tone.

But she was already scrambling down the haystack, dropping neatly into the box of Mac's truck and vaulting onto the ground.

"Come on, Mac,'' she called. "We'll go in my Jeep.''

Shrugging helplessly, he followed her, paused to lift his

denim jacket out of the cab of his truck and then folded himself into the Jeep beside her.

On the drive across the spreading golden prairie, Mac glanced over at Libby's delicate profile, her small, slender nose and firm, tanned cheek. He began to speak, hesitated, turned away to glance out the window and then looked back at Libby. "So," he said casually, "he has red hair, does he?"

Libby looked puzzled briefly and then grinned. "Well, what there is of it," she said with a quick sideways smile. "He's almost as bald as you are, Mac."

"I remember when you and Peggy looked like that," Mac said with fond reminiscence. "Fat and bald with a little fluff of red hair. Gray brought you over to see me just after you came home from the hospital, and I thought I'd never seen anything so beautiful in my whole life."

Libby smiled and reached across the seat to punch his arm lightly. "You," she said, her voice warm with affection, "were always just an old silly. Right from the start."

"And didn't you know it," he said ruefully. "Wrapped me around your little finger, both of you, even before you could toddle."

Libby giggled, remembering the games and pranks of their twinned girlhood, many of them at their beloved Uncle Mac's expense.

But they both sobered and tensed a little as they neared the high, flattened bluff in the Lyndons' West Five where the stone circles were located.

Mac, who had eyes like an eagle, squinted in the direction of the camp at the base of the cliff. "Three vehicles there today," he announced. "There's the old truck they use to haul supplies, and Warren's Jeep and..." He paused, clearing his throat suddenly. "And Dr. Coleman's Land Rover."

Libby nodded and parked beside Warren's Jeep, jumping out and beginning at once to scale the cliff. Mac followed her, his long, wiry body effortlessly keeping pace with her youthful, agile movements. Side by side they crested the bluff and paused, looking around.

Tim and Sandy worked off to the south, sifting the contents of the control pit on a fine screen and charting their findings. Warren and Alex were in the center of the largest circle near the big picture rock, deep in discussion as they stood looking down at an assortment of objects and papers on a small folding camp table.

Alex saw them first, her fine eyes crinkling warmly in a friendly, welcoming smile. Libby smiled back automatically and approached the two government consultants.

Alex, she thought, looked very nice today. The older woman wore a pair of faded blue jeans that fitted trimly over her slender, rounded hips, and a soft pink cotton shirt that set off her tanned face and her lovely silver hair, casually gathered under a little peaked denim cap.

"Hello, Libby," Alex said warmly in her pleasant, husky voice. "How nice to see you. Warren and I were just talking about you."

"Were you?" Libby asked politely, avoiding Warren's dark intent gaze.

"And Mr. Burman, isn't it?" Alex asked, turning with a courteous smile to Mac, who stood quietly next to Libby.

"Hello, Dr. Coleman," Mac said, clearing his throat again.

"Hello," Alex said. "How are the pigs?"

"They're just fine," Mac said quietly.

Libby glanced sideways at him, concerned by his tone. She knew how shy Mac was around all women, especially strangers, and how intimidating a woman like Alexandra

Coleman must be to him. He stood tense and ill at ease, his big, finely shaped hands dangling, a couple of wisps of straw still clinging to his plaid shirt collar.

Libby knew all too well how gauche and awkward Mac must look to an educated, sophisticated woman like Alexandra Coleman. But she was still disturbed by the casual, offhand way that Alex's eyes flicked over her friend, cataloging and instantly dismissing him.

He's not like that! Libby wanted to shout. Mac's wonderful! He's funny and wise and talented and well-read and full of love and dreams and philosophy, and you should show him some respect!

But all her passionate defense of Mac faded and fled from her mind as soon as Warren moved over and stood in front of her.

"Hello, Libby," he said. "How are you today?"

Again she thrilled to the warm timbre of that deep voice, and the compelling sense of his nearness. In spite of herself, she remembered the wild, searing thrill of his kiss on her lips, his strong, hard hands on her body, and the passionate, yearning response of her own body, a response she had been barely able to control.

Gathering all her strength, she looked up and met his eyes with a cool, unflinching gaze. "Mac told me, Warren," she said. "He said you plan definitely to go ahead with construction of a tourist center here on our land. Right away."

"Yes," he said, looking steadily down at her. "Yes, that's true."

"Why didn't you tell me?" Libby asked, her voice low and passionate.

"I thought you knew, Libby. I never underestimated the importance of the site in any of our talks, and I—"

"You never hinted at anything *immediate!* I thought

there would be several years of study, and then, down the road, there'd be some kind of—''

''Development will start in a couple of months, Libby,'' Alex said, interrupting their conversation, her gray eyes full of thoughtful compassion as she looked at the younger woman. ''We're expropriating eleven acres, plus a road allowance. We hope to get the basic work on the facility done before winter freeze-up, so we can complete it in the spring after spending the winter developing the exhibits and have at least a partial tourist season next year.''

''Oh, God,'' Libby muttered in despair. ''I thought,'' she murmured half to herself, ''that the government never moved this fast. I thought it took years and years to get anything accomplished.''

''Usually,'' Alex agreed with a brief, cynical smile. ''But just now there are funds in place for the development of a major interpretive site in this sector, and we've learned that it's wise to act while the funds are available. If we don't, then they could just as quickly be reallocated on someone's whim and we'd lose out altogether.''

''A couple of months,'' Libby went on, still in the same toneless voice. ''That means you'll already be starting work when my father comes home from his holiday. What a terrific homecoming surprise for them.''

''If you'd prefer, Libby,'' Warren said, ''I'll contact him in Europe and let him know what's happening. I'll outline it all for him, and—''

''No!'' Libby said abruptly, and then paused, a little abashed by the sudden vehemence of her tone. ''I'd…I'd prefer to tell him myself. Please,'' she added, glancing up at Warren.

No point in bothering Dad now, Libby was thinking.

Because, if I have my way, none of this is going to happen, and we'd just be worrying him for nothing....

As if reading her mind, Warren reached out with sudden, warm concern, taking her arm and gazing down at her. "Libby," he said urgently, forgetting the others on the windswept hilltop who stood watching them in silence. "Libby, please try to understand what we're—"

She shrugged his hand aside and moved past him, walking over to gaze at the massive petroglyph while he turned and followed her with dark, troubled eyes, his handsome, sculpted face sober and concerned.

Unaware of his gaze, Libby stood in front of the big picture stone, hearing the wild, familiar strains of music begin to rise and throb softly around her. She gazed desperately at the tiny, enigmatic symbols and designs scattered over the rough surface, still haunted by the maddening, elusive feeling that there was some secret hidden in the rock, some magic key to this whole dilemma that would solve everything if she could just concentrate hard enough to understand what the rock was trying to tell her.

She closed her eyes and swayed a little on her feet, fighting to tune out her surroundings and center all of her being on the mystery and wonder of the ancient, patterned surface.

But it was hopeless. There were too many people, too many distractions. Especially Warren McIntyre, with his wide, sensual mouth, his blunt, high cheekbones, his dark, glittering eyes, and the rough black hair spilling over his calico headband.

Libby gathered herself together and turned to face the others who stood watching her curiously.

"We'd better get back," she said calmly to Mac. "There's lots of work to do."

Then, suddenly remembering something, she paused

and smiled at Sandy, who was approaching the group hesitantly with a question for Warren.

"Sandy, would you like me to stop by later on my way home and take you with me for the evening? After all, I promised you a couple of hours in a real bathtub, didn't I?"

Sandy hesitated, casting a quick, appealing glance at Warren and Alex. "I...that would be really nice," she said to Libby. "If it's...if it's okay with Warren."

"Certainly," he said, his eyes on Libby. "It's very generous of you, Libby. She'll be free in an hour or so after she and Tim finish cataloging these deposits."

"Good," Libby said briskly. "I'll just run Mac home and help him unload his hay bales, and then I'll be right back." She started for the edge of the cliff, uncomfortably aware of Warren's dark eyes piercing her back as she walked away.

Behind her, Mac paused to cast one more wistful, furtive glance at Alexandra Coleman's trim, blue-jeaned figure, and seemed as if he might be about to say something. But Alex had already turned away, her attention caught by a small stone arrowhead that Tim was showing her, and she didn't even see him.

"WAFFLES, MADAME?" Libby asked with a dreadful French accent. "Or would ze lady prefer poached eggs on toast? Eggs benedict? Quiche, perhaps?"

Sandy giggled, sipping coffee at the table and smiling at the tall red-haired woman with the frilly apron tied over her jeans. During the previous evening of fun and laughter, their relationship had advanced quickly to this level of comfortable teasing, and they were both enjoying the break in their routines of hard work and isolation.

And Libby enjoyed the brief respite from her worries,

the merry, girlish chatter that took her mind from its dreadful, obsessive concentration on that lonely hilltop with its "singing stones," and what was soon going to happen there....

"You mean to say the woman can *cook*, too?" Sandy said in mock despair, clapping a small brown hand to her forehead. "My God, no wonder I don't stand a chance!"

Libby sobered and moved over to the fridge, rummaging on a lower shelf for the tray of brown farm eggs. "There's no competition here, Sandy," she said quietly over her shoulder. "At least none that I'm aware of."

"Oh, sure. It's easy to be unaware of a competition that you can win without even trying," Sandy said gloomily, returning to her coffee.

Walking over to the stove with a copper-bottomed frying pan, Libby glanced at the girl's bent head with concern. This was the first time Sandy had come so close to any mention of Warren, and Libby tensed, searching for words.

But Sandy soon brightened, glancing up at the other woman with a crooked little smile. "Hey, don't look so worried, Libby," she said dryly. "I'm getting over it, truly I am. I've had such a terrible crush on him for months and months, but I don't need to be hit on the head with a brick to see the light, you know. It's even kind of a relief actually. I mean," she added, looking with hungry interest at the platter of crisp bacon Libby was taking from the microwave, "he never showed any interest in me, as a woman, I mean, even before you came along. And now that *you're* in the picture, my chances have progressed all the way from unlikely to zilch."

Libby turned quickly back to her pan of sputtering eggs, feeling her cheeks grow warm. "I don't see what I have to do with it," she said lightly.

Sandy snorted. "Oh, *right*," she said with gentle derisiveness, her mouth full of bacon. "And you've never ever noticed the way his eyes get all dark and stormy when he looks at you, and the way his jaw muscles tighten right here—" Sandy pointed a callused finger at her own pretty jawline "—or the hungry, sexy look on his face, like he just wishes he could drag you into his cave and gobble you up."

Sandy shivered dramatically and gazed at the blue sky framed by soft lace curtains at the big kitchen window. "God," she muttered, "what I'd give to have the man look at *me* like that."

"He's too old for you, Sandy," Libby said, carrying the frying pan full of eggs to the table. "Put some toast slices out and I'll slide your eggs onto them."

Obediently Sandy did as she was told while continuing the conversation. "I know he's older than me. About ten years, actually. Just enough to make him interesting."

Libby opened her mouth to say something, and Sandy chuckled. "You look just like my mom, all nervous and disapproving," she said, picking up her knife and making a tentative little slit in the yolk of an egg. "Oh, perfect. Not hard, not runny. Don't worry, Lib," she added. "I've given up. Truly I have. I don't even hate you anymore, though I would cheerfully have killed you the first time I met you up on that hilltop and saw how he looked at you. But I'm not a dope, and I'm not the type to die from unrequited love. It's time for Sandy to admit defeat and look elsewhere for love," she concluded cheerfully, pausing before she stuffed an enormous forkful of egg and toast into her mouth.

"Then," Libby said with relief, "how about Tim?"

"Tim!" Sandy gazed at her new friend with astonishment, her blue eyes wide and startled.

"Well, sure," Libby said. "I mean, it's obvious how *he* feels, and he seems like a really nice guy...."

"What do you mean, 'how he feels'? About *me*?" Sandy asked, still staring in disbelief.

"Well, of course. Anybody can tell that he—"

"Oh, come on, Libby," Sandy protested. "Tim likes glamour girls, cheerleader types, homecoming queens and all that. All during the winter term he was always squiring some gorgeous, glamorous chick or other around the campus. He's not interested in plain little grubs who dig in the dirt."

Libby shook her head, amazed by the complexity of human relationships and the blindness that even intelligent people seem to experience when their own situations are involved. "I can't believe you've never noticed, Sandy," she said.

"Noticed what? Lib, these eggs are just delicious. I'll never eat plastic eggs again, I swear."

"Noticed the way Tim's eyes get all dark and stormy when he looks at you, and his jaw muscles tighten right here...."

Libby pointed at her own tanned jaw in gentle mimicry. The two young women dissolved in gales of laughter, grinning at each other across the sun-splashed oak table.

"What's the joke?" a deep voice asked from the doorway, startling both of them.

"Hi, Warren," Sandy said cheerfully, glancing over Libby's shoulder.

Painfully conscious of the man just behind her and of the amused interest in Sandy's bright blue eyes, Libby sat awkwardly in her chair, reluctant to turn around. But Warren eased the situation by moving comfortably into the kitchen, pulling out a chair and seating himself at the table.

"If I may?" he asked, smiling at Libby, his dark eyes warm with admiration. "I thought I'd come over to pick Sandy up and save you the trip all the way out to the site."

"Thank you," Libby said, still uncomfortably aware of Sandy's merry blue eyes. "That was considerate of you. Would you…like some breakfast? I could toss a few more slices of bacon into—"

"No thanks," he said cheerfully. "But a cup of coffee would be nice if you have some to spare. Tim's coffee," he added with a comical wry face, "leaves a little to be desired."

"A *lot* to be desired," Sandy amended, making an identical face. "What's happening today, Warren?"

"Routine things," he said, looking up with a smile at Libby who handed him a steaming mug of fresh coffee. "I wanted you and Tim to finish surveying the plateau so we can start the topographical charts, and I'm just going to carry on with mapping the petroglyph, I guess."

"Maybe you should put that off for a while and help Libby today," Sandy said innocently, gazing down at her empty plate and avoiding Libby's startled gaze.

"Why?" Warren asked. "Does Libby need help?"

"She certainly does," Sandy said. "You know what the woman's planning to do today? She's roping a *bull*, all by herself, so she can perform surgery on it."

Warren's dark eyes turned questioningly to Libby, who flushed in protest.

"It's no big deal," she said defensively. "He's just hurt and needs a shot of antibiotic, that's all."

Warren stared at her, astounded. "You mean, Sandy's not kidding? You're really planning to rope and doctor a bull all on your own?"

"I told you, it's no big deal. We noticed him last night

when we were driving over here. He's been fighting with one of the other bulls, and he must have caught a horn in the flank and it's gotten badly infected. I just have to put a loop on him, drain the wound and give him a little shot. Nothing to it. I've done it dozens of times.''

Warren continued to gaze at her, his handsome face amazed and concerned. Finally he turned to Sandy. ''You take my Jeep back to the cliff, okay, Sandy?'' he said casually. ''I'll help Libby with her veterinary work and then she can drop me off later.''

Sandy grinned in private amusement, pushing her chair back and getting lightly to her feet. ''Good idea,'' she said, trying unsuccessfully to stifle her chuckles at Libby's alarmed expression.

''Really, Warren, it's no problem,'' Libby said earnestly. ''I don't need help. I can manage perfectly well on my own.''

But Sandy was already heading briskly for the door. She paused, turned back to the two at the table with an impudent grin and significant, exaggerated wink and then ran down the walk to the black Jeep.

The silence in the kitchen lengthened uncomfortably after the girl was gone and Libby and Warren were left alone at the sunny table.

''This is…so embarrassing,'' Libby said in a low voice, gazing down at her hands.

''What is, Libby?'' Warren asked gently, reaching over to take one of her tanned hands in his and beginning to play idly with her fingers.

''The feeling…the feeling that you have to be the one to give me extra help, as if I'm dependent on you somehow. And Sandy's implication that…that…''

''That there's something between us?''

She nodded, unable to look at him.

"There *is* something between us, Libby," he said quietly. "Whether you want to admit it or not, it's something that both of us can feel, and something that other people can see."

"I don't care!" Libby burst out, pulling her hand away and getting up abruptly to clear the table. "I'm not ready for…anything like that, Warren. I don't want things happening to me that are…against my better judgment or beyond my control. And there are a lot of things you and I would have to settle before we could start to…to build a relationship or anything." She looked directly at him, her eyes flashing emerald fire in the morning light, her lovely face flushed with emotion.

Warren returned her look in thoughtful silence while the sun glinted warmly on the blunt planes of his rugged face. "Okay, Libby," he said gently. "Have it your way and at your own pace. All I ask is for you to accept the fact that I'm not going away and you'll have to deal with me."

"Personally or professionally?" Libby asked with a bitter little smile.

"Both," he said soberly.

Libby sank into the chair opposite him and gazed at him with desperate appeal. "Warren," she began, "why didn't you tell me about the size of the development and how soon it was happening? Why were you so evasive?"

He hesitated, toying with the small cream pitcher on the polished wooden table. "Self-preservation, I guess," he said finally. "I knew how you were going to react and I kept hoping that…something would happen."

"Like what?"

"Who knows?" He shrugged and grinned awkwardly at her. "I thought maybe Alex would decide she didn't like the potential for the site or the government funds would suddenly be reallocated or you'd come up with the alternate site you talked about.''

Libby stared at him, suddenly alert. ''Would that still make a difference even at this stage?''

''Maybe,'' he said. ''I told you before, it wouldn't keep us from doing all kinds of studies on your site. But it could draw the major development away into another area. I said *could*,'' he added hastily, seeing the look on her face. ''Or, on the other hand, Alex could just check out the new site and say, 'No soap. I like the one I've got.' There's no guarantee.''

Libby's face clouded with disappointment. She was silent for a moment, watching his strong, tanned hands as he continued to move the cream pitcher in small, precise circles on the table.

''I *hate* it, Warren,'' she said abruptly in a low, passionate tone. ''I hate the whole idea of it, of buildings and strangers on our land. It just makes me furious.''

''And do you hate me, too, Libby?'' he asked. ''Do you hate me for my involvement in it?''

''Sometimes I do,'' she said. ''After all, if it weren't for you—''

''If it weren't for me, it would be somebody else. A site like this is too important to go unnoticed forever, Libby.''

''I suppose you're right,'' she said wearily. ''I just wish that—'' Libby stopped abruptly and turned away, avoiding his dark, troubled gaze. ''Well,'' she said, keeping her voice light, ''enough talk. That poor old bull is suffering while we sit here chatting. And if you really plan to help me, we'd better get going. Can you ride a horse?''

''Certainly I can,'' Warren said with dignity, trying to match her change of tone. ''When I was a kid, I spent all my summers on my uncle's farm. I can do all kinds of cowboy stuff.''

Libby smiled bleakly. "Good. I could use another cowboy around here sometimes. Let's saddle up and ride, pardner.''

JUST IN CASE Warren wasn't as accomplished a horseman as he claimed to be, Libby chose the two gentle old mares that had belonged to the twins when they were much younger. She stole a few sidelong glances at him as he heaved his saddle into position and tightened the cinches. Then, satisfied that he appeared to know what he was doing, she finished saddling her own horse, led the two of them out into the sunlight and stepped lightly up into the stirrup.

Warren vaulted onto his mount, reined the old mare around and fell easily into step beside Libby. He hadn't been exaggerating, Libby realized. He sat the horse with careless, athletic grace, his hands casually low on the reins, his long back relaxed.

She sensed his dark eyes on her and felt an uncomfortable warmth creep up her neck and onto her cheeks, knowing what he was thinking.

"Pretty high-stepping pair of horses," he observed innocently. "Are you positive that a couple of tenderfeet like us can handle these frisky critters?''

Libby grinned in spite of herself. "How could I be sure," she asked defensively, "that you really knew how to ride and weren't just bragging? Just my luck that I'd put you on something frisky and you'd get thrown on your head and then sue us for the *whole* West Five instead of just taking the best part of it.''

"Libby…'' he began, his voice suddenly grave.

But Libby was in no mood for serious talk. She spurred

the old mare into an alarming burst of speed, bending low over the pommel and laughing as the wind whipped at her hair and sang in her ears.

Warren's mount, accustomed to a lifetime of the twin's antics, immediately threw herself into the race with astonishing energy, and the two horses flew across the golden grass toward the rising sun.

Their burst of speed was short-lived, though. Panting and heaving, the horses soon slowed to a trot and then to a long, easy walk, and their two riders chatted amiably as the miles unfolded. At last they fell into the kind of warm, comfortable silence that is possible between people who are good friends, and Libby turned to steal a glance at her companion.

His dark face was flushed with happiness at the beauty of the morning and their exhilarating run, and his black hair shone warmly in the bright morning light. With his lean, muscular body and his powerful, hawklike features, he looked more than ever like a tall Indian brave riding out at the head of a raiding party.

Now that she was getting to know him better, Libby saw more than just his striking looks. She saw the gentle, generous line of his mouth, the warm humor and intelligence in his dark eyes, the thoughtful and considerate glances that he gave her. Just the nearness of him made her heart swell and tremble with pleasure, filled her whole wide world all the way to the distant horizon.

And yet, beyond the goodness and humor and the powerful masculine appeal, like a column of ghostly figures riding just behind him, there were other images, mental pictures that made her shudder.

There were convoys of government trucks, construction vehicles and endless loads of tourists pouring noisily across this land that had been private and undisturbed for so many years....

"There he is," Libby said aloud, relieved that the bull was still near the slough where she had spotted him the previous evening. "He looks pretty droopy, doesn't he?"

They reined in side by side and gazed at the poor, suffering animal who stood at the water's edge with listless, lowered head, his wide, curving horns almost sweeping the mud at his feet. He was a big Hereford bull in his prime with short, heavy legs, massive forequarters and a glossy, curled hide. His right flank was soft and puffy, painfully swollen beneath a long, jagged gash caked with dried blood.

"The tips of their horns are razor-sharp," Libby explained. "And a horn puncture can quickly get septic." She tightened her lariat over her saddle horn, shook out the loop and turned to Warren. "I'll just drop a loop over his horns and tighten up, and then you can set your loop in front of his hind feet, okay?"

He nodded, automatically untying his own rope.

"Have you done this before, too?" Libby asked.

Warren nodded again and turned to give her a slow, deliberate grin.

She smiled back, then turned away. "Okay, okay, so you're a real cowboy and I'm an idiot. Come on, let's stretch him out."

The injured animal was too weak and feverish to put up much resistance. Almost immediately he was stretched between the two horses, one loop encircling his horns, the other tightening around his hind legs, pulling him heavily over onto his left side where he lay gasping, his big liquid eyes rolling in panic.

Leaving her well-trained horse to hold the rope tight, Libby stepped down, untied a leather kit from the back

of the saddle and walked over to the big, heaving animal
while Warren sat his horse and watched with interest.
"Do you need any help?" he asked.

Libby shook her head. "You stay up here just in case
he decides to fight this. One of us has to be mounted and
in control."

Warren nodded in understanding and watched while
Libby slashed the festering wound lightly with a long,
shining bone-handled knife. Pus and blood flowed down
the animal's side and he flung his big head about, flailing
and bellowing fiercely.

"Keep him tight, Warren," Libby called. "Don't give
him any legroom."

Warren backed his mount a little, stretching the rope
tighter while Libby poured an antiseptic solution into the
wound and then dusted it heavily with blue powder.

"Antibiotic," she said to Warren. "And I was right.
It's not deep enough to need stitches. Now I just have to
give him a little shot..." While she spoke, she took out
a syringe, filled it carefully from a small white bottle of
penicillin and plunged the needle into the huge, throbbing
vein in the bull's massive neck. Then she ran to lead her
horse forward, quickly loosened the rope around the big
animal's horns and nudged him with her boot.

"Slack off now," she called out to Warren. "Follow
him a few paces after he gets up so he can walk out of
your loop."

Warren obeyed, watching as the bull struggled unsteadily to his feet and tottered forward. He shook himself free
of Warren's loop, lowered his horns, bellowed noisily and
made a couple of angry, threatening gestures at Libby,
who ignored him and calmly went on putting her veterinary equipment back into her case.

Then, still rumbling with outrage, the bull set off toward the east, already looking relieved and less racked by pain.

Warren tied his rope back in place, dismounted and moved over beside Libby, who was scrubbing her hands with water from her canteen and drying them vigorously on a tall sagebrush.

She smiled up at him, all of her tension and worry forgotten for the moment. "He looks happier, doesn't he, Warren?" she said with pleasure, watching the bull's rapidly diminishing shape. "I love easing their pain like that and making them feel better."

She turned back toward Warren, smiling broadly. But her innocent pleasure in curing the bull fled when she saw how Warren was looking at her, his face intense, his eyes dark with emotion. Suddenly her mouth went dry, and she stood stock-still, as if mesmerized.

"Oh, Libby," he whispered. "If you only knew how you look right now, sweetheart, with the sun in your hair, and your eyes so green. Libby, you're just so beautiful."

Libby shuddered and moved into his arms, forgetting her fears, forgetting what he represented, drawn irresistibly by the passion in his voice and the burning desire in his eyes. She knew only that she yearned for him, needed him, craved this closeness just as much as he did.

Moaning softly and biting her lip, she struggled with herself, wanting to resist, wanting to hold on to her own strength and independence, but somehow unable to muster her defenses. With a reckless, yielding joy she felt his hands moving passionately over her body, unbuttoning her shirt, cupping and squeezing her breasts while he whispered to her about her loveliness, her utter desirability, his great, aching need for her....

Slowly, slowly, they sank into the sea of waving grass, their bodies pressed together, their breath coming in quick, ragged gasps as his lips roamed hungrily over her face and breasts and his hand crept lower, reaching to unfasten the zipper of her jeans.

Libby shifted and murmured against him, distressed by what was happening but lost in passion, drowning in need, powerless to stop him or herself.

Suddenly, dimly, she became aware of a gentle, insistent motion, a rapid, butting movement against her side that Warren certainly wasn't responsible for.

Confused, she opened her eyes and gazed directly into her old mare's puzzled, reproachful face. The horse was nuzzling and pushing against Libby, the metal bit clanking in her big yellow teeth, disturbed by this unusual and alarming behavior on the part of her young mistress.

In spite of herself, Libby chuckled at the anxious expression on the mare's long face and the insistent way that she continued to nudge and press, trying to put a stop to these unseemly human antics.

When Libby giggled aloud, Warren glanced up at her in surprise, his dark face still hot with passion, and took in the situation at a glance. Seeing Libby's flushed face and laughing eyes, and sensing her withdrawal, he sat up immediately with a rueful grin.

"Well," he said in resignation, "so much for romance, I guess."

"I guess," Libby agreed solemnly, fastening her shirt with shaking hands, and then bubbled with merriment again when the old mare turned aside with obvious satisfaction and began placidly to crop the long grass at her feet.

Warren glared at the horse. "Glue," he told her darkly. "That's what happens to horses like you. They go into glue bottles. Just remember that."

The old horse twitched her ears and tossed him a coy,

flirtatious glance, batting her long eyelashes. Calmly she returned to her meal while Libby shook with laughter at the expression on Warren's face.

He was unable, by now, not to see the humor in the situation, and he laughed with her, helping Libby to her feet and dusting her off tenderly, kissing her with warm thoroughness before handing her up into her saddle.

When she was seated, he stood silent and intent beside her, gazing up at her, his lean, tanned hand resting lightly on her denim-clad leg. Libby realized what his dark eyes were telling her—that she might have been saved by her horse this time, but he wasn't going to go away, and the day would come when nothing would save her.

She bit her lip ruefully and smiled back at him, reaching down shyly to touch his crisp, dark hair. Then she spurred her horse forward without looking back and started off toward the ranch buildings.

CHAPTER SEVEN

ALEXANDRA COLEMAN SAT on her little apartment balcony, gazing over the wrought-iron railing at the sprawling city bounded by rolling prairie and foothills to the west and a cloudy smudge along the horizon that was the Rocky Mountains.

The sunset was fading behind the distant range of mountains and twilight flooded the land, spreading a deep, cool blanket of purple velvet over farms and fields and city streets.

The air was heavy with summer, rich with the fragrance of roses and peonies, still warm from the daytime sun. In the hushed stillness of early evening, the city noise seemed strangely muted, as if sounds were traveling through something heavier than air. Traffic moved more slowly, and people wandered out of their houses and apartments to lift their faces to the glowing, darkening sky.

Alex shifted in her lawn chair, feeling so lonely that she could hardly bear it.

There was something about this time of day, she thought, these magical, mellow moments caught between sunset and starlight, that made her sharply aware of her solitude, made her long painfully for someone to sit beside her, to hold her hand quietly and understand her feelings.

Alex frowned, puzzled by her own thoughts, trying to analyze her deep discontent. She had always been a serenely independent and capable woman, handling her personal life and her career with good humor and intelligence, seldom feeling any need for help with either.

But these days, for some reason...

Alex sighed and looked off to the west where the glow was fading from the sky and two new stars twinkled, one above the other, in the dark violet sky.

She smiled at the stars and smoothed the letter in her hands, remembering how her unknown correspondent had told her in this, his most recent letter, the Indian legend of where the stars had come from.

"There was a new moon last night," he'd written, "and the sky was brilliant with stars. I thought of you and wondered if you knew the Plains Indian legend of how the stars got into the sky. It seems that the Great Spirit didn't like the souls up in heaven spying on the people who were still living on earth, so he put a huge buffalo robe in the sky to divide the two places. But the souls in heaven were still curious, and at night when the sun's glare was gone from the earth, they took pointed digging sticks and poked holes in the buffalo hide so that they could peek through. When the Great Spirit saw the holes, he was angry, and he sent the robe to spinning, just fast enough so that nobody could look through the holes. To this day the buffalo robe is still spinning very slowly and the bright light from heaven shines through the holes. But, like the smoke hole in a teepee, the center hole always stays in the same place, and when you look up at the North Star, there just might be a soul in heaven peeking back at you through the buffalo robe...."

Alex gazed up into the sky, waiting for the North Star to appear, smiling at the charming little story. Then she gazed down in the darkness at the letter in her hands, her tanned face troubled.

The letters were arriving about one every four or five days. This one had been in the noon-hour mail, and Alex had already read it more times than she wanted to admit.

She would have hated to confess, as well, how eagerly she waited and watched for these letters, and how much their contents had come to mean to her. Alex was a trained, competent professional with a responsible executive position and a large budget to administer. She certainly wasn't the sort of woman to get all starry-eyed and emotionally involved with a writer of anonymous letters.

But somehow she had, and the thought horrified her.

Alex knew that she was being foolishly irrational, that the letter writer was probably many years younger than she and motivated by some obscure emotion. Possibly he was even having a bit of fun at her expense. She knew as well that if she had any sense she would destroy the letters as soon as they arrived, throw them out unopened and feel nothing but relief when her mystery man finally moved on to other diversions.

But Alex found herself utterly unable to throw any of these letters away. They were so interesting, so beautifully written, so full of vivid descriptions of the subtle, changeable, lovely world of the prairies, and expressive of a shy courtly charm and grace that was both soothing and immensely appealing.

And, Alex realized, there was another quality to these letters that she found deeply satisfying…a sort of gentlemanly, considerate interest in her as a person and a warm, sincere wish to enrich her life, to entertain her with images of beauty and brighten an existence that the letter writer seemed to believe might be unfulfilled to her.

He knows, Alex thought gloomily. He knows how I feel about my life. Dear God, who is he! I wish I could know who he is. I'd give anything to know….

And there, she knew, was where the danger lay. She was reaching the point where she wanted this relationship to become real and tangible. She wanted to see her mystery man, to smile at him and touch him. Just through the power of written words on paper, Alexandra Coleman was becoming emotionally involved, and the fact astounded and distressed her. And yet, whenever she saw one of the creamy envelopes with its flowing, masculine handwriting, she felt a deep stirring, a warm, frankly physical reaction that alarmed her more all the time.

"What a *fool* you are, Dr. Coleman," Alex muttered bitterly aloud as she had so many times in the past couple of weeks. "This is the behavior of a girl of sixteen, you silly, silly woman…"

But nothing worked, not logic nor reason, not ridicule nor self-abuse. Alex still waited with rich anticipation for her letters, still carried them in secret trembling to some private place where she could devour their contents undisturbed, still longed to meet this man and look into his eyes, to hear his voice and walk beside him over the open spaces that they both loved.

"Oh, *God!*" she muttered in agony.

Briefly she considered accepting Jason's invitation to the ballet on the coming weekend. She hadn't seen Jason since the symphony and kept manufacturing excuses to put him off. Compared to her writer of letters, the man who described sunrises and sage grouse dances, who told Indian legends and quoted poetry, Jason was pretty dull company, Alex thought rebelliously.

But at least he was real, flesh and blood, an actual living person. Whereas her correspondent…

For the thousandth time Alex tried to imagine who the man could be. She had gone through all her class rosters and student records, even gone to the trouble of digging out old term papers to compare the handwriting. She had spent hours making up lists of all the people she knew at work and socially to see if any of them might fit the description of her secret admirer. And, on all fronts, she had drawn a complete blank. She was no closer to having the foggiest idea of his identity.

And yet he obviously knew *her*—knew her well, in fact, with the kind of warm, intuitive empathy that could only come from close and loving observation, coupled with a deep understanding of human nature.

Alex sighed, weary of this treadmill that her restless mind kept going over and over all through her waking hours. She leaned back in her chair, eyes closed, trying to block out her thoughts.

After a while she opened her eyes, staring blankly upward, and saw the North Star glittering high above her. Alex gazed at the point of sparkling light, wondering if some other lonely, curious soul was peeking back at her, and smiled wanly in the darkness. Then she gathered up her letter, pushed her lawn chair in place against the rough plastered wall and got up to wander inside her lonely apartment.

A GRAY SKY BROODED on the windswept, haggard expanse of land, and the cold east wind snarled and whistled up the barren ridges. Occasionally the thick mantle of clouds parted to show a pallid flicker of sunlight, rapidly extinguished by the damp morning air and the howling wind.

High on the exposed plateau among the patterns of rocks, Warren McIntyre shivered and ducked his chin into the collar of his sheepskin-lined denim jacket, flapping his arms vigorously against his body for warmth. With fingers numbed by cold he snapped the shutter on his Polaroid, taking pictures of the petroglyph from all possible angles.

The wind swirled and gusted, sending spirals of gritty soil aloft in dense clouds that stung his eyes. Rain began to fall in small cold drops driven by the wind so that they burned like tiny points of ice. Then the skies opened and the rain poured down, sluicing along the animal trails that ridged the sides of the cliff, pelting the silvery sagebrush and the swaying grasses.

Finally Warren admitted defeat, gathered his equipment and shoved it into waterproof bags, rolled his laminated charts and closed his field book. He slipped and skidded down the muddy hillside and hurried into the grove of birch trees at the base. In front of the tent that he shared with Tim, Warren paused to unlace his muddy hiking boots, then bent to enter the igloo-shaped shelter, snugly protected by the pale green leaves overhead and a broad canvas fly that shed the rain.

Inside the silent, empty tent he rolled up the front flap to let in the fresh morning scents, the delicious smell of damp earth and sagebrush, of wild roses and wet tree bark. Rain whispered and rustled in the canopy of branches overhead, and the wind sighed mournfully around the snug, curved edges of the tent.

Warren shed his damp coat and set his tiny butane stove up on its pedestal in the entryway, enjoying the surprisingly powerful burst of warmth that it generated. He seated himself on a camp stool at a little folding table in the center of the tent, unwrapped his sheaf of photographs and began to lay them out on the scarred wooden surface.

He was pleased by this set of photographs, by their clear contrast and good definition. Usually, up on the exposed plateau, the sun shone so brightly that it was difficult to get a satisfactory image of the southern-facing petroglyph, especially with Polaroid equipment.

But, on this dull and cloudy day, he had managed an excellent set of prints. And it looked like the storm was settling in, with a solid rainfall that would likely last all day. He would finally be able to get caught up on the ocean of paperwork that was always accumulating and do an intensive study of these pictures.

But even as Warren framed the thought, the images began to swim in front of his eyes and he saw Libby's face, her sparkling green eyes and sweetly curving mouth, her tanned, firm cheek and her tall, slender body.

He saw her calmly, efficiently, operating on the big Hereford bull, her lovely face intent on her work, and heard her laughter when she teased him about his riding. He felt her rich womanly body yielding passionately in his arms, smelled the sun-warmed fragrance of her hair, tasted again the dizzying sweetness of her kiss....

Restless with longing, Warren pushed the photographs aside with an abrupt gesture and gazed at the taut, luminous canvas of the tent wall. Once again his mind struggled with the problem of what he was doing, of his involvement with this archaeological development and what it meant to the woman who was growing more and more important to him.

This wasn't the first time Warren had been involved with such cases, and he knew that landowners' reactions were never predictable. Some were greedily delighted with the amount of money the government was willing to offer for a seemingly useless piece of land. Others, like Libby, felt that no amount of money was enough, and the process of settling their cases was often difficult and painful.

But this was the first time that Warren had really

viewed the situation from both sides. He had ridden with Libby across the golden expanse of her family's land, helped her as she looked after the livestock in her care, sat with her by the fireside as she rested from a day of hard, solitary work on her land. He could understand how she felt, how her concerns for the privacy and integrity of this wild sweep of prairie could match his own passionate absorption in the wondrous mysteries of the past, and the absolute obligation he felt to make them known and available to the world.

The ancient symbols in the photographs on the little wooden table in front of him were rare, precious, indescribably wonderful. They belonged to the masses, to everyone who thrilled to antiquity and lost civilizations and the mystery of human origins.

But the land...the land belonged to Libby and her family, and they loved these barren, open spaces that were touched only by the wind, inhabited only by eagles and coyotes.

Warren brooded, his handsome face somber and intent, wondering what anyone could do about this dilemma. And with growing, bitter pain he wondered if his professional integrity was ultimately going to extract from him the cruelest price of all, forcing him to sacrifice the love of a woman who was rapidly coming to matter more than he could have dreamed possible.

He took the photographs and stacked them neatly in a pile, his lean brown fingers aligning the edges absently as he pondered. Finally he pushed his chair aside, extinguished the flame in the little heater and pulled on his hiking boots again, crossing the glade to Sandy's tent where she and Tim were spending the rainy day doing charts of small artifacts from the control pit.

Warren hesitated in the shelter of the canvas fly on the

other tent, thinking about the two young people. Sandy
had been different ever since she came back from her visit
to the ranch house, he mused. She seemed much happier
and more contented, singing to herself as she worked and
smiling occasionally for no reason. Her strange black
moods and puzzling fits of impatience had passed completely, and Warren found this a considerable relief.

He wondered what Libby had said to the younger girl,
what she had done to ease Sandy's mind and increase her
contentment. Libby was a trained social worker, after all,
used to dealing with people and all their problems....

The thought of Libby made him smile again, his tanned
face creasing warmly, his dark eyes shining.

Lord, what a woman she is, he thought. What a rare,
gentle, wise, incredibly strong woman....

He noticed, as well, that Sandy was looking with more
interest at Tim these days, and wondered if Libby had
passed on his own comments about Tim's attraction to the
girl. Warren fervently hoped so. He was reluctant to play
matchmaker himself, but he knew that his camp would
run more efficiently if it wasn't so charged with emotional
tension.

Although Sandy was being a little more friendly with
Tim, the boy didn't seem to be aware of it. Tim had
adopted the habit, largely in self-defense, of ignoring her,
treating her with a kind of intense casualness that did
little, in Warren's eyes, to hide his adoration. But it
seemed to bother Sandy, and she was finally making an
attempt to draw her co-worker out, to kid with him and
get him talking to her.

Women! Warren thought with a bleak grin. How's a
man supposed to bear it? She spends a month or so ignoring him, breaking his heart, and now that he's with-

drawn from her to save his life, she starts flirting and trying to get him to react to her....

Still smiling at the absurdities of human relationships, he pulled aside the tent flap and bent to shoulder his way inside.

"Hi, kids. Any coffee brewing?" he asked, and then abruptly stopped short, becoming aware of what the pounding and rustling of the rain had hidden before.

There were three people in the tent, not two, and they were obviously having a wonderful time together.

Sandy and Tim were seated tailor-fashion on each side of a big piece of plywood covered with bone fragments, small stone tools and scrapers. Between them sat Malcolm Burman, his long, gangly body jackknifed down onto a little folding stool, his big, finely shaped hands hanging between his knees as he talked and the two young people listened in rapt, delighted silence.

"So Langley's wife was just furious, ran out to the tractor and told Langley that this lady was at the farmhouse, claiming to be married to him, too," Mac was saying. "And Langley said, 'Well, now, sweetie, I been meanin' to talk to you about that.'"

The tent rocked with laughter, and the three occupants looked up at Warren who stood uncertainly beneath the low, domed ceiling, smiling down at them.

"Mac's been telling us stories," Sandy said, reaching for the thermos and pouring a mug of steaming coffee for Warren. "This ranching country is just a hotbed of sin and corruption. You should *hear* these stories."

Tim chuckled, and Sandy smiled at him. Their glances caught and held for a moment, filling the cozy little space with an awkward intensity before Tim dropped his eyes and turned to pick up a splinter of bone.

"Serrated edge. Could have been a fleshing tool," he

said tonelessly to Sandy. "Better put it in the tentative column for now."

She obeyed, bending her golden head to write on her clipboard while Mac looked up at Warren, his vivid blue eyes smiling.

"Actually," Mac said, "I came to see you, Warren, but you were up on the hill, and Tim and Sandy here were so hospitable that I just stayed."

"I don't blame you," Warren said, sitting on another camp stool near Mac and accepting the coffee from Sandy with an absent smile. "This looks like a cozy place to spend a rainy day. What did you want to see me about, Mac?"

"Nothing in particular. Just wanted to visit a bit, see how you were doing and what's going on."

Warren nodded, sipping his coffee and smiling. Mac paid frequent visits to the archaeological site and seemed fascinated by the processes and methods of charting and mapping, of identifying and preserving. Mac was always painfully shy and tongue-tied if Alex was around, but alone with him, Warren was charmed by the older man's gentle humor and his startling intelligence, his quick, incisive grasp of scientific principles and philosophies.

No wonder Libby adored the man, he thought. There was definitely something special about Malcolm Burman, although you'd never suspect it by his looks....

"And," Mac added, his voice carefully noncommittal, "I kind of wondered if Libby might be over here."

Something in Mac's tone made Warren glance up quickly. "Why, Mac? What made you think she might be here?"

"Oh, no reason. I stopped by the ranch real early this morning and her truck was gone, and I don't know what she'd be doing out in this rain. I just thought she might have driven over here.''

Warren's face clouded with instant concern. ''Do you think we should…?''

''Don't worry,'' Mac said. ''Libby's a big girl and can look after herself better than anybody I know.''

''But if her truck—''

''Maybe,'' Mac said soothingly, ''she just went into town to do some shopping. She keeps saying there's a ton of things she needs, but she never has the time.''

''Maybe,'' Warren said, unconvinced, his face still creased with concern.

''I guess Dr. Coleman won't be out today, either, now that it's raining so hard. I think she mentioned the other day that she might be coming today,'' Mac went on casually.

Warren shook his head. ''Not likely. I think she's got a meeting today with the deputy minister and a bunch of other VIPs. Poor Alex, she hates those meetings. Any more coffee in there, Sandy?''

''Two cups,'' Sandy said cheerfully. ''One for you and one for Mac.''

Mac bent forward, holding out his mug obediently, and Warren was startled by a sudden, fleeting look of bleak loneliness and disappointment in those vivid blue eyes. But then Mac, in response to Sandy's promptings, launched himself cheerfully into another rollicking tale of prairie morality. Warren sipped his coffee, smiling as he listened and wondering if perhaps he had imagined that strange, inexplicable flash of yearning on Mac's weathered face.

LIBBY REINED IN beside a dense stand of chokecherry trees, sheltering beneath the curving foliage overhead as she adjusted a scarf around the neck of her slicker. She knotted the tattered length of fabric to keep the rain from trickling down inside her collar, jammed the old Stetson firmly over her eyes and then spurred her reluctant horse back out into the driving rain.

"Come on, Scout," she murmured apologetically, bending to pat a gloved hand on his dark, streaming neck. "It's a dirty job, but God knows somebody's got to do it, and who is there besides us?"

Libby squinted against the rain and gazed up at the sky, as hard and gray as hammered pewter while the moisture streamed down relentlessly. Every time she came to the community pasture to hunt for the other petroglyph site, it seemed to be raining, Libby mused, probably because there was so much work to do at home when the weather was fair that she just couldn't spare the time.

She knew it wasn't really wise to come out here in the rain. For one thing, the rough terrain was treacherous when it was wet, and for another, it was perilously easy to get lost and disoriented when there was no sun to sight by, just shifting horizons and gray leaden skies looking the same in every direction.

Libby shrugged, set her mouth in a firm, determined line and spurred her horse into a canter, keeping a wary eye on the ground at intervals, scanning the endless vista of plateaus and gullies for anything of interest.

As she rode, her mind wandered through the maze of troubled thoughts that was becoming so dismally familiar to her—thoughts of government development on her father's land, of Gray's inevitable return home and his helpless outrage, of stone circles and carved symbols and lost mysteries from ancient times.

And through all these thoughts ran the recurrent theme that was the most troubling and distressing of all. Libby was never really free of the memory of Warren McIntyre's lips and hands, the dazzle of sunlight on her closed eyelids and the soft, fragrant grasses beneath her body as he lay above her, stroking her breasts, kissing her with powerful, demanding passion, whispering urgent words of love.

Libby shifted restlessly in the saddle and ducked her head against a sudden gust of icy rain, trying to banish the memories of Warren. She had never felt about any man the way she felt about him, never experienced this deep, deep yearning, this absolute need for his touch and his kiss, this hungry longing for more of him that felt like an aching void at the very center of her, at the core of her womanhood.

She didn't know how much longer she could resist him, because she knew that she wanted him physically as much as he wanted her. And it wasn't just sexual desire. Libby also sensed a shy, growing urgency to know him better, to learn more about him, to understand what he thought and felt, to know his dreams and fears and find out what made him smile.

But at the same time she dreaded that kind of nearness and yielding, that communion and gentle exchange of confidences, knowing how it would form bonds that would weaken her bargaining position.

Because, more and more, Libby was coming to look on this whole problem of the archaeological site as a bargain of sorts. If she could find the alternative site, the one that she passionately believed in, here on the public land of the community pasture, then she would be in a position to negotiate with Warren. She would show him the new site only after somehow extracting his firm promise to withdraw from her own land. And, to be able to drive a bargain like that, she had to remain firmly detached. Everything depended on her strength and her wits. She couldn't allow herself the luxury of falling in love with Warren McIntyre if she wanted to keep herself in a position where she could preserve the wild serenity and privacy of her ancestral home.

But, even as she framed the thought, Libby saw his dark eyes shining, felt the crisp, springing texture of his hair against her cheek, felt the sweetness and strength of his lips on hers, and wondered if she could withstand him much longer.

Off to her right Libby saw a high plateau, just the kind she was looking for, and reined her horse around to toil up to the summit. But the hilltop was bare and windswept, with only some scattered sagebrush here and there, bending in the rain, its gnarled stems as thick as her wrist.

Aching with disappointment, Libby guided her horse down the hill again, gripping firmly with her knees and letting him take his head on the steep, sandy slope. The big bay gelding edged into a deer trail that threaded the dense brush at the base of the cliff, stepping daintily along through the dampened foliage to the edge of a little clearing. Suddenly Libby reined in, smiling with pleasure.

A female mule deer stood at the outer fringe of the poplar grove, nursing twin fawns. She caught Libby's scent, threw her head up, stamped her hind feet once and shot through the grove of trees, disappearing at once into the deep thickets of brush.

At the stamp of their mother's hooves, the two fawns dropped to the ground in a tangle of long, awkward legs, vanishing as instantly as if they had been shot. Libby sat her horse under the poplars, looking with interest at the spot in the long, wet grass where the fawns had disappeared. The mother, she knew, would be somewhere nearby, watching from a screen of brush in an agony of fear.

The fawns had clearly been trained to drop to the ground on command, but they were very small, probably only a couple of days old, and they had not yet been trained to stay in place. As Libby waited, they struggled to their feet and wobbled, one behind the other, across the hollow toward the grove of trees where their mother had vanished.

Libby grinned.

"Oh, my," she murmured aloud, "are you two ever going to be in trouble when your mommy catches you. You're supposed to stay still, you know. You're not supposed to get up and wander around."

One fawn disappeared into the brush. The smaller one, left alone, stood unsteadily on his knobby, splayed legs, looking around in confusion. Finally he faltered over to the base of a tree and sank to the ground, tucking his legs clumsily beneath him.

Libby trotted through the clearing and stopped a little distance away to look at him. She edged closer, dismounted and walked over beside him, awed by his beauty and symmetry. He was very small, his body not much larger than that of a good-sized house cat. His hide was like silk, a light tan spotted with a design of white splotches that was as individual as a fingerprint. His tiny hooves were still soft and tender, his eyes milky-blue and opaque, not fully adjusted to the light.

He lay quietly beneath her scrutiny, not yet wise enough to be afraid. Still, he was conditioned by the instincts of countless thousands of years to shrink into stillness, not to trust this strange animal. He was shivering in the rain and his little body rippled and trembled. Libby longed to take him into her arms, to cuddle him and warm him and kiss his silky head and ears. She restrained herself, knowing that a person must never touch a fawn, that the man-smell on him would drive his mother frantic and make her unable to bear having him anywhere near her.

Libby got slowly to her feet and started back toward her horse. Then she paused, turned and gazed intently into the grove of trees, searching for a bit of movement, a flash of color. But the grove was still and the fawn lay alone and shivering at the base of the tree.

"Okay," Libby called into the dense brush. "I'm leaving. You can come out and get him now. And next time," she added with a smile, shaking her gloved hand for emphasis, "you make sure he stays put when you tell him to!"

Still smiling, she put her boot into the stirrup, swung up into the saddle and rode out of the clearing and up the next hill of sand.

Soon her face grew sober again and she frowned with concentration, thinking about the doe and the fawns, the curled little body of the spotted baby, the trail through the dense brush to their clearing...

All at once she saw the patterned face of the big petroglyph and a heavy line with little stick figures of deer marching along it. Warren believed that the deer were objects of some deep symbolic importance, but what if he was wrong?

What if the *line* was the important element, and the deer were just drawn on it just to identify it? What if they were placed there specifically to illustrate that it was a deer trail, like the highway markings on a modern map?

At the word *map*, Libby's mind flared with sudden illumination, like the sun blazing through clouds.

That was it!

That was the thought that had been nagging at her for weeks beneath her fears, her struggles, her dreams of Warren and her concerns about the future. What if the big rock was just that—an ancient map? What if it was intended to serve as a guide for Stone Age travelers and it contained on its surface the directions to find the next site of worship?

Libby shivered with excitement. The idea seemed completely plausible, more so because it helped to explain the images that haunted her mind so frequently these days, little scattered memories of landmarks and symbols on the surface of the rock that seemed more and more familiar as she spent so many lonely hours riding out here in the community pasture.

The rock is actually a map of this place, Libby thought, and what I'm riding through now is the real thing. No wonder I'm starting to see similarities between the two. But I need to study the patterns a lot more before they can tell me anything....

And that, of course, was the problem. She couldn't say anything about this theory to Warren or Alex. They were specialists in the field with years and years of study and training, while Libby knew next to nothing about rock carvings or Paleo-Indian man. All she had was this crazy hunch.

I won't tell them, she decided. I'll think about it, get some books and see if I can learn anything. Most of all, I've got to find a way to get close to that rock sometime so I can really look at it.

It would have to be at night, she knew. The crew worked all during the day, every day. Warren even stayed alone at the camp most weekends and spent his free time up there mapping and examining the petroglyph.

On the coming weekend, Libby decided, after the weather cleared, she would go up to the big rock at night. There was a full moon on the weekend, and with luck Warren might be in the city along with his crew. She'd take a flashlight, climb to the summit and spend as much time as she liked studying the patterned surface. Maybe then the mysterious signs and symbols that haunted her dreams would start to have some meaning.

Feeling cheered and optimistic for the first time in weeks, Libby huddled inside the warmth of her heavy waterproof coat and relaxed to the easy, rocking rhythm of the big horse's gait. She began to sing softly aloud to keep her spirits up, dug in her saddlebag for a sandwich and rode along munching on bread and cheese, letting her horse pick his way through the rough stands of sagebrush and prickly pear cactus that gleamed like molten silver in the gentle, flowing rain.

CHAPTER EIGHT

LIBBY LED HER HORSE from the barn, latched the door
quietly behind her and tossed the rein up onto the bay
gelding's neck, pausing to pat him absently while she
gazed overhead. The stars hung low in the sky, warm and
brilliant on this mild summer night, dancing and glimmering in the velvet blackness like a celestial light show.
High overhead, the full moon shone with a calm, serene
radiance, splashing bands of platinum across the weathered sides of the barn and glittering on the rough, silvered
surfaces of the haystacks.

The blazing summer sun and warm west wind of the
past few days had dried the prairie, sweeping away all
traces of the recent rains and leaving the broad fields sere
and silent beneath the wide, cloudless sky. But tonight
even the wind was stilled, and the only sound in the quiet,
moonlit expanse was the measured, mournful hooting of
a great horned owl hunting in a nearby meadow.

Libby listened in thoughtful silence to the call of the
owl, a rough, broken note followed by two long, sobbing
ones that trailed off into a melancholy whisper on the still
night air. It was a sound of mystery, of darkness and loneliness and the ancient unknown, of secret midnight places
where man trespassed at his own risk.

She shivered a little, shook herself and zipped her
denim jacket snugly to her chin. Then she swung herself
up onto her horse, reined his head toward the west and

spurred him gently, setting him to a gentle, rocking canter that carried them rapidly into the deep, silvered vastness of the sleeping prairie.

When she reached the West Five, she swung her horse wide, circling so that she could approach the Singing Stones from the opposite side, deliberately adding a couple of miles to her journey in order to give a wide berth to the little camp at the base of the cliff.

It was a Saturday night, and Libby was fairly certain that nobody was sleeping in the tents. When she'd driven by earlier in the day, Warren's Jeep had been gone, and the place had looked utterly deserted. But she still didn't want to take any chance that he might have returned, that he might hear the bay's hoofbeats and climb the plateau to investigate...

She rode into a shallow, grassy ravine at the western slope of the cliff, reined in and slipped to the ground. As an extra precaution in the hushed midnight stillness, she clipped a loose hobble onto the bay's front legs, then slackened the saddle cinches and took his bridle off so that he could graze freely. He nuzzled fondly at her, cocked one hind leg and lowered his head, eyes drooping shut in the moonlight.

Libby smiled and caressed his rough, silvered mane. "All right, you lazy old thing," she whispered. "Go to sleep if you want to. Just don't make any noise. You hear me?"

Her smile fading, she edged from the ravine and began silently to climb the hillside, moving carefully to avoid dislodging small stones or stumbling into banks of cactus on the narrow, rough deer trail.

As she climbed, she listened to the scraps of coyote song carried on the warm night air. The coyotes were hunting somewhere in the vastness of the big field, and their calls drifted sweetly across the silvered prairie, high little piping yips of excitement followed by long, melancholy howls that sobbed and sang in the darkness, as remote and lovely as the starlight.

At the summit Libby stopped to catch her breath, then moved slowly forward into the circles of stone. All at once she stopped, gripped with awe and a sudden paralyzing fear. There was something so strangely different about this place at night, so weird and mystical.

The moonlight poured down with cold, austere brilliance, bathing the hilltop in an icy glow. Every rock shone bright silver in the cool white light, and Libby suddenly realized they were positioned so that their flat sides would catch and reflect the moonlight, leaving deep pools of shadow behind them. The big picture rock was a beautiful, forbidding column of shining platinum, its ancient, patterned face flashing a warning to intruders.

Hesitantly, holding her breath, Libby edged forward into the largest circle and stood in front of the glistening petroglyph. She felt a disturbing sense of fear and reverence, as if she were venturing into some place of indescribable holiness and circles of avid eyes were watching from the darkness, waiting for her to be stricken with some kind of divine and terrible punishment...

A little breeze began to play through the stone circles and the tall, waving grass, and the music of the stones rose around her, haunting, silvery notes that grew and throbbed, swelling finally to a towering crescendo of sound that thundered in her ears and took her breath away.

Sternly Libby composed herself and tried to study the rock. She took her small flashlight from her pocket and played it over the rough, patterned surface, noting with surprise that the incised, lichen-splashed figures were actually easier to distinguish in this thin, silvery beam of light.

She bit her lip, frowning in concentration, trying to make sense of the tiny symbols, the deer and antelope, the hilltops and valleys and winding creek beds, the suns and phases of the moon, the flights of arrows and strange geometric signs.

Her head began to swim in confusion as the music rose again, insistent and throbbing, with a powerful, primitive beat. The old spell of the place began to weave itself through her mind, and Libby felt herself sinking, whirling, drawn into that hypnotic vortex of music and rhythmic drumbeats, into a world of smoky camp fires and glittering starlight, of chants and rituals and primitive magic.

She heard the patter of dancing bare feet on the flattened grass, saw the moonlight glinting on feathers and amulets, smelled the resinous fragrance of burning wood and soft, tanned leather. She felt herself plunging, spiraling deep into the past, and sensed nothing but a great, aching, hungry yearning to lose herself in those ancient mists, to be one with the ageless mystery of the stones that surrounded her.

She wasn't even surprised when the tall brave came striding toward her through the mist, starlight in his black eyes, moonlight glistening on his high, flat cheekbones. Quietly she watched him, knowing that he came out of her dream in answer to her deepest longings. When he drew near, she reached out for him, shuddering with need, and sighed in bliss as his hard-muscled arms closed around her.

"Libby!" he whispered, his breath warm on her face. "What are you doing up here? I've been coming up at night to check the angles of the moon on the petroglyph, but I never dreamed that you—"

"Don't talk," Libby murmured urgently, lost between two worlds, drowning in the fiery passion that thundered in her blood like the wild, insistent beating of the drums. "Please…don't talk. Just hold me. Oh, hold me."

Warren's arms closed around her, his big, firm body growing taut in response to her fervor. He kissed her hungrily, and she pressed against him, moving her lips on his, whispering hushed and broken words of desire, running her hands over his face and hair and arms.

He was so wonderful, so strong and hard to her touch, so real and tangible and satisfying after the misty, haunting world of dreams and troubling half-life that he had materialized from.

Libby felt herself being lifted, carried out of the circle of stones into the soft grass at the edge of the cliff. With a wondering, soaring sense of joy, she felt his hands stripping the clothes gently from her body, laying bare her breasts and thighs to the warm, caressing moonlight. She lay in a soft nest of discarded clothing as his hands moved over her, warm as the summer wind, stroking and fondling her silvered skin with a gentle, lingering touch.

She closed her eyes, completely abandoned to her senses, wanting the soft caresses to go on forever as her heart beat in time to the drums and the firelight warmed her body.

When at last she opened her eyes, he stood naked above her, tall and beautiful in the moonlight, his lean muscular body rippling and glistening. Libby gazed up at his arrogant maleness, and her body opened to him with warm, sweet yearning, with a timeless, ancient need that only he could fill.

"Oh, my darling," she whispered, reaching up to him through the mists of time. "My darling, you're so wonderful. I always knew you would be wonderful."

"Libby," he murmured, lowering himself into the softness of the fragrant grass and gathering her into his arms. "Libby, my sweetheart, my love. Let me look at you."

He lay beside her, propped on one elbow, his tanned upper arm bulging and tensing, and gazing in wondering pleasure at the length of her slender naked body as his hand slowly caressed her breasts and her smooth, firm abdomen, cupped her hips, stroked her silken thighs, trailed gently across the delicate, fragrant softness of her skin.

The beating of her heart, the throb of the drums and the frantic rhythm of the dancing feet grew more and more insistent. Whirling through a world of dreams, Libby reached up and drew him down toward her.

She forgot who she was, where she was, what was happening to her. She knew only that she was on fire with need, aching for this man, longing for him with a hunger that transcended time and reason. With shuddering, wondering happiness she felt him slide into her, felt their bodies lock together in an ageless, primal rhythm, felt him move in her and through her in time to the music that sang and throbbed among the ancient stone circles.

The firelight leaped and danced, the chants swelled and the dancing feet pounded faster, faster, until all the scattered, brilliant images finally united in one mighty surge of light and sound that was thunderous, blinding, overwhelming. Sensations went crashing through Libby's body and left her limp, breathless, drained and empty of passion, conscious only of silence and moonlight and a calm, tremulous, peaceful happiness that flooded her whole being.

She stirred and opened her eyes, seeing Warren's face close to hers, his fine, austere features calm and relaxed, his dark, sculpted face gentle with love.

He smiled at her, his dark eyes shining. "Sweetheart," he whispered. "Oh, Libby, my love..."

Gradually she felt reality creeping back, flowing relentlessly into her mind and overshadowing all her contented sense of fulfillment with grim reminders of time and place.

"Warren," she murmured, sitting up and reaching hastily for her clothes. "Warren, I'm...I'm so sorry. I don't know what made me so..."

"Sorry!" he exclaimed, still smiling. "You're *sorry*? Dear God, the most wonderful experience of my whole life, and the lady *apologizes*!"

Libby smiled back awkwardly, warmed in spite of herself by the sincerity beneath the teasing gentleness of his voice.

"It's...it's this place," she murmured, grateful for the cool moonlight that hid the painful flush on her cheeks. She flexed her long legs and tugged on her panties and jeans, then searched frantically through the tangled welter of clothing for her shirt. Warren stepped into his own discarded jeans and moccasins, watching her in thoughtful silence.

He came and knelt beside her, holding out the shirt for her, helping her to slip it over her shoulders. "What do you mean, 'it's this place'?" he asked, bending forward to look into her eyes, his lean brown hands still gripping the front of her shirt.

"It's...I don't know," Libby said helplessly. "I told you once before, it's like magic. Maybe black magic," she added with an awkward laugh. "It just makes me come all unglued. When I'm alone up by that stone, I see things that aren't there and hear things and get...stranded, you know, somewhere between the present and the past, and completely lose my grip on reality."

Still kneeling in front of her, Warren began to fasten the top button on her shirt, then paused and lifted the fabric aside gently to bend forward and kiss her breasts, pressing his face hungrily into the silvered fragrance of her skin.

Libby shuddered with emotion, gazing down at his crisp, dark hair against her breast, feeling the warm firmness of his lips. Desire began to rise in her again, flooding her with a sweet, disturbing warmth.

"Warren," she whispered, pushing gently at his shoulders. "Warren, please, don't."

He drew aside instantly, his face calm and unreadable, and continued to button her shirt. "So, Libby," he said, "this place makes you crazy, does it?"

She nodded, looking down at his tanned hands against her shirt, unable to meet his eyes.

"And what just happened," Warren went on in that same quiet, detached voice, "was that some kind of fantasy, too? Did I just imagine it or what?"

"In a way," Libby said earnestly. "I mean, of course it happened. But I really don't think..." She hesitated, then looked up at him directly. "I don't think it could have happened anywhere else, Warren."

"Why not?"

"Because I don't..." Libby paused, unable to meet his dark, piercing gaze.

"Because you don't really feel that way about me, Libby? Is that what you're telling me?"

Libby bent to tug on her riding boots, the long plait of her ruddy hair falling over her shoulder against her cheek. "I'm not sure how I feel about you, Warren. I just know that as long as you're here on our land, doing what you plan to do, it's not possible for us to have this kind of relationship."

He paused in the act of buttoning his own shirt and cast her a sudden, sharp glance. "Libby…" he began softly. "Libby, why *were* you up here tonight, come to think of it? Did you just have a sudden craving to see the stones by moonlight?"

A little more in command of herself now that she was fully dressed, Libby gazed back at him, eyes wide, mind racing.

"Come on, Libby," he prompted her gently. "I want to know just why you're wandering around up here at midnight."

"I don't see why I should tell you anything," Libby began, shrugging into her jacket with an attempt at casualness. "After all, as I've pointed out to you before, I'm the landowner here and you're the trespasser, right?"

"You're right. We've argued that point before, Libby, and neither of us is likely to change his view. Why don't you just answer my question?"

Libby considered, gathering her scattered thoughts, and decided that the safest course of action was to stay as close as possible to the truth. "I wanted a chance to look at the rock when nobody was here," she said. "I keep having the feeling that there's some solution to the whole mess, and it's somehow hidden in the rock itself. I know it's silly," she added, looking down at the silvered grasses at her feet.

Warren watched her steadily, his dark eyes glittering in the starlight. "What kind of solution could there be?" he asked slowly. "And how could it be in the rock? You mean, some kind of message in the symbols? What kind of message could possibly discourage development of this site, Libby?"

She shrugged and turned away. "I told you it was silly. In my position you'll grasp at any straw, I guess."

He watched her thoughtfully and then drew her into his arms again. "Libby," he whispered against her hair. "Libby, please don't slip away from me again. Not tonight, darling. For tonight let's just be kind to each other. I want to hold you and kiss you some more and tell you how lovely you are."

Libby shivered in his warm embrace, struggling with her own turbulent emotions. Part of her mind urged her to run, to put as much distance as she could between herself and this sweet madness that flamed in her blood. But another part of her, wild and insistent, longed to stay with him, here in his arms forever, as close to him as a woman could be to a man.

"Stay with me, dear," he whispered again, his breath warm on her ear. "I'm all alone down there tonight. Stay with me in my tent and I'll hold you all night, and in the morning we'll get up with the sun and I'll cook you breakfast over an open fire. Please, darling. Stay with me."

"Oh, Warren..." Libby moved in his arms, trying to draw away, but he gathered her closer and his lips began to roam hungrily over her face once more.

Trembling with sudden need, Libby gave up and abandoned herself to his caress. At last she leaned back in his arms and smiled up at him. "So," she said, trying to keep her voice light, "you're offering to cook me breakfast, are you?"

"Absolutely," Warren said solemnly. "The best camp fire cuisine in these parts, my lady."

She chuckled and hugged him again. "Well," she said thoughtfully, "In that case, maybe I *could* just consider..."

"Say no more." Laughing, he kissed her and slipped an arm around her, turning her toward the edge of the cliff above the camp, and then stopped abruptly.

Libby glanced up at him in surprise. "Warren?"

"What about your horse? I trust you rode over here, because if you'd driven I'd have heard the engine."

Libby nodded. "He's fine. He's on a loose hobble down at the bottom, and the lazy old boy will probably sleep like a log till dawn, anyway."

"Me, too," Warren said solemnly.

Libby cast him a suspicious glance. "You'll sleep till dawn?"

"Like a baby. Just because the most beautiful woman in the world happens to be sharing my tent, don't think that's going to be any distraction to *me*."

Libby smiled in the darkness, warmed by his teasing words and the significant look that accompanied them. She snuggled into the curve of his arm and walked with him to the cliff edge, pausing once to cast a quick, troubled look back over her shoulder at the big petroglyph. The massive rock stood silent and immutable, flashing silver in the moonlight, guarding its secrets from her and all the world.

Wearily Libby realized that she was no closer to the solution of the mystery. But the feeling still hovered at the back of her mind, as tantalizing and maddeningly elusive as ever, that somehow, somewhere in the mass of little figures and signs lay the answer to her prayers.

Somehow, if she could only learn to read their signs, the ancients would speak to her across a gulf of countless years and ages, telling her how to protect what was sacred to her. But she couldn't unravel their mysteries, couldn't understand what they were whispering to her.

And until she could the man beside her would continue, on some deep level, to be an enemy to her. With every day that passed he was growing more dear and beloved than anyone she had ever known, but the implacable mys-

tery of the patterned rock stood between them, and Libby
was deeply afraid, even as she thrilled to the warmth and
strength of his embrace, that the obstacles might one day
prove to be insurmountable.

THE NOONDAY SUN LAY warm and rich across Mac's
broad, flat shoulders and gleamed on the faded brim of
his old brown Stetson. He leaned back thoughtfully on his
tattered green lawn chair, peering at the painting on his
easel and then out at the prairie slough in front of him.

With a small frown of dissatisfaction, he adjusted the
easel, lifting one leg clear of a little flattened clump of
cactus and straightening the wooden tripod. He fiddled a
while longer with the support bar, adjusted the piece of
masonite that held the watercolor paper and rearranged
his paints on the wooden tray.

"How come you keep fiddling with all that stuff?"
Keith asked. "Can't you get things to suit you, or what?"

"It's very, very difficult," Mac said with dignity, "to
do this kind of lighting. Noonday sun is the hardest thing
of all to capture."

"So do the painting some other time," Keith said casually.

Mac frowned again, his tanned face thoughtful. "I want
noonday light," he said. "This is the summer scene in
the group, and I want it to be warm. I want it to shine
like gold."

Keith glanced up at his uncle with great fondness.
"You're crazy, Mac," he said cheerfully. "Crazy as a
hoot owl."

"Hoot owls aren't crazy," Mac said calmly. "They're
very rational birds. And," he added, bending once more
to tug at the leg of the easel, "so am I."

Keith chuckled and went back to work. The younger

man sat cross-legged on a heavy plaid blanket littered with the remains of a casual bachelor picnic lunch. He wore jeans, a tractor cap, sneakers, heavy leather gloves and nothing else, and his muscular, tanned back rippled and flexed as he tugged at the ropes he was braiding.

Keith was making a "bull rope," a beautifully intricate construction designed to use when riding bulls at rodeos. He had a bundle of lengths of raw hemp tied to the nearby truck bumper, and he was braiding them in eight plaits, with work so tight and precise that the gloves were necessary to protect his hands from rope burns as he tugged at the coarse fibers.

The resulting rope was flat and heavy, about two inches wide, and diverged at the halfway point to form a handhold of two thicknesses with leather stitched into it for strength. The top of the handhold had been spliced carefully in with the braid, and beyond the handhold the rope thinned so that it could be wrapped around the rider's hand for extra support.

Mac glanced over with quiet approval at the boy's neat, beautiful work, watching thoughtfully as Keith set the flat, braided length aside and crawled around on the blanket to straighten the tangled, trailing ends of loose hemp.

"That's a nice job you're doing," Mac said. "Looks real good."

Keith grinned up at him impudently. "I wish I could say the same for your painting, Mac," he said, "but nothing much seems to be happening there."

"Patience, my boy," Mac said placidly, waving his brush at the paper, which was mostly blank. "The way I look at it, there's a picture in here already. I just have to let it out."

"When?"

"In my own good time. Hand me one of those dough-nuts and quit being so critical."

Keith handed over the tin of sugar doughnuts, and both men returned to their work under the vast, soaring arch of prairie sky. Mac paused, doughnut in hand, to gaze around him at the land he loved. The prairie lay rich and warm, sleepy in the noonday light that spread like a roll-ing carpet of molten gold across the endless, undulating landscape. Far on the horizon little mists of violet and pale green swirled across the darkened smudge of land where the earth met the sky, and Mac frowned at them thoughtfully, wondering how to reproduce them.

A tiny, slender-bodied ferret trotted suddenly into view from behind a clump of sagebrush and sat up to examine them, his bright black eyes deeply interested. Mac held himself carefully silent and gazed back at the beautiful little silken animal, holding his breath, already forming the passage in his mind.

"Today I saw a black-footed ferret. They are so rare as to be almost extinct, with just a few surviving here on the prairie where it's most isolated. I wish you could have been there. I know you would have loved to see him. He was glossy brown with a touch of…"

The ferret ducked his head and darted off into the tall grass. Sighing, Mac wet his brush and returned to work, thinking about his letters.

At first it had been such a wonderfully satisfying thing, writing the letters to her. Just knowing that she would hold them in her hands, read the words he had written, perhaps find her day warmed and brightened by something he had said. That had been all that Mac needed to feel perfectly happy.

And he knew that she read them. One day at the ar-chaeological site he had overheard Alex telling Warren a story about the early settlement of the region that was practically a word-for-word excerpt from one of his letters and was also a bit of history that she would have been very unlikely to pick up elsewhere. Just hearing his own words in her sweet, husky voice, knowing that a thought had traveled directly from his mind into hers, had been almost enough to make Mac dizzy with delight.

But, like all lovers, he soon found himself wanting more and more. Just as it had soon become unsatisfying to paint the set of seasonal pictures for her, now it was no longer enough to write the letters. He craved something even more real, some kind of personal contact and direct communication. But he was so terribly afraid of her reaction if he should go to her and introduce himself as the writer of the anonymous letters.

Alexandra Coleman's attitude toward Mac now was a sort of preoccupied courtesy. She treated him the same way she probably treated the paperboy or the janitor in her building or any other minor functionary existing on the fringes of her life. She obviously looked on Mac as a pleasant old codger, shy and a little simple but essentially harmless.

And no wonder, Mac thought grimly. I can't even seem to find my voice when she's around, let alone say anything intelligent enough to make her notice me....

But although her courteous, casual indifference was a cause of enormous pain to him he was afraid to admit to writing the letters. What if she was disgusted with him? Worst of all, what if she laughed at him? Mac writhed inwardly, picturing her fine tanned face, her lovely gray eyes sparkling as she tried to contain her startled amusement.

"Hey, Mac, you know that lady who works over at the archaeological site. Alexandra Coleman?"

Mac started guiltily, almost dropping his brush. "Yes," he said, forcing his voice to remain casual. "What about her, Keith?"

"Well, she gave Libby the name and address of another rancher, over east of Calgary, where they found a buffalo jump a few years ago and made a big tourist thing like they're planning here. Libby drove over there yesterday to talk to the rancher."

"Why?" Mac asked, frowning at the golden stretch of water that was gradually beginning to appear on the paper in front of him.

"Well, you know, to talk to the guy, see what it's like to have something like that on your land and how they've adjusted, how it affects their ranching operation and all that."

"I see," Mac said, adding a stand of darkened bullrushes at the water's edge. "That's a good idea."

"It stinks," Keith said gloomily, tugging on his rope with angry energy. "The whole damn thing just stinks."

"Now, Keith," Mac said mildly, "let's be intelligent about this. The government people are right, you know. You can't stand in the way of public access to something so valuable."

Keith stared at his uncle, his boyish, tanned face white with emotion. "Mac, the *land* is valuable. The *ranch* is valuable. A damn sight more valuable than a bunch of gaping tourists with their cameras and their kids and dogs and litter from their hamburgers and fries, blowing all over the countryside—"

"Whoa!" Mac said gently. "Hold on, kid. You don't know what this is going to be like. It might not be that terrible, you know."

"Libby thinks it's going to be terrible. This guy she went to talk to, he said the place is in a constant uproar.

They lost their best calving pasture, just like Gray is going to, and they always have problems with tourists trespassing, leaving gates open, scaring the livestock and teasing the bulls, all kinds of crap. After almost a hundred years on the same land, they're looking for a buyer, Mac. Libby's so upset she can hardly talk about it.''

Mac gazed down at the boy, his face troubled. "I didn't know that, Keith," he said quietly. "I'm sorry to hear it.''

They were both silent for a moment while Keith jerked angrily on the rope and Mac flicked his brush thoughtfully among the stand of bulrushes, outlining the stems.

"Funny," he said casually, "that…that Dr. Coleman would send Libby to see somebody with such a negative outlook. She must have known it would upset the girl.''

"Oh, the government doesn't know how mad this guy is," Keith said bitterly. "He's not saying anything because he wants to sell the ranch, and he doesn't want it to get around what a problem this damn tourist facility can be on a working ranch. He just told Libby in confidence because of her situation, to let her know that if there's any way in the world to stop the damn thing, she should try to do it.''

Mac glanced sharply at his nephew. "Keith," he said with a sudden edge to his voice, "there's no way to stop it. At least nothing that *you* can do about it.''

The boy was silent, gazing stubbornly down at his tangled lengths of rope.

"You hear me, Keith?" Mac repeated. "There's *nothing you can do* to stop this.''

Keith glanced up with a defiant set to his jaw and a dangerous flare in his dark blue eyes that suddenly reminded Mac of Joanna, the boy's mother.

"Maybe," Keith said quietly. "And maybe not.''
Avoiding Mac's troubled warning gaze, he dropped his eyes and returned to his braiding.

CHAPTER NINE

SUMMER DEEPENED and the prairie heat grew fierce, dancing and shivering across the brittle, waving grass at noonday in strange, silvery mirages. Rippling deep lakes flowed over the dry land and soft blue waves lapped against the horizon, vanishing in a mocking burst of heat as soon as they were approached.

The warmth brooded all day on the mountains, building up powerful thunderstorms that rolled out onto the flat land in billowing, angry clouds after the sun went down. Lightning flashed across the wide sky in jagged bolts, shaking the prairie, and the thunder boomed and echoed in great hollow explosions of sound.

Most nights the thunderstorms whipped up huge, choking clouds of dust driven on the gusty winds and then died away into gloomy, rumbling silence. But some evenings the livid mass of clouds brought rain and the skies opened, dumping countless tons of moisture on a parched and grateful earth.

During one such downpour, Libby crossed the living room at the ranch house to pull the drapes aside and peer out at the darkness. The rain pounded and danced on the veranda railing, glittering in the overhead light and flowing in dusty rivulets across the ranch yard. But her practiced eye could see the drifting and lightening in the clouds that massed overhead in the night sky, sense a gradual lessening of rain, and she could hear how the ragged claps of thunder were already drifting away to the east.

"It's not going to amount to much, Clarence. The storm's almost over," she murmured soothingly to Keith's spotted collie-cross dog, who lay trembling beneath a big armchair in the corner, wincing and closing his eyes in panic at each rumble of thunder.

"You big baby," Libby added, smiling down at the frightened dog. She bent to reach beneath the chair and ruffle his ears affectionately, poked at the dying fire and sat back in a padded leather chair, hugging her knees and frowning at the television set in the corner.

"Hi, Lib. Why so grim?" Keith asked, coming into the room with half a pizza on a dinner plate. As Keith lounged on the couch, Clarence crept out from beneath his chair, sidled across the floor with drooping tail and lay his chin anxiously on his master's knee.

Keith chuckled, patted the dog and fed him a slice of pepperoni. Clarence coughed and gulped, eyes watering, and then looked up hopefully, wagging his tail.

"Poor Clarence. He hates thunderstorms," Keith said. "Libby, how come you look so gloomy?"

"Oh, I don't know," Libby said restlessly. "This is such a stupid movie." She waved her hand at the flickering television screen. "I mean, she's supposed to really love this guy, but she suspects that he might be involved in these deep dark government crimes, so she's slipping around spying on him and getting into all kinds of ridiculous scary situations. Why doesn't she just *ask* him and get it over with?"

"Because," Keith said practically, "then there'd be no story. Besides, who can understand what goes on between men and women? Remember what it was like with my mom and your dad? I was so unhappy because they couldn't get along. They just seemed to fight all the time. I kept trying to think of ways to get them to like each other, just a little bit, and then all of a sudden, wham, right out of the blue, they announce they're getting married. It's a mystery.''

Libby grinned, remembering Gray and Jo and their stormy courtship and then thinking in spite of herself about Warren McIntyre, recalling his dark, piercing eyes, his lean brown hands....

''Yes,'' she said softly. ''It's a mystery, all right.''

''How's Peggy?'' Keith asked, detaching another slice of spicy sausage to inflict on poor Clarence.

''Radiant. Even though she claims she's only getting fifteen minutes of sleep a day because Bobby is awake all night wanting to discuss astrophysics and the theory of relativity.''

Keith laughed aloud. ''She brags so much, doesn't she? You'd think that little bald kid was just the greatest thing since sliced bread.'' He hesitated, looking thoughtfully at Clarence who was rubbing his muzzle frantically with his front paws. ''How come they're calling the kid Bobby? I thought Peg insisted he was going to be Robert, and nothing else.''

''Peggy says a lot of things, but she still can't handle Rob that easily. If he wants to call his son Bobby, then he'll do it.''

''Good,'' Keith said, his mouth full of pizza. ''Robert sounds a little too...you know...''

''School tie and blazer?'' Libby suggested.

''Yeah. Not all that macho, a kid called Robert.''

''Well,'' Libby said thoughtfully, ''there *is* Robert Redford, you know. He's certainly macho enough for me.''

Keith grinned. ''Spoken like a true woman. Funny,'' he added, ''that Peg is the mother, you know? I always pictured *you* being the domestic one with a herd of babies at your knee.''

Libby had a sudden, warm, vivid memory of Peggy's baby, drowsy and heavy and sweet in her arms. And, along with that image, she saw another one—Warren McIntyre, his dark, hawklike face soft and gentle with love, holding a tiny sleeping baby in his brown, muscular arms and smiling down at her with indescribable tenderness....

She shivered and punched the remote control to turn off the television, then gazed moodily at the fire.

Keith finished his pizza and set the plate, still smeared with warm melted cheese and tomato sauce, on the floor for Clarence to lick.

"Don't do that," Libby said automatically. "I hate it when he licks the plates, Keith."

"I'll rinse it and put it in the dishwasher right away," the boy said. "Honest."

"If I didn't watch you, I'll bet you'd put it back in the cupboard."

"Sure," Keith admitted cheerfully. "And what you didn't know would never hurt you."

Libby smiled wanly and then gazed at the smoldering embers again while Keith cast her a troubled sidelong look.

"Lib...I'm leaving early in the morning, you know. Heading down through Colorado and Wyoming. I'll be gone for a few weeks at least. Maybe more if I can hook up with some other guys who want to travel to a few more rodeos down in Texas."

Libby nodded absently, hugging her legs, her chin on her knees as she stared at the fire.

"I mean," he went on, clearing his throat, "I might not even be back before Mom and Gray get home."

"So?" Libby asked, glancing over at him.

"So you're all on your own with this government thing. If anybody's going to do something about it before it's too late, it'll have to be you."

"Come on, Keith. What can I do?"

"You've got to do *something*," he insisted. "We can't just…just sit back and let this happen, Lib. It's so awful."

"Look, Keith, I'm not a complete idiot," Libby said wearily. "I mean, I *have* researched this, you know. I got all dressed up and went into town to talk to the government agency that administers this stuff, and I looked up the legal statutes at the library, and I talked to that other rancher, who says he hired a couple of hotshot city lawyers and even *they* couldn't prevent the government from expropriating the land. So what can I do? What can anyone do?"

"There are things you can do," Keith said quietly, staring down at his dog's busy pink tongue as it carefully circled the shining expanse of the empty plate.

Struck by something in his tone, Libby looked over at him sharply, waiting in silence.

"But," Keith went on, still gazing fixedly at Clarence, "if you *were* to do something, you'd have to do it fast before they haul their equipment in and start building and set up temporary housing there and all that crap they're planning."

"Keith…" Libby began slowly, "Keith, what are you getting at?"

"Remember when Gray bought the old Colter place?" Keith asked abruptly, getting up and strolling across the living room to toss another log on the fire.

Libby watched him, puzzled. "Well, of course. That was just last fall. Why?"

"Well, he was planning to clear off all those old buildings so that he could level the yard and put some new corrals in, remember? He was going to do it this summer, but then they decided to take this big trip so that he didn't get around to it.''

Libby nodded, watching her stepbrother with a cautious, intent gaze. "So?" she prompted him finally.

Keith turned and looked at her directly, his young face taut with emotion. "Lib, I checked this afternoon. All the stuff is still out there, locked in the safe down in the Quonset. Everything's there, the blasting caps and circuits and everything."

Libby's eyes widened, and she shook her head emphatically. "I don't want to hear this, Keith. Don't say another word."

"Why not?" the boy asked passionately, crossing the room to stand directly in front of her and looking down at her with blazing eyes. "Why *not*, Lib? They're not giving *us* a hell of a lot of consideration, are they? And it's our land! If we want to do a little blasting, clear some rocks on our own land, who's to stop us? Gray's blasted rocks and old buildings dozens of times. He doesn't even need a blasting permit when it's his own land. You know that, Lib."

Libby stared up at him. "But..." she whispered, licking her lips. "But, Keith, this is...it's a heritage site. I mean, it's really valuable. They'd...probably arrest me and put me in jail for life if I blew it up."

"I doubt it," the boy said. "You could always say it was an accident or something. I mean, you were just riding there, taking the caps somewhere else and your horse shied and they fell and exploded, or something."

"Oh, sure," Libby said wearily. "Like, I just happened to be taking a shortcut up over the highest piece of land on the property, right? That's really plausible, Keith."

"Never mind that," he said stubbornly. "Nobody could *prove* you were lying, could they? And what's lost? An old rock with some dumb little pictures on it. There's dozens of them around here. Mac even says there's another one somewhere over in the community pasture. Let them go find that one and leave us alone."

"Sure, Keith," Libby said with a wan, private smile. "That sounds like a terrific idea. Why didn't *I* think of that?"

"Come on, Lib. Quit being sarcastic and give this idea a fair shake. If you just—"

A distant rumble of thunder drifted back to them on the night wind. Clarence dropped his belly onto the floor and scuttled hastily back under the chair, peering out with fearful bright eyes.

"That's it!" Keith exclaimed suddenly.

"What's what?" Libby asked, bewildered by his swift leaps of thought and deeply troubled by his proposal.

"You can blast it during a thunderstorm! In this heat we're having them practically every night. Then, right after you blow the damn thing to smithereens, you can gather up the blasting caps, get the hell out of there and say afterward that the rock was struck by lightning. The rain will wash away your tracks," Keith went on, warming to the idea, his face shining with excitement, "and it's not unrealistic to think the rock would be struck by lightning. After all, it's the highest object on the highest point of land for miles around. The whole thing is perfectly logical."

Libby gazed back at her young stepbrother, stunned and dismayed by the way his arguments were beginning to sway her. "Keith...I couldn't possibly—"

"Well, *I* sure could!" he exclaimed. "Damn, I wish I'd thought of it sooner. I could have done it tonight. Or

I could stay and do it tomorrow, but if I don't leave really early in the morning, I'll miss the Cheyenne rodeo, and I need the points to stay up there in the standings.''

"Never mind," Libby said gently, regaining control of herself at last. "Forget it, kid. Just go to your rodeos and let me look after the ranch, okay?"

"Promise that you'll at least think about it, Libby."

"I promise you," she said, trying to sound light and casual, "that I'll give the whole idea just exactly as much attention as it deserves. Now go to bed. I mended the elbows in both those shirts you put in the wash," she added.

"Thanks, Lib. Do you know the combination on the safe?"

"Of course I do, child."

"And you know how to set the caps and wire the circuits? I mean, you've helped Gray do it before, haven't you?"

"Forget it, Keith. I mean it. Put the whole thing completely out of your mind."

"Libby..." he began in anguish.

"Look," Libby said, her voice low and full of emphasis. "I said to forget it, Keith, and I mean it. If you should happen to hear, sometime in the future, that there was a terrible summer thunderstorm and this big rock was struck by lightning, I want you to be just completely amazed. I don't want Dad or Mac or anyone ever to know that we had this conversation. Do you understand me?"

The boy looked at her, his face relaxing, his eyes lighting slowly. "Libby Lyndon," he murmured, punching her lightly on the shoulder, "you're a hell of a woman."

"Get some sleep," Libby said abruptly. "All those bulls are waiting for you, and they're mean."

Avoiding his slow, triumphant grin, she turned aside to

poke the fresh log on the fire and then settled herself on
the floor beside Clarence, fingering his silky ears in deep,
preoccupied silence.

LIBBY DROVE her little yellow Jeep across the damp prairie grass, avoiding the rutted trail where pools of water
from the previous night's rain lay glistening in the hot
morning sun. At the base of the cliff by Warren's camp
she parked, swung out of the little cab and smiled at
Sandy and Tim, who were busy as usual, setting up
masses of heavy surveying equipment.

Sandy grinned and waved to her friend with genuine
warmth, while Tim gazed at Libby with his customary
frank admiration. Libby smiled back at the younger man
a little awkwardly, suddenly conscious of how she looked.

In the searing heat of these summer days, Libby tended
to abandon her customary shirts and jeans in favor of
khaki shorts, brief knitted tank tops and sandals. Her long
red hair was tied back loosely at the nape of her neck,
and she wore a casual white cotton cap with a long peak
that shaded her face.

"Okay, Tim," Sandy said tartly. "You can put your
eyes back in your head now. Just because the woman's
legs are long, tanned and gorgeous, that's no reason for
you to stare."

Tim grinned cheerfully. "Any man in his right mind
would stare," he told Sandy solemnly. "But I wouldn't
want Warren to catch me doing it. Besides," he added,
reaching out to give his shapely co-worker a brief hug,
"I'm actually kind of partial to cute little blondes, myself."

Sandy made an impudent face and then grinned back
at him, bending to wrestle a tripod into position.

Libby smiled, enjoying their mood of lighthearted, affectionate fun. "Well," she said solemnly, "it sounds like things are going well here."

Tim nodded, his blue eyes sparkling. "Things are going great," he said placidly. "Just great. Warren's up top," he added.

"Thanks, Tim. I'll be right back." Libby started up the cliff while the two younger people stood at the base watching her and then exchanged a slow, significant grin before they went back to their work.

Libby crested the plateau and walked hesitantly in among the stone circles where Warren knelt, wearing nothing but moccasins, headband and a faded, ragged pair of denim cutoffs, his bare, tanned back rippling as he traced the tiny masses of symbols on the lower portion of the petroglyph.

Suddenly overcome with turbulent emotion, Libby stood still and gazed at him. She loved the sight of him, the powerful, clean lines of his muscular body, the bulging muscles of his sun-browned thighs, the shining dark hair that fell against the nape of his neck, the spare, taut efficiency of his movements.

As she watched him, still unseen, Libby remembered that magic moonlit night among the stones, the pounding rhythm of distant drums that matched the pulsing, throbbing passion of her own body...

All at once she shivered, hugging her arms in the warm sunlight.

Warren turned, saw her and stood slowly erect, his dark eyes lighting with surprise and happiness. "Libby," he said simply, holding out his arms.

Helpless in the grip of her deep, urgent attraction to this man, Libby went to him, trembling with emotion as his big, hard-muscled arms closed around her and she felt herself crushed in his embrace. His warm, tanned skin smelled of sage and dust, and his firm, searching lips on her were hot and sweet.

"Libby," he whispered against her ear. "I'm so glad you came to me, darling. I've been thinking of you every minute, all the time, but I wanted to leave the next move up to you. I didn't want to force anything."

Libby moved in his arms, troubled by the happiness in his voice, feeling like a traitor. This man trusted her, cared about her so deeply, and all the time she was planning to—

"Warren," she said a little breathlessly, "let me go. You're crushing me!"

He grinned and loosened his embrace, smiling warmly down at her. "Just look at you, Libby Lyndon. If there was ever a girl who begged to be hugged, it's you. You're beautiful, sweetheart. Just as beautiful as this summer morning."

Libby gazed back at him, lips parted, eyes a deep emerald-green beneath the wide, shady peak of her cap, startled into silence by the glow of love on his dark, austere features and the sincerity in his voice.

"What…what are you doing today?" she asked, moving awkwardly toward the stone and away from his dark, brilliant eyes.

"Finishing my chart. I'm mapping these little peripheral symbols at the bottom edges, see? Mostly they're geometric figures."

Libby knelt by the rock, painfully conscious of his admiring gaze on her, of his lean, half-naked body so close to hers on the quiet, sun-splashed hilltop.

"Why—?" she began, and then hesitated, frowning at the symbols. "Warren…what makes you say these symbols are peripheral?"

He knelt beside her, resting a big arm casually across

her shoulders and pointing with a lean brown finger at a neat trail of parallel lines.

"Because they don't seem to have any relation to the central images. See that, darling, that little row of lines leading into that long spiral circle? That's the only image like that on the whole stone. I can't make any connection between it and the other symbols. None at all."

Libby shifted under the disturbing weight of his arm and his overwhelming nearness. "Warren..." she whispered, "it's really, truly going to happen, isn't it? Within a week or two you're going to have construction crews in here, and you'll be starting to build a tourist facility. You'll be bulldozing a road and fencing it off to divide our calving pasture."

"Oh, Libby," he began, his voice reflecting the anguish of his spirit as he gazed down at her. "Libby, I'm so sorry. I know how you feel about this, and I know that in some ways you're probably justified. But, sweetheart, you don't have to look just on the dark side, you know. There are a number of facilities like this on private land, and we seldom have any complaints from the landowners. Honestly, Libby, we don't."

"How about Al Herrold?" Libby asked. "He has a few complaints, believe me, Warren."

"He's just one case. It doesn't necessarily need to be a problem. It's possible to conduct this whole enterprise in a spirit of intelligent cooperation so that—"

"Now you sound like a real government employee," Libby said bitterly. "'A spirit of intelligent cooperation!' God, Warren, do you know how much I've come to hate that kind of talk in the past few weeks?"

"I'm sorry, Libby," he said quietly, standing up and drawing her erect to face him in the ancient stone circle. "You're right, of course. Platitudes and euphemisms don't count here. What counts...the only thing that counts, in fact, is this.''

He waved his hand, indicating the big rock with its tiny incised figures, standing within the quiet rings of stone. Libby stood watching him, her face silent and withdrawn.

"This is truly wonderful, Libby. It's a treasure that transcends time and place, and it's far more important than what you want or what I want or whatever government agencies happen to decide. It's a rare, precious, priceless bit of our shared past, and it belongs to all of us.''

Libby looked at the massive, patterned rock face. With cool detachment she noted a deep niche near the top and a long narrow crack running down from it, and a couple of crannies near the midsection that were just the right size to hold the blasting caps. If the caps were properly positioned, the whole rock would be riven, smashed to pieces, scattered over the face of the plateau in a mass of chips and small meaningless boulders.

"Libby?" Warren asked.

Libby gave a guilty little start and turned to him, forcing herself to smile. "I understand, Warren," she said. "I know how you feel about your work, and I truly do understand how precious this rock is to you.''

His face lighted gratefully and he reached for her, drawing her into his arms. "Oh, Libby," he murmured against her ear. "My darling, I hate the thought of doing anything to hurt you. I love you, Libby.''

She pulled away in sudden panic and turned aside, rubbing nervously at her arms and talking rapidly as if her rush of words could somehow unsay what he had just said. But Warren persisted, taking her elbow and turning her back to face him, reaching down to cup her chin and lift her face to his.

"Did you hear me, Libby? I'm telling you that I love you. Do you know how much that means to me?"

"Please, Warren," Libby whispered. "Please, don't say anything more."

She cast a troubled, anxious glance at the western horizon where low, hazy drifts of puffy white clouds were beginning to build and mass like distant mountains. "I'd better get home and get some work done," she said. "It looks…it looks like there's going to be another thunderstorm tonight, and I have to get the cows in out of the upper pasture and make sure that—"

"Libby," he said softly, his dark eyes intent and serious.

"Please, Warren," Libby said. "Don't say any more. Please. Not yet."

"When, Libby? When am I going to be allowed to tell you how I feel? When do I get to plead my case?"

"Later, Warren. After…after they've started building and developing up here, and I've…I've had a chance to get used to it a little, okay? Then we'll…" Libby gulped and swallowed, feeling suddenly weighed down and crushed by a miserable, aching burden of sorrow and loss. "Then we'll talk about the future," she whispered, unable to look at him, knowing that it was a lie.

Because after tonight, after she had done what she had to do, there would be no chance of a future for them. He would hate her forever and rightly so. She would deserve every bit of angry scorn that he felt. But her duty would be done, her home would be safe and her family's land would be protected.

She had no choice.

Warren was looking down at her in concern, his piercing black eyes thoughtful and sober, his tanned, sculpted features silent.

"Warren…" Libby began.

"Yes, sweetheart? What is it?"

"Warren…I want you to know…I want you to know that I'm…I'm sorry," Libby faltered. "I want you to be aware that I really do…understand how you feel about this place, and I'm truly sorry for the pain that my feelings and reactions have caused you."

And, darling, she told him silently, I'm sorry for the pain I'm going to cause you by what I have to do. I'm sorry, so terribly sorry, because I love you, too, Warren. I love you with all my heart, and I'll never be able to tell you, not now….

She gave him a sad, awkward little smile, reached up to touch his tanned cheek with a gentle hand and then turned away from him, walking swiftly out of the ancient circles and down the steep, angled cliff face without looking back.

ALEXANDRA COLEMAN SAT at her desk with a misty smile, her beautiful, finely drawn features thoughtful and preoccupied. She finished reading the mass of handwritten pages, dropped them onto her desk and rested her hands quietly upon them, gazing absently out the window at the sprawling city. For a long time she sat in silence, staring at the noisy snarls of traffic moving in the streets below her office window.

But her eyes were far away, fixed on some distant horizon that only she could see.

At last she gathered up the neatly written pages, folded them with gentle hands and put them lovingly into their envelope, which she tucked back into her handbag. Then she shouldered the bag, touched her silvery hair briefly with a comb and left her office.

Two floors higher up in the massive government building, Alex hesitated in front of a big oak door identical to her own, knocked and stepped inside. Mark Whitby, the young sandy-haired government naturalist, glanced up with a harried look from a towering mass of documents and charts on his littered desk.

"Hi, Mark," Alex said cheerfully. "Idle as usual, I see. What a shameful waste of public funds."

He chuckled, grimacing wearily at the mass of documents and pushing his chair back.

"Alex, Alex, you're so cruel. Look at me, buried under studies and abstracts. I'll never, ever again see the light of day."

"What's it about?"

"Research on the burgeoning mule deer population. The gun clubs want the hunting controls eased, and the environmentalists want the herds protected. And I'm supposed to decide who's right."

Alex grinned, her wide gray eyes sparkling with humor. "At least," she said in her warm, husky voice, "you can comfort yourself with the knowledge that whatever you decide, it's going to be wrong and you're going to get all kinds of vicious, bitter criticism. That's the really nice thing about being a government employee."

"Now I remember," Mark said sourly, "why I've always liked you so much. That's a pretty dress," he added, waving an ink-stained hand at Alex's soft sage-green corduroy shirtdress. "Like you, Lady Alex. Classy but warm."

"Listen to the child!" Alex scoffed. "Just for that, how about if I take you away from all this and buy you a glass of vegetable juice down in the cafeteria?"

"Sorry, Alex," her colleague said, shaking his head regretfully. "If I don't put together some kind of preliminary bar graph by the end of the day, I'm sunk. I'm just ready to feed a few figures into the computer and see what it does with them.''

"Oh," Alex said, hesitating by the door.

"So why don't you just come clean?" Mark said cheerfully. "Come on, Alex. Shoot."

"I beg your pardon?" Alex asked, startled.

"Come on, sweetie. There's something you want, and I owe you so many favors that you don't have to bribe me with vegetable juice. Just ask me."

Alex blushed faintly and laughed, looking all at once so young and lovely that the youthful naturalist grinned at her with warm, startled approval, waiting for her to speak.

"No favors, just some information. I just wondered," Alex began diffidently. "I wondered if you could tell me the range of the black-footed ferret. I mean, where exactly would you be likely to see one near the city?"

"Near *this* city?" Mark asked, glancing up at her with quick interest.

Alex nodded tensely.

The naturalist leaned back in his chair, hands locked behind his head, frowning in concentration. "I doubt that you *would* see one," he said finally. "The black-footed ferret is very close to extinct, you know, and it has no natural range here in the settled area. At least not anymore. If you were to see one anywhere in this part of the province, it would likely be much farther south in the open semidesert country down near the border."

"Oh," Alex said, her mobile face reflecting her disappointment.

"Why do you ask, Alex?" Mark said curiously.

"Well, it's nothing, really. It's just that…a friend of mine in…in a letter he wrote mentioned seeing one, and

I had the impression it was somewhere near the city. I just wondered where, exactly, it might have been.''

''I wish you'd ask him,'' Mark said, his eyes lighting with excitement. ''I'd be really interested in knowing if the ferrets are managing to move back into this area. I haven't heard of any for quite a few years. Would you ask him, Alex, next time you see him?''

''Yes,'' she said, her smile fading, her lovely eyes growing distant again. ''Yes, Mark, next time I see him I'll ask him.''

She smiled absently, gave her colleague a little distracted wave and left, trudging back down the hall and up to her own office.

Safely inside, Alex closed the door and wandered across to gaze out the window with a brooding expression.

So much for that, she thought. Another clue that's turned into a dead end.

She continued to stare down at the gray, grimy city, shimmering in the afternoon heat. But her mind was far away once more, musing over the newest letter, grappling with her painful, aching yearning to meet the man who wrote those letters.

By now Alex no longer even tried to pretend that the letters weren't the most important and precious thing in her life. She lived for them, longed for them, received them and read them with breathless anticipation. And almost all of her waking hours were devoted to restless, endless speculation about their author.

If it was possible for an educated and intelligent woman to fall in love with a faceless entity, with a person who existed only through words on paper, then Alexandra Coleman was in love with the man who wrote these letters. The thought both thrilled and appalled her, but she knew that there was no longer anything she could do about it.

She was doomed to wait for the letters, to search them frantically for clues to their origin, to watch and try to be patient until somehow, somewhere, he would choose to reveal himself or make a slip that gave away his identity. And when that happened, Alex would see him face-to-face, be able to look into the eyes of mystery and hear the voice that she longed to hear.

"You silly woman," she murmured aloud to herself as she often did these days. "You silly, silly woman."

But the words were no longer harsh. Alex had long since given up castigating herself for her behavior and had come to accept it as something she couldn't help. She grimaced tolerantly at her own weakness and feminine fantasies, then moved back to her desk, stuffing charts and diagrams into her big leather briefcase.

She locked her office, paused in the outer vestibule and smiled at the receptionist. "I'll be gone for the rest of the day, Gloria. I'm going to run home and change my clothes, and then I'll be going out to Warren McIntyre's petroglyph east of the city. Just take calls, please."

"Sure thing, Dr. Coleman," Gloria said placidly, smiling up at her employer. "I broke my nail," she added, lifting one glossy, well-manicured hand for Alex's inspection.

"Poor baby," Alex scoffed fondly, bending to examine the ragged painted nail. "You should come out with me to the site. We're digging pits to check the foundation areas for artifact levels, real pick and shovel work. You could break the others so they'd all match."

Gloria chuckled and shook her well-coiffed head. "I think I'll pass on that, thanks. Oh, Dr. Coleman..."

"Yes, Gloria?"

"What should I tell Mr. McKellar if he calls again? I

mean, last time you said to tell him you'd be here this afternoon, but if you're not going to be..."

"Oh, yes." Alex paused. "Yes, I guess we have to tell Jason something, don't we? Tell him..." she said, her gray eyes sparkling with mischief, "tell him that I've gone out hunting for black-footed ferrets, and I don't know when I'll be back."

CHAPTER TEN

WARREN STOOD ERECT, wiping an arm across his hot face and glancing in concern at the bank of fluffy clouds, pearl-white tinted with pink and violet, that were building slowly on the western horizon.

"Some pretty big thunderheads there," he said to his companion. "Do you think we'll have a storm again tonight, Mac?"

Mac Burman, who was busy digging with a trowel at the bottom of a wide, shallow pit, glanced up from his work and squinted at the horizon with a quick, practiced eye. "Yes," he said briefly. "I think we will. Look at this one, Warren. What do you think it is?"

Warren knelt again and looked at the dainty fragment of serrated flint on Mac's callused palm. "Could be a piece of an arrowhead, Mac, but it's almost impossible to be sure," the younger man said, lifting the shining piece of flint and holding it up to the light. "Sometimes the flaking can be quite distinctive, but you still can't accurately put a name on any projectile point unless the basal portion is there to identify it."

"It's fascinating, isn't it?" Mac observed, sitting back on his heels with his trowel dangling from one hand, "how they all used their own patterns to make their arrowheads? I didn't realize you could date them just by the way they were shaped. I always thought they were all the same age, you know, and the different shapes just reflected...creative license, you know?''

Warren chuckled. ''Thank God you're wrong,'' he said cheerfully, ''or archaeology in the Western Hemisphere would be an even more difficult business than it already is.''

''I never dreamed it was so fascinating,'' Mac went on, returning to his careful trowel work at the bottom of the pit. ''I'd like to learn a lot more about it,'' he added shyly. ''I wish I could go back to school, take courses, get some training in this. I love it.''

''There's no reason you couldn't, Mac,'' Warren told him, setting the stone fragment in position on a big chart pinned to a board nearby and tracing rapidly around its outline. ''But you can learn a lot just by practical field experience, too, you know. I mean, you've been helping me off and on for what...just a month or so?''

He glanced down into the pit at Mac, who nodded and took up a brush to work carefully at a piece of projecting bone.

''And you're already a valuable assistant. You learn incredibly fast, Mac. I'd be happy to train you and give you the field credits if you're really interested.''

Mac grinned ruefully up at the younger man. ''The problem with me,'' he confessed, ''is that there's so many things I find interesting, there's just never time to do all of them. I wish every day was ninety hours, and every life was three hundred years. Then there'd be time to learn all the things I'd like to know.''

Warren looked down with affection at Mac's broad shoulders and his dusty tractor cap as he labored at the bottom of the pit. ''That's what makes you such a great guy, Mac,'' he said with quiet sincerity. ''That kind of interest and enthusiasm for life in general makes you a pleasure to be around. No wonder Libby thinks you're so terrific.''

Mac smiled awkwardly and then returned to his careful excavation of the bone fragment, frowning thoughtfully as he worked. "Speaking of Libby," he said in a casual tone, "how's my girl doing these days? I don't see much of her anymore."

"Neither do I," Warren said gloomily. "I wish there were some way I could—"

"It'll be all right, Warren," Mac said, glancing up quickly at the somber note in the young archaeologist's voice. "It really will. You just have to understand Libby. She's always been such a..." Mac settled back on his heels, looking earnestly up over the rim of the pit.

Warren set his chart aside and watched the older man silently, waiting.

"There were two of them, the twins, you know, and they were as different as night and day. Peg was always wild and carefree, charming and irresponsible, and Lib was just the opposite. If she had a job to do, she'd move heaven and earth to do it. Even when she was a tiny little girl, I can't ever remember her breaking a promise or neglecting a duty. She's always taken those things so seriously."

Warren nodded thoughtfully. "And now she feels it's her duty to protect this place in her father's absence, and she thinks she's letting him down by allowing us in here. That's the problem, isn't it, Mac?"

Mac nodded. "Exactly. And, being Libby, she can't just let go of it. She can't just decide there's nothing she can do, give it up, be easy on herself. Libby's not made that way."

"So, if she can't get rid of us, she can at least satisfy

her own sense of honor by having nothing to do with me, right?'' Warren asked, his dark face full of pain.

Mac looked at the other man with quiet concern. ''You really care for her, don't you, Warren?''

''I love her,'' Warren said simply, surprising himself by the ease and rightness of the words. ''I love her, Mac. I've never felt this way about anyone.''

Mac stood erect and stepped out of the pit, seating himself beside Warren on the grass in thoughtful silence.

''I think about it all the time,'' Warren went on, his voice low and strained. ''All day when I'm working up here, and all night when I'm lying down there in my tent, I think about this whole damn mess and how it affects Libby and what could possibly be done to straighten everything out.''

''And what conclusion do you arrive at?'' Mac asked gently.

''None,'' Warren said in despair. ''My thoughts just keep circling around and around on the same old treadmill. I know she doesn't want us on her land, and I can understand why. I understand it perfectly. In fact, if I were her, I wouldn't want this development here, either. And yet I look at this site and the amount of interpretive information that's available here, the illuminations about Paleo-Indian man that have never been developed anywhere else in the hemisphere, and I know absolutely that the world has a right to see it. I know that one family's landowning rights shouldn't stand in the way of public access to something like this. And, Mac, I just don't know what to do.''

Mac looked at Warren's face, at his fine, dark features drawn with the weary anguish of his conflict. He reached out a hand, dropped it onto the younger man's shoulder and squeezed affectionately. ''Don't take it so hard, son,'' he murmured. "You're doing the only thing you can do, being true to your training and your own feelings about heritage. And in time I believe that Libby will come to understand how you feel and agree with you."

"You really believe that, Mac? You really, honestly think she'll change her views and come to believe that a development here is a good thing?"

Mac stood up, dusted off his jeans and stepped lightly back down into the pit, picking up his brush again to attack the tantalizing piece of bone. "What if she doesn't?" Mac asked, his blue eyes suddenly shrewd. "Is there anything you could actually do to change the course of events here if you decided she wasn't going to change her stand and you couldn't bear to lose her?"

Warren hesitated, gazing intently at Mac's wise, weathered features. "I don't know," he said slowly. "I suppose if I were to argue passionately enough, I could convince Alex to hold off for a while, by promising her to find another site in the area in the near future...or, failing that, I guess I could remove myself from the project, at least refuse personally to have anything to do with a development that's causing so much pain to somebody I care about. Should I do that, Mac?"

Mac returned to his thoughtful probing of the soil around the bone, his big hands deft and gentle. "Well, Warren, let me tell you," he said at last, glancing up from beneath the peak of his dusty cap. "This is the way I look at it. Now, God knows, I've never had much to do with women myself, and I certainly don't claim to understand them all that well. I don't really believe," Mac added with a brief smile, "that *any* man can claim to understand them all that well. But I've spent a lot of years of my life sitting back and watching people, just being observant, and I've noticed a couple of things."

Warren knelt near the edge of the pit, listening carefully, knowing from experience that when Mac spoke like this, in thoughtful, measured tones about the mysteries of human interaction, he was worth paying attention to.

"Now women usually have strong feelings about things," Mac went on. "They know how they want things to be, and they can be really passionate and relentless about trying to get what they want. They can try real hard to force a man to see things their way and do what they want. But if they're successful at it, if they can get their man to go against his own convictions, to knuckle under and do things their way, then they often lose respect for him in the long run. It's a strange kind of paradox, actually."

Warren considered this, his dark hair falling across his forehead, his face thoughtful. "You mean," he began slowly, "if I go ahead with an active involvement in this development, Libby will hate me for what's being done to her family's property. But if I withdraw from it just out of consideration for her, then ultimately she'll come to despise me for being too weak to uphold my own principles?"

Mac nodded briefly. "That's about it. In a nutshell," he added.

"Talk about a hopeless situation," Warren muttered. "Heads I lose, tails I lose."

"Not necessarily," Mac said briskly. "You should give some credit to Libby for her own good sense. It could be that things will turn out the way you're always telling me, that this development will go ahead without any real problems or inconvenience to the Lyndon family, and Libby will eventually see that you were right and admit that she was all concerned about nothing. And, knowing Libby, if she really believes that, she'll come to you and tell you so. She's the most honest girl in the world.''

Warren nodded slowly, looking down at Mac's skillful hands as he set the brush aside and gently lifted the loosened bone fragment.

He thought about Mac's words and realized that although they had an undeniable ring of truth, they were still small comfort. He didn't want to wait for the passage of time to vindicate him in Libby's eyes. He didn't want to wait for anything. He wanted her now, tonight, wanted her in his arms and in his life, as close to him as his own heartbeat. With a vivid clarity that was almost painful, Warren remembered the wondrous beauty of her slim, silvered body on the moonlit hilltop, the wild, rich pleasure of her passionate response, the feeling of utter peace and fulfillment when their bodies merged.

She was the woman for him, the one he'd searched for all his life. His attraction to her and his yearning for her went far beyond the purely physical. All the qualities that Mac saw in her, the loyalty and upright truthfulness, the deep sense of honor and responsibility—these were attributes that Warren prized above all else, and that he had almost come to despair of finding in a mate.

Now that he had found Elizabeth Lyndon, had walked beside her and laughed with her, looked deep into her heart and held her close in his arms, there would never be another woman for him. And yet Mac was telling him that he could do nothing about his feelings, could only wait and see if the woman he loved might ultimately decide to accept him, if her feelings and reservations would somehow change with the passage of time.

He shifted awkwardly on the grass, his dark face tense with emotion.

"Patience, son," Mac said gently, as if reading his

mind. "It's a long life. We have to be patient to get the really good things. Now what about this, Warren?" he added in a more businesslike tone. "Look at all these little marks."

Warren reached down and took the bone fragment into his hand, forcing himself to concentrate on it. All at once his dark eyes kindled with excitement. "It's a fleshing tool, Mac. It's been incised and sharpened, and...look at this! There are ornamental designs carved on the haft, and some of them match the geometric symbols on the petroglyph! I'm sure I've seen that odd-shaped triangle...and that other..."

Still murmuring aloud, Warren leaped to his feet, turning eagerly to head for his tent and his charts while Mac stood in the pit and watched him, beaming with pleasure.

"Wait till Alex gets here!" Warren called back over his shoulder. "She's going to be wild about this."

Mac glanced up quickly, his smile fading. "Is Dr. Coleman coming today?" he asked anxiously. "I didn't know...you didn't say..."

Struck by the panic in the older man's tone, Warren paused and turned back toward the pit. "Yes, she's coming. She should be here anytime," he said. "Come on, Mac, don't look so scared. Alex is really a very nice person, you know. If you'd just force yourself to talk to her a bit, you'd find that out."

Mac looked back at him in awkward silence, the brush dangling helplessly from his hand.

"For a man who has all this wisdom about human relationships," Warren went on in a gentle, teasing voice, "you sure don't apply it sometimes, Mac. I meant what I said, you know. You'd probably get along really well with Alex if you'd just make the effort to talk to her a bit."

Mac gazed at the younger man, his face a strange mixture of emotions. "Well, now," he said finally, finding his voice at last. "Maybe I will. Maybe I'll just do that."

While Warren watched, Mac pushed his tractor cap back with slow deliberation, brushed a hand cheerfully across his bald head, then replaced the cap and returned to his work, whistling softly under his breath.

ALEX GAZED DOWN, enchanted, at the small bone fleshing knife that Warren placed in the palm of her hand. With reverent care she ran a fingertip over the incised figures on the ancient yellowed haft, then turned the tool gently to examine the other side.

Mac watched her, feeling the same kind of wondering delight in her appearance as she obviously felt for the beautifully carved little tool. On this hot, brooding summer day Alex wore cool khaki slacks, a loose white cotton shirt and soft, broad-brimmed khaki hat. Wisps of silver hair escaped from under the hat, blowing around her tanned face as she examined the dainty artifact.

On this windy hilltop, with the golden prairie spreading all around her and the sky darkening above her, Mac thought her entirely lovely, as rare and beautiful a sight as he had ever known in a whole life dedicated to a love of the beautiful. He turned aside hastily, hoping that his face hadn't given away his thoughts, and returned to his careful work at the bottom of the shallow pit.

"Oh, my," Alex breathed. "Look at the delicacy of the carving, and these geometric symbols... Warren, they're almost pre-Columbian, aren't they? I've never seen anything like this so far north, have you? I can't wait to get back to the office and look up—" She broke off, gazing raptly at the bone tool again. "Who found it?" she asked without looking up.

"Mac did," Warren said. "Right there in his pit."

"Mac?" Alex asked blankly, looking up at the young archaeologist. "Oh, you mean Mr. Burman," she added, her face clearing.

"Alex, call him Mac," Warren said cheerfully. "Every-one calls him Mac."

The subject of this conversation continued to labor silently and with great energy, keeping his face averted, knowing she was looking at him.

"I didn't know Mr. Burman... I didn't know Mac was a field-worker," Alex said hesitantly.

"Technically he isn't," Warren said. "He's just really interested in the dig, so I decided to give him a little training and let him help me."

Warren grinned suddenly, gesturing to a second pit on the far side of the plateau where Tim and Sandy were laughing over something, their golden heads close together in the sunlight.

"Those two," he went on, "seem so cozy and giggly these days that I can never be sure how much work I'm going to get out of them. So I'm grateful when Mac can come over to help me."

"That's one good thing about those of us who have attained a certain age," Alex said briskly, giving Mac a polite smile as she walked over to the edge of the pit. "At least our employers can be certain that we're not going to be constantly preoccupied with affairs of the heart. It makes us *much* more reliable workers."

Warren chuckled at this, and even Mac grinned faintly, but kept his face averted, continuing to dig busily.

"Did the fleshing tool come from this pit?" Alex asked, leaning in to examine Mac's work. "What was its positioning?"

Mac glanced in sudden panic at Warren, but the young

man's broad back was turned and he was apparently deeply absorbed in a study of his artifact chart, so Mac had no choice, short of actual rudeness, but to answer her questions himself.

"It was on…on the floor of the pit," he said, clearing his throat awkwardly and pointing at the damp soil at his feet.

"Horizontal or vertical?" Alex asked.

Mac considered, searching for words to describe the slanting orientation of the bone tool, the mysterious, exciting way that it had first appeared and then begun, gradually, almost shyly, to emerge from its ancient, concealing shroud of earth.

"Sort of…half and half," he said lamely.

Alex nodded absently, and then turned to call Warren who folded up his charts and came over to the edge of the pit.

"Warren, how rich is the artifact level over here? Should we be planning an alternate position rather than placing a walkway right here?"

Warren shook his head. "The whole plateau is rich in artifacts, Alex. We can't preserve the whole thing and still allow public access. I think the only thing we can do is position the walkways, preexcavate like this to salvage anything really valuable and then go ahead with the development."

Alex gazed sadly at the tool in her hand. "I just hate to think," she said with sudden rebellion, "about people running around over soil that's filled with things like this."

Warren patted her shoulder. "This is your job, Alex. And if we plan well enough, and provide them with adequate, controlled walkways, then they'll certainly be doing less damage to the rest of the site."

Alex nodded glumly. "I know," she said. "I know you're right. Sometimes I'd just like to forget the whole thing and be completely selfish for a change. I wish this hilltop could stay forever just the way it is and be left alone by everybody to guard its own secrets, the way it's done for thousands of years."

"Then you and Libby have a lot in common," Warren said with a grim smile. "That's the way she feels, too."

Alex gazed at him, her gray eyes troubled. "Yes," she murmured, "I suppose she does. Poor Libby. I can understand her feelings perfectly. But then I can't just neglect my position and my responsibility to the public, can I?"

"No, Alex," Warren said gently. "I don't believe you can."

Alex placed the finely carved bone tool in Warren's hand and glanced down into the pit where Mac was working on his hands and knees, carefully remaining aloof from the conversation above him.

"Mr. Burman...Mac!" Alex said suddenly. "What's that you're working on?"

Mac looked up from his careful brushing of a roughened object protruding from the lower edge of the pit wall. "I think it's a piece of pottery," he said shyly. "I can't tell how big it is, though."

"Oh, my God," Alex breathed, jumping down into the pit and kneeling beside him.

Holding her breath, she leaned forward to peer at the little patterned lip of the pottery shard and then turned to Mac, her eyes blazing with excitement. "Give me a brush!" she called to Warren over her shoulder. "And a dental pick!"

Mac moved aside and leaned forward to watch as she excavated the piece of pottery, so fascinated by her expert, precise work that he almost forgot to be paralyzed by her nearness.

After about fifteen minutes Alex paused to let Warren make a sketch of the positioning of the shard in the earthen face, then lifted it reverently free from its bed of dirt and turned it in her hands.

The curving piece of pottery was surprisingly substantial, a portion of a container almost twice as big as Mac's fist, including part of the lip and the base, and a rounded bowl decorated with strange, precise markings.

Warren leaned over Mac's shoulder, gazing at the pottery fragment, and began a rapid-fire technical conversation with Alex about its shape and patterning that went far beyond Mac's grasp. But he understood their excitement and the awed, hushed feeling of reverence that came with an understanding of the antiquity of this artifact. Mac closed his eyes in the sunlight, dreaming a little, trying to visualize the pair of hands that had fashioned this exquisite object and the last time it had been held and used.

He pictured someone dropping it here on the hilltop, feeling a surge of irritation when it broke in half on the coals of the fire, tossing it aside impatiently into the dust, where it lay for untold centuries and millennia before once again being held up to the light of the sun....

"I'll take it down and catalog it," Warren said to Alex, "and see if we can find anything similar on the charts. But I'm sure those markings are a complete anomaly here on the Plains. I've never seen anything similar."

"They're all related," Alex said thoughtfully. "The markings on the petroglyph and on the bone fleshing tool and on this pottery shard. There's some kind of significance, Warren. It must be...I don't know...ceremonial or something."

She hesitated, the small, sun-warmed creases deepening

around her fine gray eyes as she pondered the shard of pottery. "There's...something here," she said slowly, looking up with a troubled expression at both men, who watched her in silence. "Something...all connected somehow. We're missing it, Warren. There's some kind of significance that we're missing...something vast and marvelous that's just beyond us, that we can't seem to catch hold of...."

She fell silent, still gazing in brooding silence at the scrap of pottery in Warren's lean brown fingers. Finally Warren broke the silence by getting to his feet and dropping a hand on her shoulder. "We're just doing our jobs, Alex," he said, "the best way we can, that's all. I'll be right back. You two get to work, and maybe we can find the other half."

His warm grin broke the spell in the silent pit beneath the wide, brooding sky. Alex turned to Mac with a smile and held out his brush. "Well, I guess we're field partners, Mac," she said cheerfully. "You take that side, I'll take this one, all right?"

Mac accepted the brush, his hands trembling a little, turned away and went back to work. He felt a deep, surging happiness just having her there so close to him, working with her in placid harmony on a project that interested both of them. In fact, his fantasies had often included scenes like this, times when they were together, side by side at the hearth or in his bright, warm little kitchen, each of them deeply and contentedly absorbed in some private pursuit.

He saw himself working on a painting while she sipped coffee and read from a book propped against the milk jug at the kitchen table...saw himself playing his violin by the fireside on a winter's night while she sat at the old oak rolltop desk, writing letters...each of them warmed and fulfilled by the other's quiet, undemanding presence....

"So you enjoy archaeological work, do you, Mac?"

He stiffened a little and gripped the trowel in his fist, wounded by the tone of gentle politeness in her voice. It was so obvious to Mac that she was just trying to make conversation, trying to be courteous without having any knowledge at all of what he was like or how he felt.

And how was she supposed to know anything about him? He'd never, ever been able to converse with her, to talk freely and laugh with her and let her see into his thoughts at all. No wonder she looked on him as a sort of harmless village idiot.

Mac frowned, disgusted with himself for his cowardice.

This is a wonderful woman, he told himself sternly. A warm, interesting, intelligent woman. And if you ever want to get closer to her, Malcolm my lad, you're going to have to drum up some courage. Otherwise you don't even deserve to think about her....

"Mac?" she was saying politely, glancing over at him with concern.

"Pardon? Oh, yes," Mac said with an awkward little laugh. "You were asking about archaeology. Yes, I enjoy it a lot. It's kind of—"

He wanted to go on, to enlarge on his feelings, to tell her about his mystical sense of unity with the ancient craftsmen who made these tools and carvings, the wonderful bond between creative people that could reach all the way through the centuries and the ages to forge a warm perfect understanding. "It's...very interesting," he finished lamely.

"Yes," Alex said, turning back to her work. "It certainly is."

Mac looked at her slender body in the soft khaki slacks,

at the warm curve of her tanned cheek and the bright strands of silver hair escaping from beneath her hat. His mouth went dry and he cleared his throat nervously. "Dr. Coleman..."

She glanced up, smiling politely. "Yes, Mac?"

"There's actually a lot...a lot more I'd like to learn about archaeology. Warren said that you teach a class at the university and have all the books and things, and you could tell me...tell me a lot about the people who've occupied this site down through the ages. He said—"

"Yes, of course," Alex said with quick kindness, seeing how difficult it was for him to frame his request. "Warren's right. I have all kinds of books, and I'd be happy to lend some of them to you and give you some of my lecture notes, too. Sometime when you're in the city, if you'd just stop by my office..."

"When...when would be a good time, Dr. Coleman?"

"Oh, most any afternoon. I often have meetings in the morning..." Alex paused, making a little wry face to show how she felt about those meetings, and then continued. "But I'm usually in my office in the afternoon. Just check first to make sure I'm not scheduled to come here that day, all right?"

Mac nodded gratefully and drew a deep breath, steeling himself to do the hardest thing in all his life. "If I were...if I were to come and take up a lot of your time some afternoon, answering my questions, then I'd like to pay you back somehow, Dr. Coleman. I wondered if I could...if I could take you out to dinner afterward, maybe?"

Mac finished, hot and tense with embarrassment at his own awkwardness, and stole a quick glance at her from beneath the dusty peak of his cap.

She was startled, he could see, but at least she didn't

look amused. She wasn't laughing at him, although he was painfully aware of how ridiculous he must look in her eyes—a nervous, inarticulate old balding pig farmer, stumbling and blushing as he invited her out for a date.

Mac writhed inwardly with humiliation, wishing himself a million miles away from the quiet scrutiny of her beautiful gray eyes.

But her face was kind and her voice was gentle as she answered him. "Why, Mac, that's very kind of you, but…"

She hesitated, searching for words, and Mac understood suddenly that this was by no means an unusual event for her. Women like Alex Coleman experienced a lifetime of invitations they couldn't accept, of men yearning for their company who had to be refused with tact and consideration.

Mac hesitated, his head lowered, waiting humbly for her to finish.

"You see," Alex said at last, "I'm not…not going out socially…like that…not these days. I'm…" She paused, and Mac was surprised to sense that she, too, seemed awkward, even a little shy. "Actually I'm…kind of committed, in an emotional sense, I mean," she finished, her voice trembling slightly.

"You are?" Startled and dismayed, Mac glanced up at her to find her gazing off at the cloudy horizon with a dreamy little smile playing about her mouth.

"Yes," she confessed with a nervous laugh. "It's…someone who's just come into my life recently…someone who's come to mean quite a lot to me in a very short time."

"That's…that's very nice, Dr. Coleman. I'm really glad, for your sake."

Mac's stomach knotted with searing, bitter pain. He

nodded abruptly, turned aside and began scraping blindly at the floor of the pit, mortally afraid that he might begin sobbing aloud.

Alex watched him for a moment with quiet concern, began to speak, thought better of it and went back to work, as well, brushing carefully at a piece of shining flint projecting from the wall of the pit.

CHAPTER ELEVEN

RAIN HAMMERED like steady bursts of gunfire on the curving, corrugated metal roof of the Quonset, and the crashes of thunder out on the darkened prairie sounded as grim and ominous as cannon fusillades.

The noise of the storm was a fitting accompaniment to what she was doing, Libby thought desolately. The ranch was like a war zone, isolated in darkness at the vortex of a violent, whirling storm, and she felt as if she, too, were going off to war, arming herself and preparing to strike a mortal blow against her enemy.

She shivered a little in the dusty chill of the big storage building and glanced in sudden panic out one of the darkened, rain-smeared windows, then squared her shoulders and went back to her task. Carefully she wound the long red and black circuit wires on their spools, packed the heavy blasting caps and the control panel in place and set the whole mechanism on the floor of the Jeep.

Libby refused to think, to let her mind dwell on what she was doing. She knew that it was horrible, unspeakable, an act that she would regret bitterly all the rest of her life. But with equal clarity she understood that it was inevitable. They had left her no option, because she was the sole person in charge of protecting this land. All the responsibility rested squarely on her shoulders, and she could only remove the threat of strangers on the property by removing the reason for their interest.

No other course of action was available to her.

Her face tense and grim with purpose, she checked the caps and circuits once more, tossed a covering of waterproof oilskins over them, locked the safe and climbed into the Jeep, pulling it carefully from the Quonset into the rain and getting out to latch the big front door of the storage building. Then, shivering with cold and fear, she climbed back behind the wheel and set off into open country.

The thunderstorm had started well after sunset and was now raging full force. Long, searing bolts of lightning set the sky on fire, glittering through the jets of pounding rain that lashed the earth. Thunder crashed and hammered at the rolling land, shaking the hills with its force.

Occasionally sheets of lightning danced and played in the darkness, illuminating the landscape with a weird, eerie glow and shining on the streaming, silvery flanks of the cattle that pressed together in silent panic, heads lowered, backs turned to the storm.

As she drew close to the plateau, Libby killed the lights and drove in tense silence, peering out the window with rain pelting against her face, trying to stay on the trail. She knew that the roar of the storm would cover the sound of the Jeep's engine, but if anyone happened to be watching, they would be able to see the lights.

But it was also dangerous, driving blind like this on the prairie while the rain flowed and sluiced across the trail, obliterating it completely in places, and big jagged boulders lurked in the tall grass, ready to puncture the oil pan or tear off the undercarriage, even on a vehicle as rugged as the Jeep.

Libby drove as near as she dared to the plateau and then, with a knot of tension in her stomach that made her feel sick, she turned off the ignition, got out, wrapped the

blasting equipment carefully in its oilskin covering and
set off on foot toward the silent hilltop.

Rain pounded on the heavy waterproof canvas of her
slicker, crept in around the edges of the hood, trickled
down her neck in slow, icy rivulets. Her boots sank into
the mud with every step, dragging and pulling at her legs
until her chest heaved with exhaustion.

At last she reached the base of the plateau on the side
opposite the camp and began the long, arduous journey
up the slippery incline. As she climbed, the downpour
began to moderate into a rapid, steady rainfall while the
electrical storm swirled close again, rumbling and crashing all around her, illuminating the whole wide landscape
with each bolt of lightning.

Finally, stumbling with weariness, her arms aching
from the weight of the blasting equipment in its waterproof covering, Libby gained the crest of the plateau. She
made her way through the circles of stone, silent and still
in the quiet rainfall that rustled through the sagebrush.

Suddenly a huge dagger of lightning split the sky from
west to east, hovering on the night air for a long time
before it began to fade. In the weird silver glow Libby
could see the ancient, enigmatic stones, their faces wet
with rain, silent and somehow terrifying in their timeless
mystery.

She shivered, lowering her burden carefully to the
ground, then hugged her arms and danced awkwardly
from one foot to the other on the damp grass. Her mind
worked rapidly, reviewing the procedure that she had
planned with such care.

The first cap, the primary circuit, would go into the big
crevice near the top of the rock. Two secondary ones
could be placed lower down. They'd hook up together to

the control panel, so they could all be retrieved at once after the blast. She would have to...

Libby paused, squinting through the rain at the shadowy outline of the massive petroglyph, calculating how much fuse she needed for her own safety, balancing caution against the need to do the job efficiently and then get back in time to recover all evidence of her circuits and make her escape from the hilltop before the crew would arrive, alerted by the sound of the detonation.

Finally, satisfied that she knew how to arrange the wires, she picked up her burden again and began to walk slowly toward the petroglyph.

As she worked carefully, inserting the primary caps into the upper crevices of the big rock, a jet of lightning tore the heavens open in a blinding red-gold thrust that drove straight from the sky overhead to the prairie near the plateau. While the chilly, sulfurous glow lingered, Libby gazed at the face of the petroglyph, at the tiny mass of cryptic symbols that had stood for countless ages on this hilltop, had witnessed ice storm and blazing sun, fire and flood and drought.

Libby stared, mesmerized, at the patterned rock face. The glow faded, casting the world into darkness again, and still she lingered, reaching out a trembling wet hand to touch the rough, lichen-splashed granite. Suddenly her hand fell away and she drew a deep, sobbing breath.

She couldn't do it.

No matter what was at stake, no matter what the cost would ultimately be, she realized in an illumination as sudden and blinding as one of those lightning bolts that she could never be the one to destroy this precious thing. It was too much to ask of anyone that they be the agent of so terrible a destruction.

Libby drew another deep, shuddering breath, assailed

by a heavy wave of despair, of sorrow and anger and hopelessness. Then, touching the stone once again with a gentle, trembling hand as if in apology, or a silent benediction, she began to recoil the spools of wire and wrap them carefully back into their oilskin covering.

She stood erect, clutching the damp, slippery bundle, and reached up to remove the caps she had already placed in the rock. Intent on her task, she wasn't aware of anything else until she felt something clutching at her arm with terrifying strength, sensed a large, solid presence near her in the darkness. A voice shouted close to her ear, harsh with anger. Libby dropped her hands, screamed aloud with almost uncontrollable fear, then took control of her emotions and forced herself to be calm.

"What the hell," the voice was saying furiously, "do you think you're doing up here? And who are you? Answer me, goddamn you!"

Her arm was gripped brutally once again, her whole body shaken by that large, angry presence. Libby turned, raising her head in the soft rainfall so that her hood fell back from her face. She looked into the beam of a big flashlight and heard Warren's voice, stunned and disbelieving.

"Libby! It's you! What are you…? I saw the lights of a vehicle out on the prairie. Then the lights suddenly went off, and I was afraid that somebody…" he began, stumbling awkwardly in his amazement.

"Hello, Warren," Libby said, licking her lips nervously, conscious of the damning burden that was still clutched in her arms and the primary cap that she had not yet removed from the rock crevice. Her mind raced frantically, trying to think what to do, how to explain her presence up here, how to get away from him somehow before he found out that she—

"What are you doing up here in this storm?" he asked again, a little more calmly as he began to recover his composure. He lowered the flashlight so that it illuminated the space between them. Libby peered cautiously up at his shadowed face and his big body in a streaming black raincoat, his dark hair plastered sleek against his head. She hesitated, still searching for words.

"How about you?" she said finally, with an awkward, forced little laugh. "What are *you* doing up here in this storm, Warren? Do you always spend every night up here in these old stone circles? Don't you archaeologists *ever* sleep?"

Warren ignored her attempt at levity and kept regarding her steadily, his dark eyes narrowed and thoughtful. Around them the rain slowed even more, moderating to a gentle, rustling drizzle that slanted softly on the midnight breeze. The electrical storm drifted off to the east, rumbling and flashing distantly, taking most of the swirling, angry clouds with it. As it passed, silvery shafts of moonlight began to beam through the ragged traces of cloud cover.

In the muted glow of the flashlight, Libby could see Warren's stern, sculpted face, quiet and shadowed in the dimness. She moved uneasily, conscious of his thoughtful appraising glance, the grim humorless line of his mouth. Gently he reached for the bundle in her arms, and she grasped it close to her, struggling against his quiet strength.

"No!" she said abruptly. "No, Warren, I don't want—"

But her wiry agility was no match for his calm, powerful determination. He turned her around with gentle firmness, pinning her arms together behind her back, then bent swiftly to peer at the oilskin-wrapped package that dropped from her grasp.

Libby stood watching in grim silence as Warren kicked the package softly to one side and knelt to play the flashlight over the shiny wet covering. Slowly he folded the oilskin back to reveal the neat spools of wire, the blasting caps and controls.

Stunned, Warren rocked on his heels and stared in silent disbelief at the blasting equipment. At last he stood slowly erect, moving his beam of light over the face of the rock, lingering on the cap with its trailing ends of wire that protruded from the rock face. He stiffened and turned to shine the light in Libby's face again.

She blinked against the glare and shifted on her feet, holding an arm over her eyes to block the direct glow of the flashlight.

"Warren!" she said sharply. "Put that thing down, okay? You'll blind me."

Slowly he lowered the flashlight until it once more illuminated the space between them—a space, Libby felt with hollow, aching misery, that in the past few seconds had grown into a gulf as vast as the Grand Canyon.

"I can't believe it," he said at last, his voice hushed and cold. "I just can't believe it."

"Warren..." Libby began, looking up at him helplessly, searching for words to explain her weeks of desperation, Keith's suggestion and her own terrible decision, and then, finally, the ultimate, overwhelming knowledge that she couldn't do it, after all.

But his dark eyes were beginning to kindle with anger, and his handsome face was set in harsh, dark lines.

"What an accomplished liar you are," he said bitterly. "You know, you even had me convinced. All that pious talk about how precious this place was to you ever since you were a little girl, how it seemed so sacred, like a church, and how you could even hear this magical music up here among the stones.''

"It's true," she whispered, staring at him while the errant night wind blew damp tendrils of hair around her face. "It's all true, Warren. Everything I said about this place—"

"And I was completely taken in," he went on as if she hadn't spoken, still in that same cold, expressionless tone. "God, what an incredible fool I've been. I actually fell in love with you partly because when you talked about these stones, it was as if you were putting my own feelings into words. I loved you for your wonderful empathy and understanding."

Libby gazed at him in silence, knowing at last that there was nothing at all she could say to stem the tide of his words, to ease his bitter, angry pain and disappointment.

"Understanding!" he repeated with a hollow, mirthless smile. "Can you believe it? I sensed *understanding* in a woman who's capable of destroying one of the most precious things in the world just to achieve her own selfish ends."

"Selfish!" Libby interrupted angrily. "How can you accuse me of selfishness when I—"

"You're a terrific actress, Libby," he said, his face still cold and impersonal. "You really had me convinced that you loved this place and cared about it."

"I do!" Libby began hotly, stung at last by his bitter, accusatory tone. "I care about it more than you could ever imagine. In fact, I—"

"Pardon me if I find that a little hard to believe," he said with a brief, sardonic smile. "It's too much like the mother who kills her own children because she loves them too much to let them bear all the sorrows of the world. Somehow it's just a hard story to swallow, Libby.''

"All right. Believe what you want," she said coldly, too furious with him all at once to care any longer what he thought or what she said to him. "You're going to, anyway, so why should I waste my time trying to convince you otherwise?"

She turned, her eyes flashing in the dim light, and walked away from him into the darkness at the edge of the cliff.

"Libby," he called.

"Yes?" She paused, her heart pounding, and looked back at the golden pool of light where he stood alone in the darkness, aiming his flashlight toward her.

"Aren't you forgetting something?" he asked curtly, playing the beam of light over the blasting equipment that still lay on the ground in the folds of yellow oilskin.

"I guess," Libby said, looking directly at him, "that I don't have any more use for it, do I? You can have it, Warren. In fact—"

She choked suddenly, overwhelmed with a desperate, hot anger that flowed through her body and welled up inside her, bringing her dangerously close to tears of outrage and frustration. She paused, terrified that she might begin to cry, and he would misunderstand and think she was ashamed or remorseful.

Finally, not trusting her voice to say anything more, she turned and began the descent of the slippery trail, knowing miserably that there was no danger, now or ever again, that Warren McIntyre might want to follow her.

As THE SUMMER DREW ON the prairie air mellowed, grew clear and crisp and shone in the twilight with a soft golden glow. And at last the cycle of steaming hot days and wild lightning storms at night broke. In the evenings the harvest moon would slip over the horizon, a huge, shimmering globe of reddish-bronze, and in the early morning the air was sweet and tangy with just a hint of frost.

Libby went through her days weighed down by an aching burden of sorrow, desperately lonely and yet reluctant to seek anyone out for comfort. She even avoided Mac, making excuses when he called to express his concern, telling him how busy she was and how little time she had to visit.

She was growing more and more weary of the grinding, solitary responsibility of the ranch work and longed to be free of her chores. Yet she dreaded the thought of her father's return, knowing what he was going to find on his land and how he was going to feel about it.

And she dreaded the end of the summer for another reason. She found herself thinking all the time about her job and her city apartment, about the need to move back there, very soon, and pick up the threads of her life. Libby was surprised and troubled to find how reluctant she felt about it all, how much she hated the idea of that other existence, of being plunged back into the crowded, depressing world of people and all their problems.

Doggedly she plodded through her daily round of ranch work, thinking about her job and her future, wondering what she really wanted. Almost in spite of herself her thoughts kept turning to the lonely hilltop over in the West Five, to the ancient circles of stone and the vivid, enigmatic symbols on the big petroglyph.

Maybe that was what she really wanted. Maybe she should go back to college, take the necessary courses, get the training to be an archaeologist, like Warren or Alex.

"Oh, sure," she said bitterly to her reflection as she stood alone at the mirror in her room, brushing her long, fiery hair. "Wouldn't Warren just love that, to have *you* appear in his world and announce that you've decided to become a colleague!"

Her face darkened and she turned aside to gaze into her closet with a distant, brooding expression.

Warren was never going to believe her, she thought, leafing impatiently through her clothes. She could try for the rest of her life to convince him of the truth...that she had been driven by her own sense of responsibility to a foolish, desperate act and then on the verge of doing it she had caught herself and pulled back from the brink.

Libby knew she would never have been able to love Warren so much if he didn't have his sense of passionate conviction, his absolute integrity and belief in what he was doing that marked all his actions. But those were the very qualities that made it so hard for him to make allowances, to be casual and forgiving about moral issues. He set high standards for himself and expected others to do the same. And now that he truly believed Libby to be capable of such a criminal and destructive action, he simply wouldn't allow himself to be drawn toward her ever again.

Libby gulped and swallowed hard, almost overcome by another bleak surge of misery. Only now, in these past few days, had she come to the ironic realization of how very much she loved Warren McIntyre, how much he had grown to mean to her over the course of this long, troubled, sun-drenched summer. She knew that he was lost to her, but she also knew, with weary certainty, that no other man, as long as she lived, would ever move her as he had.

At last she selected a soft chambray sundress and pulled it over her head, buttoning the skirt and tugging the straps into place. The dress fit tightly on the bodice, displaying her shapely bosom and tanned shoulders, and flared seductively over her slender hips as she moved, but Libby was concerned only with comfort, not appearance. She tugged on a pair of leather sandals, clipped her hair back with a big carved silver barrette, grabbed her handbag and ran down through the house to her truck.

On the way into the city Libby gazed out at the vast soothing expanse of land, golden and dreaming in the late summer sun, watching as the miles slipped past her window and trying not to think about anything. On the outskirts of Calgary she pulled into the snarling city traffic and wended her way expertly through the complex stream of vehicles that glinted and flashed under a bright noonday sun.

Barely taking time to exchange pleasantries, she did her weekly errands, stopping at the mill to pick up sacks of dog food and calf meal supplement, and at the hardware supply for a dozen big, heavy blocks of salt for the cattle. Everywhere she went men stared with warm, admiring glances at her slim, tanned body and vivid red hair, but Libby remained absorbed in her own thoughts, completely oblivious to them.

Finally, after all her errands were done and she'd finished a quick submarine sandwich, she parked downtown and walked up the wide stone steps into the silent, cavernous depths of the city library.

Libby paused at the entrance to the reference section, sniffing the pleasant, soothing fragrance of books and paper, enjoying the peaceful stillness of this place devoted to learning and human wisdom. She found a vacant study carrel, deposited her sweater and handbag and went to the microfiche, smiling politely at a bald little man next to her who was researching Hungarian cuisine.

Without hesitation Libby sought out her own topic,

gathered up an armful of books, took a pen and notebook from her handbag and settled down to her work.

As she read and pondered, made notes and leafed rapidly back and forth through her mountain of reference books, the summer sun slipped lower in the western sky, tinting the clouds with pink and sending long, slanted shadows across the green lawns outside the window. But she was unaware of the passage of time, of the empty library and the waning afternoon light, of everything but the symbols and figures and words that swam before her tired eyes.

As so often happened when she set out to research something, Libby was amazed by the amount of material she discovered on petroglyphs and their symbols, by the huge mass of study and documentation that had already been done. And, with growing excitement, she began to recognize a certain uniformity to that strange jumble of symbols that marked the central monolith of the stones in the West Five. Slowly but steadily patterns and meaning seemed to emerge. From studying the reference books, she found that many of the symbols on "her" stone were identical to petroglyphs found elsewhere.

It had to be more than mere coincidence, she thought, paging feverishly through the largest reference volume and glancing up nervously from time to time at the clock. There had to be something here, some kind of definite meaning, like an alphabet that could be read quite simply once the symbols were understood.

But, without a key, how could you ever learn the meaning of an alphabet? And, even if you had a clue to help you break the code, how could you step into the mind of someone who lived hundreds of centuries ago? How could you know how he saw things and how he interpreted his own symbols?

Libby paused, dimly aware of her own fatigue, her empty stomach and her burning, tired eyes. She rubbed the small of her back, stretched wearily and then turned back to her notes, to the sketches she had made from memory of the symbols on the face of the petroglyph, and others that she had copied from the reference books. She stared at them, willing her thoughts to focus, forcing her exhausted mind to bend into a shape that was completely alien.

I'm living off the land, a hunter and gatherer, she thought. My life is regulated by the sun and moon and stars, by the cycles of seasons. I've never heard of physics, I've never seen a wheel, I have no concept of geometry. I haven't developed any real form of written language, of symbolism or phonetic representation. Now, if I want to give pictorial directions to someone else, someone just like me, how do I go about it? How do I make him understand what I'm talking about, and where to find it?

And suddenly, as clear and dazzling as one of those prairie thunderbolts, the answer was there on the page in front of her.

Libby stared in amazement, stunned by the beautiful simplicity of it, reluctant to trust her own eyes. But, no matter how often she checked it, how many times she referred to the books and compared them to her own sketches, it was still there—simple, obvious and crystal clear.

Libby shivered and drew a deep, calming breath, got up to walk around a little on the thick pile carpet and then returned to her desk, gazing once more at the orderly mass of symbols.

This is crazy, she thought. Why should I be able to see something that all the experts have missed in all their lifetimes of study? How can I possibly be so presumptuous?

And yet she knew she was right. Maybe it was her weariness that had finally lifted her out of her own mindset and into another one. Maybe it was her painful, conscious effort to look at the world of the plains through ancient eyes.

Or maybe, she thought with a small, sad smile, it was just because she loved the prairie so much and had spent so many solitary dreaming hours on its vast, lonely expanse that she had managed to establish some kind of direct spirit communion with those ancient first inhabitants.

Whatever the cause, she was convinced she had stumbled onto the key to the symbols and that she could now read them almost as easily as a modern road map. Barely daring to breathe, she riffled through the mass of papers, studying them closely.

The most important symbols were the odd, misshapen triangles, topped always by circles. Warren thought they represented human figures, possibly female, but Libby knew now that he was wrong. The triangles showed where the sun was positioned relative to the landmark at noon, which made them as reliable as compass readings.

Libby knew absolutely that she was correct in this assumption. She already knew some of the landmarks that were represented on the face of the petroglyph, and she had ridden over all of them dozens of times, squinting up at the sun as she gathered cattle or searched for strays. She understood now, without question, that the triangles were drawn to serve as simple but wonderfully effective guides for other travelers.

The parallel lines represented animal trails, which always led toward water. The arrows were simply directional and also showed inclines, hills and valleys, up and down. The "snake," as Warren called it, was the creek bed that wound through the community pasture, and here, on its banks....

Time sped by, and Libby continued to read and jot notes and ponder. Eventually one of the summer student assistants at the library drifted close to Libby's study carrel, holding a bottle of glass cleaner and a polishing cloth.

"Excuse me, miss," the girl murmured shyly, her face flushing bright pink, "but my supervisor says to tell you that we're almost ready to close."

Startled, Libby glanced up, gave the girl a quick distracted smile and nodded. "Okay," she whispered. "I'm just...I'm almost finished here. Can you give me...fifteen more minutes?"

"Sure," the girl said cheerfully. "We'll all be here for another half hour, anyway, just cleaning up and putting books away."

"Thanks," Libby said. "I promise I'll be out of here before then."

She returned to her books, leafing frantically through the massed pages of symbols, frowning as she searched her mind for something that still nagged at her memory. Maybe something she'd seen on the rock face...or could it be something that Warren had said...

The sun dipped below the wide overhanging eaves on the west side of the library and beamed across the carpet in the reference room, mellow and golden, dancing with dust motes in the quiet evening stillness.

Suddenly, in one of those dazzling, unexpected moments of total recall, Libby was back up on the hilltop in the blazing light, and Warren was beside her, muscular and tanned, pointing at the incised designs on the petroglyph. The memory was so vivid that she could feel the prairie breeze on her face, hear the muted song of a pair of meadowlarks nesting under the chokecherry trees, smell the sweet, pungent fragrance of crushed sage in the sunlight.

"They're peripheral geometric figures," Warren was saying. *"See these parallel lines, and then this long spiral? I can't figure it out. There's nothing like it anywhere else on the rock face...."*

Libby's eyes widened and her face went white with shock.

"Oh, God," she whispered aloud, staring down at her pages of notes. "Oh, my God...."

With trembling hands she checked a couple of other pages, consulted a marked article in one of the reference books and then sat and gazed blindly at the beam of sunlight on the dusty carpet.

"Oh, God," she murmured once more, her voice shaking. At last, as if in a dream, she gathered her notebook and pen, stacked the reference books neatly on the desktop and got up to leave.

In the foyer the little student assistant was down on her hands and knees, busily scrubbing masses of children's smeared fingerprints from the glass front of the dinosaur display case. She looked up as Libby approached, about to say a cheerful goodbye, but Libby passed her with a quick step and a tense, preoccupied expression, too deeply absorbed in her own thoughts to be aware that anybody was nearby.

CHAPTER TWELVE

ALEX HURRIED ALONG the carpeted hallway, sparing only a hasty smile for the receptionist. She rushed into her office, closed the door behind her and grasped the pile of mail on her desk. Sinking into an armchair near the window, she thumbed eagerly through the stack of envelopes and circulars, her hands shaking a little in her excitement.

Then, more slowly, she went carefully through the entire pile once more, searching for that familiar creamy stationery, the beautiful, flowing handwriting.

At last, gripped by a bitter, aching disappointment, she tossed the untidy stack of mail back onto her desk and gazed out the window with a brooding expression.

The letters had stopped coming.

The last one, now almost two weeks old, was still folded lovingly in her purse. And, although she checked the mail every day, waited with pent-up breath and pounding heart for new letters to replace it, they never arrived.

Alex stirred restlessly in the chair, her elegant features drawn and troubled as she stared down at the street below.

This whole episode with the letters had distressed her more than she cared to admit. In fact, strangely enough, it had shaken her existence to its very foundations. It wasn't just her surprising surge of feeling for the unknown letter writer—she was intelligent and mature enough to be able to write that off as a bit of summer madness, one of those brief, silly reversions to adolescence that all women are capable of, but from which Alex knew she would soon recover.

I had a terrible crush on him, whoever he was, Alex thought with a small, ironic smile, swinging her slender, well-shod foot. But I'll certainly get over it. I'm a big girl now, after all.

The real problem was the uncomfortable revelation that her unknown correspondent had caused her to perceive about her own life, the clear and relentless light that he had shone on her deepest dissatisfactions. He had forced her to recognize and acknowledge her own unhappiness, even, tentatively, to consider some alternative life-styles. And then he had just lost interest in the game, dropped her cold.

Alex had an irrational feeling of being cheated and abandoned. She had often thought, during these past two miserable weeks while she waited for another letter, that her friend had been rather unfair. He'd started something he wasn't willing to finish, gotten her all stirred up and discontented with her life and then quietly faded from the scene.

Alex fingered the soft fabric of her silk collar, smiling at her own foolishness.

The letter writer hadn't intended anything of the sort, she realized with the blunt honesty that was an integral part of her nature. He had just been some lonely young soul, some shy and distant student admirer who had set out to relieve the loneliness of his existence by a brief, safe, imaginary dalliance with an older woman. He couldn't have any knowledge of the bitter accuracy of his perceptions or of her own overwhelming response to them. The whole incident had been one of those unhappy coincidences, an unfortunate combination of circumstances that started out as a small, harmless amusement and then somehow acquired a great deal more significance than it really should have.

"And I'm glad it's over," Alex muttered aloud, glaring at the ragged pile of mail on her polished desktop. "I'm really tired of all that silliness."

It was true. She was tired of emotional turmoil, of waiting for the mail with shivering, girlish anticipation, of having her whole day ruined when there was no letter. She was sincerely glad that the whole episode had come to an end.

So why, then, did she feel this desolate emptiness? Why did she feel this loss of hope, this haunting sense that nothing ever again would be able to make her as happy as those beautiful written images...?

"Today I found the end of the rainbow. There was a shower just at noon and a rainbow in the east when the clouds passed away. The rainbow arched across the prairie onto a hilltop not far away, and the hillside was covered with prickly pear cacti in bloom. The colors of the flowers were all the colors of the rainbow, gold and pink and violet, glittering like jewels with the raindrops on them. All around, the nesting birds were singing, the way they love to sing after a rain shower. I wish you could hear them. Sometimes I think that if the rainbow had a song, it would sound just like the larks...."

Alex shook her head, trying to clear the letter writer's haunting words from her mind, and got up to pace restlessly around her office, slim and dainty in a cream-colored dress skirt and royal blue silk blouse. With sudden decision she took a small overnight case from under her desk, went into her adjoining washroom and changed into her khaki slacks and T-shirt. Then, tugging her soft denim cap over her silvery hair, she left the office.

"Off to the petroglyph site," she said briefly to her receptionist. "Take calls, okay?"

"Again?" the girl asked in surprise. "I thought you said you wouldn't be—"

"The crews will be arriving soon to sink the first foundations. I want to double-check just to make sure we've got all the—"

Alex paused, her face withdrawn and thoughtful. Then she gave the girl a quick, absent smile and entered the elevator, feeling the same sense of release and freedom that always crept into her soul when she was leaving this office building and heading for the open country.

She enjoyed the drive out of the city across the silent golden prairie and felt a warm sense of anticipation as she turned her Land Rover onto the rough trail that crossed the Lyndon ranch land. Then, as always, she felt a stirring of excitement when the plateau came into view, rearing up flat and stark against the incredible blue arch of prairie sky.

Alex parked near the archaeological camp at the base of the cliff, noting in surprise that Warren's tent was gone.

She stared at the neat, empty space of flattened grass where the tent had been, wondering what was going on. The other tent, the one belonging to Sandy, was still in position, with a few feminine garments fluttering quietly from the makeshift clothesline in the warm afternoon breeze.

Maybe, Alex decided, the tent floor had gotten wet or something and Warren had dismantled it and staked it out to dry in the sun somewhere. Still, the whole thing seemed a little strange....

Alex climbed the hill with quick, wiry agility, pausing at the top to shade her eyes with her hand and look around. The crew, she observed, was still hard at work on the pits being excavated beneath the proposed walkways. But, despite the meticulous nature of the work and the pressure of their impending deadline, they all looked remarkably cheerful.

Tim and Sandy were busily screening shovelfuls of dirt from their pit at the far side of the plateau, singing a silly, repetitive folk song at considerable volume, their young voices carrying warmly on the soft summer wind. In the other pit, nearer the petroglyph, Warren labored, his lean, tanned back and dark head visible above the surface of the sod. While Alex looked on, another head, wearing a dusty tractor cap, popped over the edge of the pit, as well, and Warren bent close to it, obviously in consultation.

Alex's smile faded and she felt a brief stirring of unease, realizing that Malcolm Burman was in the pit with Warren.

Doesn't he ever stay away from this place? she thought with some irritation. It's not as if any of this was his business, after all....

Instantly she regretted her lack of charity. She supposed that Mac Burman was probably a very nice person. At least she knew that the others all seemed to think so. But, confronted by the reality of his presence, Alex still felt that sense of troubled embarrassment that any woman feels in the company of a gentle man whose advances she has been forced to refuse.

With warm discomfort she recalled his shy, clumsy dinner invitation and her own words: *There's somebody in my life at the moment....*

Alex squirmed with embarrassment. Somebody in my life, indeed! Some anonymous letter writer who'd now lost interest. How could she have been such a fool?

With uncharacteristic sharpness Alex wished that Mal-

colm Burman would just stay at home with his pigs and
not make such awkward and unnerving approaches.

She sighed and collapsed inwardly with relief when she
saw that she was at least going to be spared the chagrin
of meeting him again, of trying to be tactful and make
some kind of polite conversation. As soon as the two men
became aware of her approach, Mac stiffened in alarm,
said something hastily to Warren as he climbed from the
pit, gave Alex a small, shy wave and then practically galloped across the plateau and out of sight over the brow
of the hill.

Alex watched his tall, gangly body as it disappeared
into the blue horizon and felt a twinge of rueful sadness.
He really seemed to be a very nice man, and she was
sorry to have had to hurt and embarrass him, she truly
was…

But, she thought, squaring her shoulders and taking a
deep breath, a single woman couldn't go around accepting
every invitation that came her way just to keep from hurting people's feelings, could she? She'd had to learn to say
no and say it often. That was just the way life had to be.

Still vaguely hot and uneasy, Alex crossed the plateau
to stand near Warren's pit and gazed in brooding silence
at the face of the petroglyph.

"Hi, chief," he said cheerfully, his handsome face
creasing warmly as he smiled.

"Hi," Alex said, still staring at the rock face. "Your
friend is awfully shy, isn't he?" she added without turning
around.

Warren shook his head in rueful agreement. "Poor
Mac," he said. "Not much of a ladies' man, I'm afraid.
But," he added with warm sincerity, pausing to smile at
Alex again, "he's actually a terrific guy. I'm really going

to miss old Mac when this is all over. He sort of…grows on a person, you know?''

"I'm sure he does," Alex agreed absently, returning to her study of the patterns carved in the rock face.

Warren leaned on his shovel, his powerful biceps flexing and rounding, glistening with sweat in the noonday sun. He glanced at Alex thoughtfully. "Are you seeing something there, Alex?"

"I don't know," she said, frowning. "Warren, I just can never shake this feeling that there's something here right under our noses that's really vast and momentous, and we're *not* seeing it…maybe even because it's just too simple and basic for us to grasp."

"Like some kind of key? Some kind of clue to break the code and tell us what the symbols mean and where to find a whole chain of similar sites scattered across the prairie?"

Alex glanced at him, startled. "Yes," she said finally. "Something like that. Why?"

"Because that's what Libby believes," Warren said briefly, bending to his work again.

"Libby?" Alex asked in surprise. But Warren avoided her gaze, bending to lift careful deposits of dirt from the cleared floor of the pit and toss them into a pile on the surface that was waiting for screening.

Alex watched him a moment longer, her eyes narrowed and thoughtful, and then turned back to her examination of the rock face. "You know what I think it is?" she said suddenly.

"What do you think it is, Alex?" Warren echoed.

"I think it's the triangles. There's something about the triangles, Warren."

"Everyone agrees that they're human figures," Warren said, looking at her in surprise and then indicating some of the shapes on the petroglyph. "They're irregular shapes, but they always have heads attached. See?"

"Then why is the orientation so different?" Alex argued. "Why isn't the head on top all the time?"

"People fall down," Warren said cryptically. "Sometimes," he added with a private, bitter smile, "they even lose their heads altogether."

Alex glanced at him sharply, but his dark, hawklike face was calm and unrevealing. "You're camping up here now," Alex said suddenly, noticing all at once that his gray dome tent was pitched beneath the stand of chokecherry trees near the other pit.

"Yes," Warren said briefly. "I am."

"Why?" Alex asked.

"Security reasons," Warren said, bending to his work, his strong, tanned back muscles rippling as he plied the shovel.

Alex's eyes widened in alarm. "Warren! Have there been…threats or anything? You never told me!"

"Don't worry," he said. "I was just afraid that word might be getting around, and I don't want to take any chances with vandals or curiosity seekers when we're so close to the start of development."

Alex relaxed a little, nodding her head in agreement. "That's a good idea. You just never know what people might get it into their heads to do."

Warren smiled grimly, standing erect and squinting off into the cloudless expanse of blue sky.

"Speaking of security," Alex went on thoughtfully, "is it a good idea, though, for you and Tim to be sleeping up here and leaving Sandy all alone down there at the base of the plateau, Warren? Maybe you should—"

"She's not sleeping alone," Warren interrupted.

"But how—?" Alex began, and then paused, looking

over at Tim and Sandy, who had stopped singing and were sitting close together on the edge of their pit, tanned legs swinging, sharing a drink from Tim's canteen.

"Oh," she said, grinning. "I see."

Warren grinned back at her, holding up a piece of black fine-grained rock that glittered brightly where the sunlight caught one of its carved facets.

"See this, Alex? An obsidian knife. In fact, there's a fair amount of hand-worked obsidian up here."

Alex leaned forward eagerly to study the small beautiful object. "I wonder where they got the obsidian?" she said.

Warren shrugged. "Through the established trading routes, I suppose. Up through the Dakotas…maybe even the Eastern Woodlands."

"But this looks like a Cody knife," Alex argued. "That would put it in the Scottsbluff complex, Warren. Would there have been such elaborate trading routes that long ago?"

Warren's dark eyes kindled with interest, and the two archaeologists gazed thoughtfully at each other. "Let's mark it down," Alex said finally, handing the artifact back to him, "and then I'll take it back with me and have it checked."

"Okay," Warren said, indicating the roll of field charts nearby. "You might as well make yourself useful, kid, since you came and drove my other helper away."

Alex chuckled and moved around the pit to begin making notations. "How's Libby?" she asked without looking up. "I haven't seen much of her lately."

"Neither have I," Warren said. "I don't think Libby likes us very much, Alex."

There was something in his voice, a slight, bitter edge,

a shading of pain that made Alex set her pen aside and look over at him in quick concern.

But he kept his dark head carefully lowered, studying the smooth, damp pit face with grim concentration.

"Poor Libby," Alex said. "I feel for her, Warren. I really do. If there were anything at all we could do to make this easier for her, I'd—"

"It was a mistake," Warren said abruptly, "to send her over to the buffalo jump. Al Herrold is so bitter about the development, and he said a lot of things to her."

"I know," Alex said. "She came to see me afterward and told me all about it. I didn't know Herrold was so upset," she added. "He seemed happy enough to take his big check, and he kept making up excuses to pad it even further with easements and water rights and stock crossings and property depreciation—everything one man and seven lawyers could think of."

"In my opinion," Warren said judiciously, pausing to gaze off at the horizon again, "Al Herrold is just one of those men who'll never be happy about anything. You can't satisfy a man like that. He'll always have complaints."

"That's my impression, too," Alex said promptly, "and I told Libby so. But she's so unhappy about all this, poor girl— Warren," she interrupted herself abruptly, "why do you keep staring off into space like that? Are you looking for something or what?"

Warren turned around, a little abashed, and Alex looked down at him in surprise. "I keep thinking," he confessed, his voice low and strained, "that I'll see her out on the prairie, riding out to check cattle or taking salt to the fields or something. I just keep hoping I'll catch a glimpse of her, that's all."

Alex gazed at the younger man, her fine, austere features softening. "Libby's a wonderful girl, Warren," she said softly.

His wide mouth tightened. "Maybe," he said. "Maybe not. After all, how much do any of us really get to know about each other in the normal course of events? It's awfully hard to judge other people properly, Alex."

"Maybe," she said quietly, thinking about her beloved writer of letters, "we shouldn't try to judge them at all, Warren. Maybe we should just enjoy them while we can."

He glanced over at her quickly but made no reply.

"I wish," Alex went on, her face drawn with concern, "that there were something we could do about Libby. I wish there were a different site."

Warren dropped his shovel and stared at his colleague, dumbfounded by her words. "Alex, you're kidding. You mean you'd actually abandon this site in favor of another one after all the research and planning that's already gone into it?"

Alex returned his gaze thoughtfully. "I don't know. I mean, I can see it all here." She waved her hand at the silent hilltop. "I see the cairns and walkways and didactic panels, and the interpretive center down below with teaching displays and classrooms, a film center and a museum, and I know it would be a wonderful facility, Warren. It just makes me shiver with excitement when I picture it, you know?"

He nodded, still watching her carefully.

"But then," Alex continued, "I think of the Lyndon family and the things that Libby has told me about their history and their ties to this piece of land, and I wish—"

She broke off, staring moodily at the horizon while Warren waited in silence. "Let's put it this way," Alex said with an awkward little smile. "I'm fully committed to this site, and construction is going ahead inside of a matter of weeks. But if Libby could pull something else out of her hat, something that was, say, twice as big and three times as significant, well, then I just might be persuaded to take a look at it.''

Warren shrugged. ''The chances of that happening,'' he said flatly, ''are absolutely nil, Alex. And we both know it.''

''Yes,'' Alex said sadly, troubled by the bleak hopelessness in his voice, and the lonely droop to his powerful shoulders. ''I guess we do.''

LIBBY RODE ACROSS the silent, moonlit prairie, lifting her face to the soothing breeze that carried sweet, spicy nighttime fragrances of sage and dew and damp earth. A softly rounded moon drifted in and out of its lacy cloud veils, ringing the tattered edges with a nimbus of bright, glowing light.

She frowned, still haunted by the memory of a troubling dream she'd had the night before, a shatteringly real nightmare with a deep, terrible premonition of darkness and death. Shaking herself a little, Libby gazed up at the warm, radiant sphere so high above her. Suddenly she realized that the moon was almost full, that it had already been close to a month since that beautiful night on the plateau by the rocks when Warren had made love to her.

She shivered and clenched the reins tightly in her fingers, remembering the feeling of his lean, muscular body in her arms. Hungrily she tried to cling to that memory, to clasp it nearer to her, but its sweet warmth drifted away to be replaced by the terror of her dream once again and the cold harshness in Warren's face when he discovered what she had carried up to the hilltop the night of the thunderstorm.

Sadness flooded over her again, the same desolate,

hopeless pain that filled her mind and heart these days through all her waking hours. She spurred her horse into an easy gallop, her face taut and expressionless in the moonlight, and soon covered the remaining distance between herself and the plateau.

Near the base of the cliff Libby slowed her horse to a cautious walk and approached the little camp, observing with a small, unpleasant shock the empty place where Warren's tent had been. The other tent, the one belonging to Sandy, glowed with a soft interior light like a rounded dome of gold, warm and welcoming in the darkness.

A man's voice sounded from within the tent, saying something in soft, indistinguishable tones, answered at once by Sandy's sweet, clear laughter.

Sitting her horse quietly in the moonlight at the edge of the camp, Libby felt a quick stab of hot jealousy followed by a great helpless rush of sorrow. But then the man laughed, too, raising his voice delightedly at something Sandy said. Libby recognized with relief that it was Tim, not Warren, who was inside the tent with the girl.

She reined her horse aside, trotted him around the base of the plateau and hobbled him carefully in the same thicket she'd used the last time, removing the bridle and leaving him free to graze.

With a painful sense of déjà vu, Libby climbed the winding, shadowed path to the cliff top, knowing what she was going to see up there before she even neared the summit. Warren's tent was pitched next to the grove of chokecherry trees, angled so the opening commanded a clear view both of the picture rock and of the surrounding circles of fieldstone. Libby stood on the crest of the plateau, gazing at the darkened tent with miserable unhappiness.

He's afraid I'll try it again, she thought bleakly. Oh,

God, he's moved up here to protect his treasure from *me*. Oh, Warren, I'm so sorry, darling....

She choked, brushed briefly at her eyes and then slipped silently across the cliff face, coming around to the petroglyph on the shaded side out of the moonlight. When she was close to the base of the massive rock, she drew a small flashlight from her pocket and glanced anxiously over her shoulder at the silent, silvered tent.

Finally, taking a last deep, shuddering breath, Libby edged around to the face of the petroglyph in full view of the tent, squatted in front of the rock and shaded the beam of the flashlight carefully with her hand, playing it over the images at the bottom of the pattern.

She stared, dazzled by the power and clarity of the little carved figures. Now that she knew what to look for the message seemed impossible to miss. She could read most of the figures as easily as a child's primer, see exactly what they represented.

Hastily she drew a notebook from her pocket and jotted down the orientation of three of the triangles, working with careful precision to get them exactly right, knowing how crucial they were to her quest.

All the time while she worked, she fought to hold the memory of her dream at bay, but it flooded back over her as she read the clear and unmistakable message in the little symbols. She relived the nightmare, feeling herself once again stepping into that great void, swallowed up in a hot, pressing, whirling mass of darkness, falling...falling into nothingness, and so terribly alone that nobody in all the world could hear her final anguished screams of terror.

At last, shivering, she switched off the flashlight, stuffed her notebook back into her pocket and turned to go. But at the brow of the cliff she hesitated, staring back at Warren's tent. Slowly, almost reluctantly, she crossed the surface of the plateau again, knelt in front of the tent and gently pulled the flap aside.

A long shaft of moonlight flowed over the interior of the curved little shelter, lying warmly across Warren's long, beautiful body. He lay on his back on top of his sleeping bag, naked except for a pair of brief undershorts, his powerful body deeply still, his chest rising and falling with a slow, even rhythm.

Libby gazed in at him, her heart bursting with love. She wanted to memorize every detail of him—the way a lock of dark hair fell boyishly across his forehead, the fine, sculpted shape of his lips, the blunt, high cheekbones, flat and silvered by the glancing light, the broad, powerful chest and arms, the long, straight legs...

His eyes opened, glittering in the darkness, and he stared up at her in alarm, his body tensing instinctively, his hands clenching into fists.

"Who's there?" he demanded in confusion, pulling himself hastily up onto one elbow, peering directly into the diffuse beam of light. "What is it?"

Speechless, Libby knelt in the entryway and gazed down at him, waiting in silence while his eyes adjusted to the moonlight.

"It's you," he said finally, relaxing a little, though his voice was still cold and cautious. "What do you want, Libby?"

Still unable to trust her voice, Libby edged closer to him, kneeling beside him while he rested back on his elbow and gazed up at her with a guarded, careful expression.

"Don't worry, Warren," she said finally, her voice low and husky. "I'm not up to...to any mischief tonight. I just wanted...I wanted to see you once more, that's all."

In spite of herself, drawn by a force too powerful and elemental to resist, she reached toward him, biting her lip as she caressed his broad chest, gently ran her fingers through the soft mat of dark hair, touched his cheek and lips, delicately stroked his long, steel-hard thighs.

He shivered at her touch but held himself rigidly in check, watching her face as she bent silently above him in the moonlight.

"Oh, Warren," Libby murmured brokenly. "Warren, darling, you're just so…"

Beyond her conscious control her hands wandered up along his thighs and across his lean hips, caressing his flat belly and gently, softly brushing the rising hardness just below. Libby leaned over him, lost in love and desire, her face deep in shadow, her long silky plait of hair falling forward onto his skin.

He moaned and arched toward her, murmuring something incoherent, reaching blindly upward, but at last she managed to compose herself and drew away, still gazing down at him with an intent, unreadable expression.

"I'm sorry, Warren," she whispered. "I…I didn't mean to do that. I just can't help…" She paused, gazing in anguish at the beautiful male body that was taut and rigid with arousal.

Warren lay still and watched her in silence, his dark eyes brilliant and piercing in the moonlight, waiting for her to speak.

"Before I go, Warren," she went on finally, "I just wanted to tell you two things. I want you to know that the other night even though I came up here intending to…to destroy the stone…" She stopped again, her voice breaking a little, and then forced herself to continue. "I couldn't do it, Warren. By the time you got there, I'd already realized I couldn't do it. It's important for me now that you know that, Warren. Do you believe me?''

She looked down at him anxiously and he returned her gaze, his face still quiet and cautious in the silvery light. "I don't know, Libby," he said finally. "I don't really know what I believe anymore."

"All right," she said, stung by the measured coolness of his voice. "I guess that's a fair, honest answer, anyway. I'll go now, Warren."

"Just a minute." He reached up to grasp her arm as she turned aside toward the entryway. "You said you had two things to tell me. What's the other thing?"

She settled back on her heels, looking at his face in silence. At last she freed her arm gently and turned to go once more, pausing to bend and smile bleakly down at him on her way out of the tent. "The other thing, Warren," she said in a soft, sad voice, "is that I love you."

Then she was gone, running away from the tent, moving as swift as the wind through the silvered grass to the cliff edge.

WARREN LAY ON the warm surface of his sleeping bag, stunned and silent, wrestling with his turbulent emotions. His body still ached and throbbed, on fire from Libby's gentle, feather-light touch, and his mind was whirling.

Part of him hungered for her, yearned for her, desired her with a white-hot, thrusting passion more intense than anything he had ever felt before in his life. But on another, deeper level he still mistrusted her, suspected her motives, wondered if she might, after all, be capable of lying with such deep sincerity, of professing a love she didn't feel just to achieve her own goals.

Slowly he calmed himself and lay with hands behind his head, gazing up at the slender, arched ribs of the tent and the delicate tracery of leaves cast on the taut canvas by the glow of the moon overhead.

Warren frowned, thinking about Libby, shivering when he remembered the painful, disturbing sweetness of those final moments with her. Suddenly he sat upright, his face twisted in concentration as he tried to recall her exact words. There was something about her...something in the way she'd spoken...

With shaking hands he reached for his jeans, hurried from the tent and pulled them on, zipping them hastily. Then he slipped into his moccasins and ran to the face of the cliff, peering down into the darkness, shouting her name.

"Libby! Come back! Libby, I'm sorry. Please don't go away. Come back and talk to me."

His voice carried and died on the still night air, and he gazed into the blackness, desperate with hope. But there was no answer, just the distant stars winking impartially overhead and the mellow glow of the moon spilling across the silent landscape. Warren stared into the velvet blackness for a few more minutes and then turned, his shoulders slumped with despair, and made his way back to his tent.

Maybe he'd been wrong, Warren told himself as he lifted the flap and stepped back inside. Maybe he'd imagined that look in her eyes, the strange tone to her voice. At any rate there was nothing to be done about it tonight. Tomorrow, as soon as the sun came up, he'd drive over to the ranch and have a talk with her.

Shivering with a sudden chill, he climbed inside the soft, padded cocoon of his sleeping bag and lay on his back, his face bleak and somber.

Once again he tried to convince himself that he'd only imagined what he was frightened of. But he was certain it had been there in Libby's face and voice. Warren had the troubled, terrifying impression that Libby didn't expect to see him ever again. She hadn't been making peaceful overtures or trying to get him aroused so that they could make up their quarrel.

There in the summer moonlight, with gentleness in her fingers and sorrow in her voice, Elizabeth Lyndon had been saying goodbye.

FOR THE FIRST TIME since Libby could remember, it wasn't cloudy or raining in the community pasture. She rode across the dew-sparkled freshness of the prairie with the rising sun at her back, gazing at the life and color all around her.

Resolutely she kept her mind from dwelling either on what she had left behind or what she was setting out to find. The thought of Warren, naked and beautiful in the moonlight, staring up at her with such cautious coldness, was too agonizing to bear. And Libby felt such a strange sense of foreboding that she was equally reluctant to think about the future, so she forced her mind to dwell instead on safe and pleasant things.

She gazed at the little mammals and insects frisking and playing all around her in the warmth of the late-summer sun and wondered how they all managed to survive the winters, when the temperature could plummet suddenly to forty below and stay there for weeks on end, when it was so cold that a trickle of water spilled from a canteen would freeze before it touched the ground.

Libby shivered, touched her bay gelding with her knees to urge him into a canter and squinted at the horizon.

There, in the misty clouds to the west, she saw Warren's face, his dark, brilliant eyes and that powerful, sensual mouth, heard his voice saying, "I don't know what I believe anymore."

Libby swallowed hard and made a conscious effort once again to banish his memory from her thoughts, to concentrate on the task at hand.

She consulted the scrap of paper in her jacket pocket and glanced around her at the rugged landscape, chilled by the forbidding strangeness of it, wondering what ancient cosmic upheavals had created this rough tract of mighty hills and deep coulees, of shallow, winding creek beds and jagged, brush-filled ravines in the middle of the prairie.

Possibly a series of earthquakes, she thought, or especially severe glacial action. At any rate, there was no doubt that the rugged terrain of the community pasture had been created by some awesome, isolated force that had left the flat grasslands around it relatively untouched.

She looked at her careful little map once more, concentrating on the high, flat-topped image, spilling "raindrops" from its edge, which she now knew was a representation of a buffalo jump.

It was surprising, she thought, that Alex and Warren had failed to interpret this image as a jump. After all, the Plains Indians had used buffalo jumps for hunting for countless thousands of years. They used to drive herds of buffalo toward a high, sheer cliff, then stampede them so that hundreds of them hurtled over the cliff to their deaths.

There were only a few bluffs in the pasture high enough and sheer enough to serve as buffalo jumps, and Libby knew exactly where they were. Possibly her interpretation of the petroglyph had been influenced by the fact that she had such an intimate knowledge of this pasture, which she was sure was the area depicted on the stone, and that was why she had been able to see things the experts couldn't.

Or maybe, she thought, her success with the symbols was simply due to the fact that she *was* an amateur and could look at them with a clear eye, unaffected by any previous knowledge or by the interpretations of others.

Deep in her thoughts, she reached the base of a sheer cliff that stood close to the creek bed, and urged her horse slowly to the top.

"Good boy," she murmured aloud, bending to pat his sweating, heaving neck as he jerked impatiently at the bit. "You've been a really good old fellow, carrying me through all this. After today we'll never need to come back."

Libby gave a sudden, involuntary little shiver, assailed by the same dark sense of foreboding that had haunted her ever since she'd first grasped the significance of the little spiral figure on the petroglyph. Then she shook herself, sat erect in the saddle, pulled her hat low over her eyes and took out her chart, examining the orientation of the second triangle.

Now, she thought, reining the horse carefully around, I align myself so that the sun would be there, over my left shoulder at about thirty degrees, just at noon, and I face this way...

She situated the horse carefully, holding his rein and patting him to get him to stand.

Now I sight in that direction, find the portion of the creek where it divides around an island, and just beyond it, there should be a hill....

Libby stood up in her stirrups, gazing into the misty distance and, many miles away, saw the outline of a hill— situated exactly where the symbols had indicated. Her heart gave a great surge and then began to pound noisily while her face drained of color.

Oh, God, she thought, there it is, as surely as if they were talking to me across a span of ten thousand years, telling me exactly where to go....

The terrain between her and the distant hilltop was almost impassably rough. Libby sweated and swore, urging her big bay through treacherous, sucking alkali flats, through stands of buck brush with brutal, raking thorns, through shifting sand dunes that made the powerful horse slip and stumble.

She was reluctant to avoid obstacles by veering off course, afraid that if she did she might lose her bearings and have to go all the way back to the buffalo jump. So, patting her horse, shouting encouragement in his ears, getting off at times to lead him when the going was at its worst, Libby finally emerged, hours later, into the brush-filled ravine at the base of the hill.

When she had first seen it from far away at the top of the buffalo jump, it had looked like any other hill in the pasture, a smoothly rounded dome with one sheer side carved over countless ages by the action of the water in the creek as it drained the melting glaciers.

But, close to the hill, Libby could see that this one was different, steeper and more rugged, covered with well-established growth all the way to the top.

I probably would never have gone out of my way to check it even if I'd ridden this far east, Libby thought. I always pictured a high, flat, bare plateau, like the one on our land. Not something like this....

A little daunted by the steep incline and the roughness of the terrain, she gazed upward for a while, frowning in deep concentration. Finally she slid from the saddle, slipped off the bridle to replace it with a hackamore and tied the big gelding on a long rope to a nearby tree.

Then slowly with pounding heart and ragged uneven breath she began to climb.

At the crest of the hill Libby found her way through a shoulder-high stand of ragged sagebrush that tore at her hair and clothing. She stood still for a moment, chest heaving, staring at a grove of stunted trees choked with undergrowth that stood at the top of the hill against the wide blue sky.

Finally she forced her way forward through the brush and undergrowth, the clinging trailing vines and branches, to the center of the grove.

The foliage was so dense and tangled that she almost stumbled against one of the rocks before she was even aware of it. Libby stopped short, gaping in stunned amazement, her eyes wide and fearful.

There were two rocks, she could see now. Or, more accurately, two halves of the same massive boulder that had somehow been neatly split down the middle to expose a pair of gleaming, cut faces. The two halves were each taller than Libby, separated at right angles and positioned so that the shining, carved surfaces faced each other.

Shivering in the gloom of the tangled thicket, Libby drew her flashlight from her pocket and played it over the smooth gray surfaces. Many of the figures carved there were the same ones she'd seen before and looked as familiar as old friends. But there were unfamiliar ones, as well, hundreds of intricate symbols carved with exquisite care and detail into the faces of the two huge monoliths.

Hardly daring to breathe, her throat constricted with fear, Libby ran her flashlight down the face of the rocks until she found what she was looking for. At the bottom of each panel was one figure, all by itself.

The image was a careful, heavily incised spiral.

Libby gazed at the spiral image in awe. Finally she slipped the flashlight back into her pocket, touched one of the big stones with a trembling hand and then struggled back out through the sagebrush, running and stumbling down the steep hillside.

At the base of the hill she worked her way around through the dense, tangled undergrowth to the side opposite her tethered horse. This face was rough and rocky, huge black granite outcroppings splashed with vivid lichen, supporting tiny, tenacious bits of vegetation in the rock crevices.

Oblivious to the branches that slapped at her face and tugged her long plait of hair, Libby continued to edge her way doggedly along the cliff face until, at last, she found what she knew would be there.

Libby shivered violently, although the sun was warm on her back. Staring straight ahead with a fixed, unseeing gaze, she took a moment to think wistfully of the peaceful land behind her, her horses and dogs, her treasured girlish dreams and yearnings. She thought of all the people she loved, picturing them fondly in her mind, one by one— Gray and Jo, Keith and Mac, Peggy and her fat little baby son...and Warren. Oh, Warren....

Stifling a small moan, Libby clenched her hands into fists, squared her shoulders and stepped forward into darkness.

CHAPTER THIRTEEN

THE DAY AFTER Libby's journey, the tall waving prairie grasses lay parched and sere beneath the late summer sun, as dry and powdery as golden dust. A heavy gray sky brooded on the vast land, and the wind howled over the plains, driving tumbleweeds before it to mass in the ditches along the barbed wire fences.

Just as the midday light began to fade, a big, luxurious car pulled off the main highway and began the long drive down the road to the Lyndon ranch. Even the massive weight of the car was no match for the gusting wind that buffeted the heavy vehicle about like a child's toy.

In the driver's seat Gray Lyndon gripped the wheel tightly, frowning as he peered out through the dust-smeared windshield and then turning to give his wife a wry smile.

"Looks like the welcoming committee has arranged a really nice homecoming for us," he observed, his eyes sparkling cheerfully. "Just a really nice day on the prairie to show us what we've been missing all these months."

His wife, Joanna, smiled placidly back at him, gazing with great fondness at his rugged features, his curly graying hair and the substantial muscular breadth of his body.

"I love you," she said impulsively, reaching over to pat his leg. Then, remembering his words, she added, "I enjoy days like this when the wind blows on the prairie.

It feels so cozy when you're inside the house, listening to it howl and snarl outside, trying to get in, and knowing that you're safe.''

Gray chuckled, ruffling her short dark hair with a big hand and gathering her small body close to his for a moment.

"You're crazy, Mrs. Lyndon," he murmured against her dark curls. "Did anybody ever tell you how crazy you are?''

"Many times," she said with a grin, and then sobered. "Gray...do you think we should stop in at Mac's for a minute? Just to...to see what he says?''

Gray considered, and then shook his head. "I don't think so. I doubt that we'd get any more out of Mac in person than we could on the phone."

"It was such a strange thing for him to do," Jo said thoughtfully. "Calling and telling us we should come home early. Mac doesn't do things like that without a reason.''

"I know, but he said Libby should be the one to tell us about it, whatever it is.''

"And he *did* say," Jo went on for the hundredth time since Mac's disturbing call the previous week to their hotel room in London, "he did say absolutely that everybody's all right—Peggy and the baby and Libby and Keith? He said they're all fine, didn't he, Gray?''

Gray gave his wife a warm, tender glance, his face soft with love. "Yes, sweetheart, Mac said they're all just fine. It's some trouble with the operation of the ranch, and he thought we should come to help Libby with it. That's all.''

"I wonder what..." Jo began again, her face creasing with worry.

"Well, don't wonder," Gray said briefly. "In a few

minutes we'll be home, talking to Libby, and then we'll know all about it, whatever it is that's going on. Probably," he went on soothingly, "she's just finding the work a bit much and won't admit it, but Mac can see she's getting worn out so he thought we'd better come home a couple of weeks early."

"Probably," Jo said, unconvinced, turning to frown out the window again at the desolate sweep of land.

They drove slowly into the ranch yard, both gazing around hungrily at the dear, familiar scenes, both searching secretly for anything amiss or troubling. But the buildings lay neat and silent beneath the leaden sky, and the only sound was the snarl of the wind around the outlying corrals and haystacks.

Jo ran into the house, followed more slowly by Gray, who was lugging a couple of heavy suitcases and a bulging garment bag.

"Libby?" Jo shouted into the depths of the big house. "Libby, are you in here?"

But the house was empty, the kitchen gleaming and still. The wind sobbed around the eaves with a cry like a wailing child, and Jo shivered with sudden, irrational fear.

Gray stepped out into the yard and came back inside, his rugged face full of apprehension that he couldn't hide.

"Gray?" his wife asked anxiously.

He looked at her, his big body taut and still, his eyes dark with worry.

"Maybe we'd better call Mac," he said.

"Gray...what is it?"

"The morning chores haven't been done," Gray said. "The pets haven't been fed, and the horses in the barn haven't been turned out on water."

Jo stared back at him, her deep blue eyes wide and

strained. "Maybe...maybe she went into the city for the
night," Jo whispered. "Maybe she wanted to see the baby
or something and then had trouble on the road."

Gray shook his head. "Not Libby. You know what
she's like, Jo. When she has a responsibility, she'll move
heaven and earth to get it done. If she were away and
couldn't get back to do the chores, she'd call Mac or one
of the other neighbors to come and look after the animals."

Jo nodded miserably and slumped into a chair. "I
know. I know you're right. But that means...oh, Gray..."

She watched, wide-eyed and silent, while he strode
across the room and picked up the telephone, dialing with
tense impatience.

"Damn!" he muttered. "No answer at Mac's. Who
else should I try, Jo? Who else in the neighborhood might
have some idea what's—"

Joanna jerked her head up, pushed the chair aside and
ran to the window, leaning over the counter to peer out.
"Gray, somebody's coming! It's...a vehicle I don't
know...a black Jeep...and there's two men in it. Gray,
one of them's Mac!"

"Thank God," Gray said fervently. "Now maybe we
can start making some sense out of all this."

Jo went over beside him, hugging him, trying to warm
all of his big body with her love, and he gathered her into
his arms, patting her tenderly.

They were still standing quiet and close together when
Mac came into the kitchen, followed by a tall, lithe young
man with a dark, hawklike face, wearing jeans and a
heavy denim jacket.

"I'm glad you're back, kids," Mac said, smiling wanly

as Jo ran into his arms and giving her a brief, awkward hug.

"Mac, what is it? What's going on? Where's Libby?"

Mac hesitated, his gentle, weathered features full of concern. "You've been outside?" he said briefly to Gray. "You saw that the chores haven't been done?"

Gray nodded.

"I stopped by a couple of hours ago to see how she was," Mac said, "and when I realized she wasn't here, apparently hadn't been home at all since yesterday, then I got worried and went over to see if Warren knew where—"

"Wait a minute," Gray interrupted. "Who's Warren?"

"Warren McIntyre, Mr. Lyndon," the young man said, stepping forward and extending his hand. "Mac told me that he called and asked the two of you to come home early. I'm very glad."

"I still haven't figured out who you are, Mr. McIntyre," Gray said politely, "or where you fit into all this."

"Well, I think I'm a major part of the problem, Mr. Lyndon. You see, earlier this summer…"

Warren launched into the story of the discovery and preliminary exploration of the archaeological site while Jo and Gray stood silently watching him and listening to his words.

Sparing himself nothing, Warren told of Libby's worry that rapidly escalated into real concern and finally into anguish and of the implacable refusal of the government team to consider her pleas. The only part of the story that he kept to himself was their magical night of lovemaking and the stormy midnight when he found her on the hilltop with her blasting equipment. That part of the story, he thought, was between himself and Libby, and nobody else.

"So that's what's been going on," Gray said finally. "My poor girl. She must have gone through hell."

Warren nodded, his fine, austere features shadowed with pain. "I know she did. I hate myself for having a part in it."

Gray stared at the younger man with cold eyes and a quiet, expressionless face.

Warren's jaw tightened, and he met the big rancher's gaze, his face pale beneath his tan. "Look, you may not believe it, but I care a great deal for your daughter, Mr. Lyndon. And if she's hurt or something, I can't…" His voice broke and he waited quietly, his powerful features clenched and still.

Mac clapped an awkward hand on Warren's shoulder, and then looked at the others who stood tense and silent in the middle of the kitchen. "So now you know the whole story," he said with relief. "I'm sure glad you're home, Gray."

"Why didn't somebody tell me sooner?" Gray asked. "The poor kid, dealing with that all summer…."

"When things started to get really serious, I wanted to call you," Mac said, "and so did Warren. But Libby wouldn't hear of it. She didn't want to spoil your holiday, and she kept hoping that something would happen to make it all go away, I guess."

"I can't stand this!" Jo interrupted suddenly, her blue eyes bright with pain. "We're all standing around here talking, and meanwhile Libby is—" She waved her hand helplessly. "Where is she? Nobody knows. She hasn't been home overnight, and her chores aren't done. And we all know that she'd *die* before she'd willingly leave those animals neglected!''

There was a long moment of tense silence in the kitchen while the four of them stood and stared at one another. Gray was the first to recover.

''You're right, sweetheart. We have to get busy,'' he said, pulling Jo close to him and giving her a brief, comforting hug before he released her. ''What vehicle is she using? And who saw her last?''

''I think I did. It was the night before last,'' Warren began. ''She came over to the site to—''

He paused, his dark face taut with pain, but before he could begin again they heard, over the roar of the wind, the unmistakable sound of another vehicle entering the yard.

''It's Clem,'' Gray said, glancing out the window. ''And he's in a hurry.''

They all stared out the window, watching as a small, plump man leaped from his truck and came running across the yard, moving with clumsy, rolling speed, like a child's toy on wheels. But there was nothing comical about the man's face when he appeared in the kitchen doorway and found them all standing silently waiting for him to speak.

''Gray! Thank God you're— Gray, I need to tell you—'' the fat little man began breathlessly, stumbling over his own words in his haste. ''Thank God you're home. I was afraid there'd be no one—''

''Okay, Clem,'' Gray said soothingly, patting his plump neighbor on the shoulder. ''It's okay. We're home and we're going to look after things. Now tell me what the problem is.''

''It's...it's Libby,'' Clem panted, casting an appealing glance first at Jo and then at Gray.

Warren tensed and took a quick step forward, his dark eyes brilliant and piercing. Gray caught the younger man's glance, giving him a small, reassuring nod, and Warren subsided, waiting.

"What about Libby, Clem? What is it?"

"That saddle horse of hers, that big bay gelding, the one she calls Scout?"

Gray nodded, his face unreadable, his eyes grim. "I know the horse, Clem," he said gently. "What about him?"

"He...he came wandering into my hay meadow about an hour ago just after I got back from town. All ganted up and wire-cut, lathered real bad, still saddled with the cinches tight."

"Oh, God," Gray muttered, closing his eyes briefly. "If her horse is in such bad shape, then that means that wherever she is, she's already been out overnight."

"Your hay meadow, Clem," Mac said tensely. "You say Libby's horse came into your hay meadow? From the north?"

Clem nodded, gazing fearfully from one face to the other.

Gray looked over at his old friend. "What are you thinking, Mac? Do you have some idea where she is?"

"I don't know where she is," Mac said, looking at the others with bleak sorrow. "But I think I know where to start looking."

THE SUNLIGHT FADED with terrifying suddenness, sinking beyond the western horizon in a blowing pall of dust. The wind increased steadily until by nightfall it was blowing at gale force with a keen knife edge of frost. By the time the chill tide of darkness flowed across the prairie, most of the neighboring ranchers were involved in the search for the missing woman.

On the outer fringes of the community pasture, near the place where they had discovered Libby's abandoned truck and horse trailer, a welter of trucks and Jeeps were drawn into a rough circle in the darkness. In the center, two gas-powered barbecues were set up. Coffeepots bubbled and steamed on one grill, while hamburgers and potatoes roasted on the other.

The people back in the hills were hunting in pairs, and from time to time a team would struggle in from the blowing sand to rest for a while by the vehicles, have a hot drink and some food. Then they would pick up their rifles and flashlights and plunge back into the howling darkness.

Joanna Lyndon stood in the circle of light by one of the barbecues, her face tight with suffering. Mechanically she lifted a spatula to turn the hamburger patties and looked around for the barbecue sauce. The bottle was beyond her reach on a small folding table full of sandwiches and cakes contributed by the women from nearby ranches. Alexandra Coleman, who was buttering buns at the table, rushed forward and handed Jo the sauce. The two women exchanged a look that was full of anguish and eloquent with unspoken concern and sympathy. Then they returned quietly to their own tasks.

Lights beamed out of the darkness, and an engine rumbled nearby. Jo tensed and ran around one of the Jeeps to look, her heart pounding wildly. Her shoulders slumped in disappointment when she recognized Jim Harding's big four-wheel-drive truck and saw Jim himself climbing down from behind the wheel. Steve Moen, a high-rigger working on one of the oil wells near the ranch, got out the other side, and the two men walked into the circle of light.

Jo stood silently, looking at the young neighboring rancher.

"I got my plane put away," he told her. "I'll go back and get it out again as soon as it starts getting light."

"There'll be no need," Jo said. "We'll find her long before then. There are at least fifty people in there, Jim." Her face was taut with conviction, her blue eyes blazing.

Jim looked down at her in sympathy. "Sure, Jo," he said. "Of course we'll find her." He took a hamburger and began to munch on it. "Help yourself, Steve," he said to the burly young man beside him. "Might be a while before we get a chance to eat again."

While his partner joined him at the barbecue, Jim swallowed the last of his hamburger and took a flashlight and rifle from his truck. "Okay, Steve, let's go. Where do we start, Jo?"

Jo consulted a rough map taped to the door of a truck. "Over here," she said. "Straight north about a mile and then a half mile west." She marked Jim's initials in the block on the map.

Both men zipped their jackets up and pulled scarves over their mouths to protect them from the blowing dust. They turned to go, and Jim paused, pointing to the east. "See, Jo? Full moon coming up. It's gonna be bright as day in a little while."

The two women turned to look at the bloated orange moon glimmering through a thick pall of dust and blowing sand. Jim and Steve plunged off into the ravine and were swallowed up in the swirling dust clouds before they topped the first ridge.

Rifle shots echoed in the hills, carrying faintly on the

wind. Jo strained her ears, listening for the three shots in rapid succession that would signal, "Found," but they never came. All she heard were single shots, isolated and empty of hope. Back on the open prairie a coyote howled from some lonely hilltop, a sound so melancholy and bleak with despair that it was all she could do not to give in and sob in helpless misery.

A pair of lights came winking down a hill off to the west, distorted by blowing sand until they resembled will-o'-the-wisps, diffuse and erratic. Jo stood erect and stared at them in wide-eyed, straining silence. The lights drew nearer and dark shapes materialized behind them, hazy and mysterious against the moonlit sky.

They stumbled wearily into the circle, almost close enough to touch before Jo recognized them as her husband and Warren McIntyre. Their clothes and heads were caked with dust, their eyes white and staring in their blackened faces. The two men staggered forward and sank into lawn chairs near the barbecues, setting down their flashlights and stretching their hands toward the warmth as Jo and Alex rushed about, serving up plates of food and hot coffee for them.

"Oh, Gray," Jo murmured. "Oh, darling, look at you. You're so tired."

She knelt by his chair, clutching his dusty sleeve, while he patted her hair awkwardly. Alex came over, bringing another tray of rich cake, and both men smiled at her gratefully, their teeth flashing white against their grimy faces.

"I wish I could go out there," Alex said abruptly. "We've got all the food organized now. I'd like to help look."

"Dr. Coleman," Gray began in protest, "it's not an easy thing to—"

"Don't worry, Gray," Warren interrupted, trying to sound cheerful. "There probably aren't many men out there who are as tough as Alex. That's why I called her. If Jo has things under control here, then Alex is perfectly capable of taking a shift in the hills as soon as someone comes along to partner her."

"Mac will be back soon," Jo said. "He went over to pick up the Simpson boys. When he comes back, Alex can go out with him if she likes."

"Good," Alex said. "I'll hunt up a scarf and put on my hiking boots, so I'll be ready when he gets here."

She disappeared in the direction of her dusty Land Rover, and the other three sat silently, gazing at one another.

"Gray," Jo whispered. "I keep thinking how cold it is and how long Libby's been out there. Do you think...?"

"Don't think, sweetheart," he said huskily. "We can't afford to think. We just have to keep going till we find her, and then we'll deal with what has to be done, that's all. Your only job is to stay here and keep people warm and fed and allocated to the right areas, and we all have to keep looking. We'll comb every inch of this place, darling. We can't help but find her."

He stopped speaking, his voice slurred with weariness, and they were all silent, each of them thinking of the vastness of this rugged tract of land and how long it would take, even for an army of men to comb every inch of it.

"Well," Warren said abruptly, getting to his feet, "are you ready, Gray?"

"Ready as I'll ever be," Gray said, lifting himself from his chair with dragging slowness. "All that easy living and holiday time makes a man soft,'' he added, trying to smile at his wife.

She hugged him, choking back a sob of despair, and then stood back and watched in silence, her eyes wide and full of pain as he pulled himself erect, bent stiffly to pick up his rifle and followed the younger man wearily into the darkness.

WARREN TRAMPED ALONG the shallow deer trail beside Libby's father, his mind a frantic, tortured whirl of thoughts. He couldn't force the images from his mind—dreadful pictures of Libby's slender body, crushed and broken, chilled and slipping from consciousness, the life slowly, relentlessly draining from her while they all searched in vain through this howling, dusty inferno.

Then, superimposed mockingly on the scenes of pain and terror and death, he saw other images—the warm, gentle fullness of her mouth, the ruddy glow of her hair, her emerald eyes, the soft, rich curve of her breast, and he felt her melting into his arms with a sweet, burning rush of desire....

"Oh, God," he murmured aloud in agony.

"Pardon, Warren?" Gray said, turning to the younger man, straining to hear him over the wind.

Warren hesitated.

He liked this sturdy, practical, intelligent man. He liked Gray's quick grasp of situations, his innate fairness and kindness that kept him from casting blame, and his obvious, deep love for Libby. If Gray had any thoughts about arriving home to find a crew of government people invading his land, he hadn't expressed them. His only concern right now was for his daughter. All other considerations were secondary.

United by their concern, he and Warren had rapidly become friends, and Warren found that he yearned to tell Gray how he felt about Libby, about the warm, rich tide of feeling that, ironically, he was only now beginning to comprehend in all its fullness. Even more, he wanted desperately to confess to Gray how harsh he had been with her and how his harshness had probably contributed to this rash flight of hers.

But he knew that such confession would be a selfish indulgence on his part. Gray Lyndon was already burdened enough with concern for his daughter, without having to deal with Warren's private agonies.

"Warren? Did you say something?" Gray repeated, turning to peer through the darkness at his companion.

"Nothing, Gray," Warren said wearily. "Just thinking out loud."

"Libby!" Gray shouted in a tired, hoarse voice, turning to face into the darkness. "Libby! It's Dad! Where are you?"

But there was no answer, just the mocking snarl of the wind in the blackened void beyond them...and the rustling of dust as it snaked through the tall grass.

MAC DROVE INTO the lighted circle by the rows of dusty vehicles and unloaded the two teenage Simpson brothers, who worked evenings at a service station in a nearby town and had expressed a wish to join the search party when their shift was over.

Jo made sure that the two gangly youngsters were warmly clothed and fed, gave them some brief instructions and dispatched them to a marked portion on her map. Then she turned to her uncle, and all her taut efficiency suddenly melted away.

"Oh, Mac," she whispered, burrowing into his arms, her shoulders shaking with despair.

"Now, Joey," Mac whispered tenderly, holding her close, patting her curly hair and her dusty, heaving back. "Now, Joey, don't you start giving up on us. We all need you to be strong, Jo. Come on, that's my girl. We'll get through this."

He bent close to her, whispering something in her ear while she clung to him and grew calmer, standing quietly in his arms.

Nearby, Alexandra Coleman looked on, her beautiful gray eyes full of surprise and sympathy as she watched the two of them.

Finally Jo regained control of herself, drew away from Mac with a damp, rueful smile and turned to the other woman, who had already become like an old friend to her. "Sorry, Alex," she murmured. "There's just something about Uncle Mac that makes me fall apart. He's always so comforting in a crisis."

"I see that," Alex said, tying a big cotton scarf around her neck and giving Mac a warm smile that made him feel a little dizzy. "I'm going to be your partner, Mr. Burman—Mac, I mean," she said hastily.

Mac stared. "You don't mean—" He waved his hand vaguely at the howling, dusty void beyond the circle of lights. "You don't intend to…?"

"I certainly do," Alex said calmly. "And I don't think we should waste any more time, do you?"

Stunned and disbelieving, Mac moved over to his truck, took out his rifle and a big flashlight and returned to find Alex waiting for him, warmly bundled in a heavy duffel coat, her scarf carefully raised over her mouth.

She glanced up at him, and her gray eyes creased

warmly so that he could see she was smiling under the scarf. Awkwardly he smiled back, feeling clumsy and foolish next to her. They waved to Jo, who was brewing a fresh pot of coffee, and then plunged off into the darkness.

"Where do we go?" Alex shouted over the wind.

"We'll be working next to Gray and Warren," Mac shouted back. "Straight north about two miles, then east. Are you finding it hard going? The footing's pretty rough here."

Alex didn't even bother to answer, concentrating on keeping up with his long strides.

As they swung forward through the rugged terrain, she thought of the scene by the fire, of how tenderly and competently this strange, shy man had dealt with Joanna's pain. They all loved each other so much, these reserved, self-sufficient people of the prairies. It made Alex feel isolated and a little wistful to see the warm affection and concern they showed to their own.

She thought about Jo and Gray, who had come home from a lovely long holiday to such turmoil and heartache, and of Libby, whose long summer of lonely anguish had finally culminated in this night of terror.

I should have done something, Alex thought wretchedly. I was so callous and unthinking. I should have talked to her more, helped her deal with it. All I did was send her over to see Al Herrold, and he just made her feel twice as frantic and miserable as she'd been before....

Suddenly and surprisingly, Alex's eyes burned with tears. She didn't even know what she was crying for— for Libby, lost and wounded in the darkness or for Warren and the people in Libby's family, who stood to lose someone so dear to them, or for herself, for Alexandra Coleman, because she was just beginning to realize how terribly, miserably solitary and inadequate she really was.

Alex choked and stumbled, blinded by tears. Mac grasped her elbow to steady her and then paused to look down at her in concern, playing the flashlight over her face, frowning with alarm when he saw the muddy tracks on her dust-smeared face.

"Dr. Coleman?" he said tentatively. "Is...is something wrong?"

Alex shook her head impatiently and turned away from the glow of the flashlight. "For goodness sake, call me Alex," she said, sniffling.

"I'm sorry," he said humbly.

Alex glanced up at him, saw the gentleness of his face and the worry in his eyes and tried to smile. "I'm the one who should apologize, Mac," she said. "I didn't mean to snap at you. I just feel so... I mean, all this is just too..."

She floundered, drowning in misery, and was grateful when he lowered the flashlight and took her elbow gently, guiding her forward into the darkness again.

"You know, Dr....Alex," he began hesitantly, "none of this was your fault, you know. There's no reason in the world for you to blame yourself."

Alex tensed and glanced up quickly, but it was too dark to see his face. "What makes you think I am?"

"I...I just thought you might be feeling a little bit to blame," Mac went on gently. "And it's not right. You were just doing your job, and so was Warren. You weren't doing anything wrong."

"But Libby felt so—"

"She was really upset. And I feel bad about it, and so do you. But it's not your fault. You didn't set out deliberately to hurt Libby or her family. And nobody thinks you did.''

Alex walked on in silence, thinking over his words, feeling warmed and grateful. He really was a strange, enigmatic man, this gangly, awkward rancher whom she'd always dismissed as being of absolutely no consequence, almost a figure of fun. But this, she realized, was no comical, foolish pig farmer. This was a man to be reckoned with. Alex remembered his tenderness when he comforted Joanna and the way he always seemed to be at hand when anybody needed him.

She felt a disturbing tug at her mind, something from the past that needed her attention, and wished she had time to think things through more deeply. But the important thing, the vital task right now, had nothing to do with her. It was Libby who mattered now, Libby who had to be found before any more hours passed, before the night got any colder.

Alex shivered and plunged on into the moonlit darkness, barely able to keep pace with Mac's long strides. Although she was athletic and well-conditioned, she was getting tired and painfully short of breath by the time Mac stopped, fired a single shot into the air and waited until an answering shot sounded quite nearby, off to the west.

"Are we there?" Alex asked, trying not to show how short of breath she was. "Is this where we start hunting?"

"I guess so. I think that's Warren and Gray who fired the answering shot from the west. Are you all right? Would you like to rest for a few minutes?" he asked with concern, looking down at her as she stood beside him, slender and dainty even in her heavy outdoor gear.

"I'm fine," Alex said. "How shall we do this?"

"I think," Mac began, frowning into the darkness,

"that we'd better stay together. Let's do a sweep back and forth over this section about twenty or thirty feet apart. That way we can cover a lot of ground in a hurry without fear of getting separated."

Alex nodded. "Sounds good. Mac…?"

"Yes?"

Alex hesitated, struggling with her own fears. "Do you really think…" she began, and paused, feeling a stab of pain. "I mean, what chance is there of finding her, really? This community pasture is so huge. How can we even know we're looking in the right place?"

The wind had died down a little, and the clouds of dust no longer obscured the moon. Alex, looking up at the man beside her, could see his craggy features silvered by the light and read the cautious fear in his shadowed eyes.

"I don't know, Alex," he said. "I just don't know. There's no reason she should be this deep into the pasture, and it's awfully rugged country. But her horse trailer was parked over in this section, and she had to be either leaving it or coming back to it, so we don't have much choice but to hunt in this area."

"But, Mac," Alex whispered, "it's getting so cold, and it's been so long."

"I know," he said, looking down at her steadily. "But the wind is dying down, and there'll be a fair, bright moon for a few hours now, so I think we have a good chance."

Alex hesitated, still gazing up at him in mute, desperate appeal. Then, recognizing the futility of speech, she squared her shoulders, turned and plunged off beside him into the rough tract of land.

Patiently they crossed and recrossed the section allocated to them, half running to cover as much ground as they could, calling Libby's name at intervals.

The wind had subsided, so they could hear other voices calling, as well, carrying faintly on the crisp night air, and other single-spaced shots ringing through the darkness.

Half-blinded by fatigue, Alex stumbled on a tangled root of sage and sprawled headlong, crying out with pain as her hand fell into a mass of cactus. Instantly Mac was beside her, kneeling close to her, helping her to her feet and examining the throbbing, stinging hand.

Alex stood like a child, shivering and biting her lip with pain while he skillfully extracted the needle-sharp cactus spines. She trembled, coming slowly to a full realization of how exhausted she was, how weary and dirty and drained of hope, and then set her jaw and drew a deep breath, determined not to let Mac see her weakness.

Alex continued to stare fixedly over his shoulder while he tugged at the cactus spines. Suddenly she grasped his arm with her free hand and pointed.

"Mac!" she whispered.

"What?" he asked in alarm, turning to look behind him.

"Shh! Look at the owl, Mac. Watch it for a minute."

Mac's long body grew taut and still and he stood beside Alex, still holding her hand, gazing at the massive horned owl. The big bird was drifting on the soft air currents that still sighed over the prairie and sent little clouds of dust snaking in silent trails across the rugged landscape. The moonlight glanced on his outspread wings as he circled and swooped with soundless grace, looking down at the ground.

There was something different about the owl, Alex realized. He wasn't hunting or following prey; he was just circling and looking with mild curiosity at something on the ground—something strange and unusual....

Side by side, hardly daring to breathe, Mac and Alex edged forward toward the soaring bird, and he lifted and wheeled, flying straight up into the full moon with a flare of silver. Mac raked the flashlight back and forth over the sage and grass while Alex held her breath and walked beside him, gazing intently at the ground.

"Mac!" she whispered urgently. "Oh, Mac...!"

He hurried over beside her and stared in the direction of her pointing finger. Immediately in front of them was a huge stand of gnarled sagebrush, gleaming like molten platinum in the midnight glow of the moon.

From behind the massed sage they could see something lying on the ground. As they moved closer, details became clearer—a pair of slender, denim-clad legs and neat, small riding boots, an outflung arm, a plait of blood-soaked hair and a face, pale and still as death, glowing like fine marble in the moonlight.

CHAPTER FOURTEEN

WARREN ACHED WITH WEARINESS, and his mind was numbed with long, sleepless hours of worry and sorrow. He moved through the dusty terrain like a man in a nightmare, knowing with agonized helplessness that his love was in danger, that she was slipping away from him into the darkness and he was powerless to help her.

He shook his head and blinked his stinging eyes, trying to focus, to stay alert, to concentrate on what he was doing. A few feet away Gray Lyndon stumbled along beside him, still calling Libby's name hoarsely at intervals, but Warren could see that the man was on the verge of exhaustion.

No wonder, he thought. After a shock like this and a long, sleepless night on top of a bad case of jet lag, it's a miracle he's still on his feet at all.

Warren glanced at the big man again, his face drawn with concern, and paused. But before he could speak he heard something, carried on the chill night air. He lifted his face tensely toward the stars, straining every nerve in his body, listening. The sound came again from the east, muffled but unmistakable in the dark stillness.

It was three shots fired in rapid succession.

Warren stood rigidly, his body in the grip of a shuddering wave of emotion that he could scarcely control. He sobbed once, briefly, brushed a hand over his eyes and plunged forward into the darkness.

"Gray!" he shouted. "Gray, wait!"

Too tired to hear or understand, Gray trudged doggedly forward into the night, his big shoulders slumped, his body drooping with weariness.

Warren caught up with him and grasped his arm. "Gray! Listen!"

Gray turned a blank, uncomprehending face to him, and Warren gestured him to silence. They stood staring at each other in the moonlight while the three shots rang out again.

Gray's face crumpled. He sagged for a moment and would have fallen if Warren hadn't put a strong arm around him.

"I'll go over there now, Gray," Warren whispered. "Do you...do you want to wait or come with me now...?"

"I'll come," Gray murmured huskily. "I'll come with you, son. She might...I think she'll be glad to see me if she's—"

He choked, and Warren tightened his arm, half supporting the big man through the grass and brush in the direction of the three shots.

They were the first to get there, and they could see from some distance the little glowing pool created by the two powerful flashlights, the big stand of sagebrush and the two shadowy figures bending over something lying on the ground.

Warren's throat tightened, and his heart began to pound. He left Gray to make his own way and rushed forward, recognizing Mac and Alex, then turning his eyes to the still form on the dusty, moonlit grass.

"Oh, Libby," he whispered aloud, moving slowly to her side and dropping to his knees. "Oh, my darling..."

He looked down at her still, crumpled body, her lovely face so calm and composed in the silvery light, and in that moment he knew absolutely and with blinding, heart-breaking clarity, that this woman was his love for all time, that no other woman would ever be able to fill his heart and soul as she had.

He reached out a trembling hand, touching her face and her long plait of hair that was filled with grass and bits of twigs, matted with dried blood. Tears ran down his face unheeded, making dark streaks through his dusty face. Tenderly he cupped her cheek in his palm, stroking her face with his fingers. And suddenly he realized with a shattering flood of hope that although her skin was cold and clammy, her lips were moving and her eyelids fluttered occasionally.

Immediately his clouded, weary mind grew crystal clear, and his despair gave way to a burning urgency, a surge of energy, an overwhelming masculine need to protect and save and defend.

"She's alive," he said. "Mac, get back to the trucks and have Jo call everybody in and radio for the air ambulance. Get them to find an open area and park their vehicles with headlights illuminating it so that the helicopter can land."

Mac stood up at once, nodding tensely, poised and ready to run like a deer across the hills.

"Mac!" Warren called without turning around, absorbed in a careful examination of Libby's still body.

"Yes?"

"Tell them she's got a ragged, superficial scalp wound, probably from hitting her head on a sharp rock when she fell, but she's lost a lot of blood. She's also got a badly sprained ankle, and…'' He paused briefly, touching Libby's forehead and neck with gentle, exploring fingers, and then went on. ''And she's in shock, and no doubt seriously dehydrated. Have you got all that?''

''I've got it,'' Mac said.

''She's an incredible girl, my Libby is,'' Warren murmured, gazing down at her. ''She's survived out here for all these hours. Hang on, kid,'' he whispered to her quiet, still face. ''You've made it this far. Just hang on till we can get you some help, sweetheart.''

Alex glanced over at Mac as he prepared for his swift journey across the hills. ''Now, Mac, you be careful,'' she said sternly. ''That's some pretty rough country out there, you know. You just be sure you don't try to go too fast and stumble or something.''

Mac looked at her in mock surprise. ''Why, Dr. Coleman,'' he said with a weary, teasing grin, ''haven't you noticed what a graceful, fleet-footed young fellow I am?''

The others smiled back at him, feeling silly and lightheaded with relief, and Mac turned to plunge off into the darkness.

Still smiling, Alex moved over beside Warren, carrying a canteen of water, and handed it to him. Warren uncapped the canteen and lifted Libby's head gently on his arm. Then he noticed Gray, kneeling silently opposite him, his eyes full of anguish as he gazed down at that quiet, lovely face.

''Here, Gray,'' Warren said, handing the canteen over to him. ''See if you can get her to drink a little.''

With a tired, grateful smile Gray took the canteen and held it to Libby's mouth, tipping it gently, trying to force a trickle of liquid between her parted lips. They all watched in tense silence as she took a tiny bit of the water, then a little more, and her eyelids fluttered again.

Suddenly her eyes opened wide, gazing at all of them with a blank, unseeing stare, moving from face to face. "Dad?" she whispered in confusion, seeing her father's face close to hers. "Dad?"

"Shh, honey, it's me," Gray murmured, tears running down his weathered cheeks. "It's me, Libby. Jo and I got home just yesterday, and you were…"

But she wasn't listening. Her eyes were roaming restlessly again, searching vaguely through the shadows and pools of light, staring at the moon, the stars, the silvered sagebrush, at Alex's tired face, smiling encouragement.

Then Warren bent close to her again and she saw him. "Warren," she whispered.

Suddenly her face blazed with emotion, with depths of love and adoration that were dazzling in their small circle of darkness and pain. Warren gazed down at her in awe, stunned and humbled by that single, revealing moment of illumination, his heart aching with love.

But as quickly as the look had appeared on her face it vanished, leaving him wondering if he had perhaps only imagined that shining transformation. Her face settled into a cold, composed mask, gazing up at him with a detached, measured look that chilled him to the bone before her eyes dropped wearily closed once more. She sagged in Warren's arms, and he laid her back gently on the ground, pulling his jacket off and folding it beneath her head.

From far away they could hear the sounds of people approaching, of running feet, shouts and confusion, the roar of engines.

Libby's eyes flickered open once more. She searched for Warren and looked at him for a moment with an expression as remote as the stars winking overhead in the blackness of the sky.

"I found it," she said.

Then she turned her head aside, gave herself up to pain and exhaustion and lost consciousness again.

ALEX LEANED HER CHEEK against the chill blackness of the window, trying to stay awake, fighting a gritty, helpless feeling of unreality and dismay. "This is terrible," she muttered aloud. "Just terrible."

Mac, who was beside her, driving his truck along the graveled road to his ranch, glanced over at her in concern. "What's terrible?"

"This," she said, waving her hand vaguely. "Bothering you like this and...and everything."

"You're just being silly," Mac said comfortably, smiling at her briefly and returning to his driving. "Look at you. You're absolutely worn out. There's no way you could drive back to the city tonight. You'd be a hazard to other motorists. And there's nowhere else for you to go, because Gray and Jo will be at the hospital all night and so will Warren. So it makes sense for you to just stay at my place. I've got all kinds of room."

"Really?" Alex asked dubiously. "You're absolutely certain this is no inconvenience to you?"

"Absolutely," Mac said calmly. "Joanna lived with me almost a whole year, you know, before she married Gray. And she had a little room and a bathroom to herself, and after she left, I just kind of left it, you know, as a guest room. You can have that room with no problem at all."

Alex sighed in exhausted bliss, thinking about a bathroom all to herself and a soft warm bed.

She glanced over at Mac, grinning wearily through the

dust that coated her face. "Look at you. Fresh as a daisy," she complained. "How do you do it when everybody else is dropping from fatigue?"

He grinned back, his face creasing warmly with humor. "Oh, I'm a tough old bird," he said cheerfully.

Alex frowned at him. "You're not old," she said, "Or, to put it another way, if you're old, then so am I. We're about the same age, we two, I believe."

"Well," Mac said gallantly, "if *that's* the case, then I'm...younger than springtime."

Alex chuckled and then sobered. "Mac...do you really think she's going to be all right?"

"It sounds good," Mac said, gazing thoughtfully at the lightening band of sky to the east where the sun was about to rise. "The paramedics pretty well confirmed what Warren said, didn't they? No serious damage, just shock and dehydration and a lot of blood loss..."

"She looked so...I don't know," Alex muttered, staring up at the murky gray sky. "Mac, did you see the look in her eyes? She looked like someone who's...who's traveled to the ends of the earth and back, or looked on something unspeakable."

Mac nodded soberly. "She seemed strange, all right. Really strange."

"Well," Alex said briskly, "at least she's safe. Did you happen to see Warren's face, Mac, when she opened her eyes and saw him that first time? I almost cried. I knew there was something going on there, but I had no idea it was so...so intense."

"I knew it was," Mac said briefly. "I think I knew about it even before they did, but then I'm a natural romantic."

Alex laughed again, earning a stern, reproving frown

from her companion that set her off, tired as she was, on another burst of giggles.

Laughing with her, Mac pulled his truck into the yard, parked by the gate and turned off the ignition. "We're home," he said. "Now, you can sleep as long as you like, and tomorrow whenever you feel like it, we'll drive back out there to get your Jeep. The first order of business," he added, "is a long hot bath for you."

"Lead me to it," Alex said humbly. Suddenly she was drowning in fatigue, almost too tired to be aware of where she was or what was happening, grateful to allow herself to be helped from the truck and half carried up the walk to the little house.

ALEX WOKE to a hazy half-light that was puzzling and disturbing and lay for a moment in the soft bed, staring at the ceiling, trying to remember where she was. Then it all came flooding back—Warren's urgent, desperate call and her long drive out to meet him and Libby's family at the community pasture, their dark, frantic search and the terrible, bone-numbing weariness that had washed over her after they found the girl.

Dimly she remembered the later events, as well—Mac's shy kindness and the surprisingly gracious and tactful way in which he had made her comfortable, given her a clean white shirt to sleep in, quietly provided for all her needs before she could even think of asking.

What a nice man he is, Alex thought drowsily, stirring and stretching in the warm bed. Funny how I never noticed him at all before last night....

She propped herself on one elbow and saw that her clothes had been washed and pressed and set carefully on a chair just inside the door.

Alex grinned and then blinked. Still confused by the strange morning light, she got out of bed and crossed the room to draw the curtain aside. The farm buildings lay silent and sleepy in the warm golden glow, and Alex gazed at them, charmed by the beauty of the place.

The farmhouse stood in a green yard full of carefully tended lawns and flower beds, surrounded by big old poplar trees that cast a cool shade. Under one of the trees there was a lawn swing, a set of cedar chairs and a table that appeared to be well used. And beyond, the prairie rolled off into the sky on all sides, quiet and ageless and deeply peaceful.

It's beautiful, Alex thought with a catch in her throat. It's just so beautiful. What would it be like to live here in all this peace and beauty? And work here…?

She shook her head and glanced at her wristwatch, which stood at just after six. But it seemed much too light for six o'clock.

Suddenly Alex realized in horror that it was six o'clock in the *evening* and she had slept for more than twelve hours.

She hurried across the room and slipped into her clothes. They were so clean and fragrant that she could tell they had been dried on a clothesline out in the prairie breeze, and they bore crisp lines where they had been neatly, faultlessly ironed.

Absently Alex fingered the fabric of her shirt, gazing at it in thoughtful silence. Then she collected herself, slipped across the hallway to the little gleaming bathroom and observed with a rueful smile that everything was once again provided for her—a fresh toothbrush, toothpaste, a jar of face cream, tissues, hairbrushes, everything she could possibly want.

What a man, she thought again. What a surprising, amazing man.

She returned to the charming guest bedroom with its shining maple furniture and delicate flowered wallpaper, slipped on her heavy socks and padded down the hallway to the kitchen. As she neared that part of the house, she realized simultaneously that a number of delicious aromas were filling the air and that she was absolutely famished.

Alex stepped into the kitchen, startling Mac, who was stirring something on the stove with a big wooden spoon. "That smells just delicious," Alex said fervently. "And I'm starved."

"It's a beef stew," Mac said, smiling at her before he turned back to the stove. "I thought you should have some substantial nourishment. How do you feel?"

"Wonderful," Alex said. "Absolutely wonderful. And so I should, sleeping for over twelve hours. Why didn't you wake me?"

"I thought you'd wake up when you'd slept enough," Mac said comfortably, dropping generous mounds of dumpling batter into the bubbling stew. "These will be done in about ten minutes," he added. "We can have our salad while we're waiting."

Alex smiled at the table, beautifully set for two with place mats, wooden salad bowls, a little crystal jug of dressing and a basket filled with warm slices of home-made bread. "This is lovely, Mac," she said sincerely. "Just lovely."

He smiled shyly, drew a chair out for her and then seated himself, spreading a napkin carefully over his jeans.

"So," Alex said, biting a generous chunk from a slice

of bread and chewing blissfully, "how is she? Have you heard anything?"

Mac nodded, pouring dressing over his salad. "Warren called earlier today. She's going to be fine, although she really did lose a lot of blood. Warren says she's got a splitting headache, and it took them awhile to get her fever down after she was settled in the hospital."

"How long was she out there, Mac? Has she talked to them at all?"

"Just a little, I guess. More bread?"

Alex smiled guiltily and took another large slice of bread.

"Libby told them," Mac went on, "that she'd been riding in there all day and was on her way back to her truck in the early evening. She was worn out, too tired to be careful and her horse shied at something. She wasn't sure, thought it was probably a rattlesnake."

Alex shuddered, gazing wide-eyed across the table.

"He reared and threw her, and she hit her head on the rock, and that's all she can remember. But her hands and knees are all scratched and torn. She probably tried to walk a bit and couldn't because of the sprained ankle, so it looks as if she tried to crawl for quite a distance before she passed out again. She can't remember anything about it."

"Oh, the poor girl," Alex whispered, her gray eyes bright with pain as she stared at him. "So she was out there...how long? Over twenty-four hours?"

Mac nodded. "Closer to thirty hours, I guess. Warren says it's really lucky we found her when we did, Alex."

"I can't bear to think about it," Alex said, watching as Mac got up and returned to the table carrying the kettle of stew, mounded with golden feather-light dumplings. "I can't bear to think about what might have happened if—"

"Don't think about it," Mac said gently, spooning the rich stew onto her plate and adding a couple of dumplings. "There's no need at all to think about it. She wants to see you," he added. "Tomorrow, Warren said, she should be strong enough to have a little company, and she's asked to talk to you."

"To me?" Alex said, startled. "Why?"

"I don't know," Mac said. "Warren doesn't know, either." He was silent for a moment, staring thoughtfully at his plate.

"Mac?" Alex prompted him. "What is it?"

"Warren seemed so…unhappy, you know?" Mac said, glancing up at Alex. "I mean, he's delighted that she's not badly hurt, and she's going to be all right and all, but he still seems kind of down and really worried about things."

Alex ate her stew silently, looking at him with questioning eyes.

"I think it's the way Libby's acting," Mac went on. "I think it's got Warren really concerned. He says she doesn't seem to want to talk to him…or to anybody, actually. She just seems so strange and withdrawn, he says. He didn't go into any details, but I think he's really worried."

Alex cut a potato carefully into tiny pieces, considering. "Mac," she began finally, "what she said to Warren last night after we found her…remember…about finding something? What do you suppose she meant?"

Mac was silent, gazing at his dinner companion with thoughtful blue eyes. "I think," he said gently, "that you're probably going to find out tomorrow, Alex. I think that's what Libby wants to talk to you about.''

Alex's gray eyes widened, and she opened her mouth to speak, but Mac shook his head.

''Now that's enough about all that,'' he said with gentle firmness. ''Let's not speculate anymore. Tell me what you think about my cooking.''

Relieved, Alex laughed and praised him, and their conversation turned to lighter things. Alex relaxed, enjoying her meal, delighted by this strange, solitary man with his shy, perceptive insights and his gentle wit.

She watched as he lifted his tall, spare body from the chair, noting that he seemed not nearly as awkward in her presence now. Still laughing and chatting with surprising ease, as if they were old friends with a whole world of things to discuss, they cleared the table and did the dishes. Finally Alex hung up her dish towel and looked around regretfully at the snug little house and the sunset fading beyond the poplar trees.

''Well,'' she said with reluctance, ''I guess we'd better go out and get my vehicle before it's dark again, Mac. I'm so sorry to trouble you, but…''

''Do you really have to be back tonight?'' Mac asked. ''Couldn't you spend one more night and drive home tomorrow? You've been so worn out. I think another night's rest in the country would do you good.''

Alex gazed at his blue eyes, wavering. ''This is awful,'' she said, trying to laugh. ''I've bothered you enough already, and I really should be—''

''Come into the living room,'' he said comfortably. ''Relax by the fire for a little while and we'll think about it.''

Amazed at herself, wondering what on earth was happening to her, Alex followed him into the cozy little room and watched as he knelt, expertly laying the fire and lighting it. The flames caught and licked up onto the dry cedar logs, crackling cheerfully while the wind began to howl again outside the windows.

"This is so nice," Alex said, looking around the little room and sighing with pleasure. "Just so nice."

While Mac carefully swept the hearth and restacked the logs, Alex wandered around the room, looking with pleasure at the well-read books, the warm, comfortable furnishings. Her glance fell idly on a little table tucked out of sight in an alcove, where something square and bulky was covered by an oilcloth sheet. Alex peeped over at Mac, whose back was still turned, and edged the sheet aside curiously. Then, forgetting herself in her astonishment, she lifted the loose piece of fabric and stared. The object beneath the oilcloth was a small easel, and on it was a delicate watercolor painting, nearly finished.

The picture was an autumn scene, the exact mate of the spring scene hanging on the wall in Alex's office.

Alex whirled to find Mac looking over at her, his tanned face hot and flushed with embarrassment.

"But..." she whispered, her mind spinning in wild confusion. "Mac...I don't understand. How did you—?"

He shifted nervously on his feet, staring down at the braided rug by the hearth, unable to meet her eyes.

"Mac...*you're* the artist? *You* painted the spring scene in my office?"

Mac nodded awkwardly, still unable to look at her.

"And when I said...all those months ago, when I mentioned it to you, then you decided to paint the others...."

"They're all done," he murmured. "This is the last one."

"But why...why didn't you tell me?" Alex asked, still struggling to understand, to grasp this amazing reality.

"I thought you...might not like the painting as much if you knew I'd done it," he said humbly. "I wanted to surprise you with the others. I was planning to send them to you anonymously, you know, when they were finished, just to give you pleasure without the embarrassment of having to know they came from me or thank me or worry about...about payment or anything...."

Send them to you anonymously...anonymously. The words registered in her mind with a crushing impact, and she stared at him, thunderstruck, her slender body trembling.

"Mac!" she whispered. "*You wrote those letters!* It was you, wasn't it? It was you."

Mac went white beneath his tan and glanced up at her in agony. "I'm so sorry, Alex," he muttered. "I'm really sorry. I know it was stupid of me, but I just wanted so much to...to tell you things and let you know how I felt and how I lived my life and bring some happiness into your days, and I didn't know how to go about it, so I just..."

Alex continued to stare at him, her body tense and still though her mind was racing, recalling the letters and reliving everything she'd ever seen or known about the man in front of her in the light of this stunning revelation.

"Why did you stop?" she asked abruptly.

"Pardon?" he asked, looking up at her in bewilderment.

"The letters," Alex said. "They were coming so regularly and then they just stopped. Why did you quit sending them?"

Mac shook his head in disbelief and stammered a little

as he tried to reply. "Well, because you…you said…you told me that you had…somebody in your life. And I didn't want to embarrass you or make even more of a fool of myself, so I just…"

He looked at her in alarm. She was laughing, her gray eyes shining, her elegant features warm and glowing. "Oh, Mac," she said, clutching the edge of the table and sagging against it. "Oh, Mac…"

"What?" he asked, bewildered and hurt by her laughter.

Alex came slowly across the room toward him. Her smile had faded, but her eyes still shone with a glow that dazzled him, that soothed his pain and took his breath away.

"Mac," she whispered, stopping in front of him. "Mac, look at me."

Humbly he raised his eyes and gazed into her face, holding his breath.

"Mac, when I told you I had somebody in my life, do you know what I meant?"

He shook his head, still gazing at her beautiful, smiling face.

"I meant," she murmured, "that I've been so lonely for so many years and then suddenly I'd fallen completely in love with this mysterious man who was sending me the most wonderful letters. *That's* what I meant, Mac."

Mac stood in front of her, stunned and silent, while a great, wondering joy began to dawn in his eyes.

Alex moved into his arms, hugging his lean, strong body, laughing and crying. As his arms closed around her, she snuggled against his chest and gazed at the cozy room with the firelight casting warm shadows on the walls and ceiling, savoring the rare, rich feeling that for the first time in years she was in just the right place at exactly the right time.

WARREN SAT in the small padded armchair by Libby's hospital bed, watching her calm, sleeping face. He wore casual white cotton slacks and a pale yellow short-sleeved shirt, and the afternoon sun shone warmly through the window behind him, gleaming on his straight dark hair.

Nurses and their young assistants passed regularly in and out of the room, doing housekeeping and routine checks on the woman in the high, narrow bed and pausing occasionally to glance wistfully back at the tall man by the window, at his muscular, tanned arms, his lean, powerful body and handsome, intent face.

But he was completely oblivious to them, conscious only of the pale, still face swathed in bandages that lay on the white hospital pillows.

Warren shifted wearily in the chair, still gazing at the beautiful face that looked so peaceful and gentle in sleep. But when she opened her eyes, he knew that her face would close and her expression would become remote and guarded once again, shutting him out, hurting him so deeply.

He looked at his watch, checking the time, wondering when Gray and Jo would be back. They had finally gone home the night before once they were confident that Libby would be all right, assuring Warren that they intended to sleep the clock around and have a really good rest before they came back to the city.

They were both such nice people, he thought, his dark face suddenly shadowed. Gray had been so kind and generous, concerned only for the welfare of those around him. But when he was fully assured of Libby's safety, he'd finally begun to express his shock and outrage about the massive government development on his land that was now scheduled to begin construction within days.

Once again Warren stirred uneasily, still looking at Libby's silent face. A small movement out in the corridor distracted him, and he glanced up to see Alex in the doorway with Mac close behind.

Warren smiled, delighted to see them. Alex had obviously been back home since the night of the search, because she wore high heels and a soft fawn-colored suede dress with heavy copper jewelry, and looked gracious and lovely.

Behind her Mac stood crisp and handsome in a pair of charcoal-gray dress slacks and a black cashmere sweater. Warren looked at him in surprise that turned to startled amazement as the two of them entered the room hand in hand, smiling warmly at each other before they turned to Warren.

"We brought some prairie flowers," Alex whispered, holding out a delicate little bouquet. "We thought they'd make her feel at home."

Warren still gazed at them, trying to take it all in—their obvious rapport, the warmth and tenderness they showed to each other, their shining happiness.

"When did all *this* happen?" he whispered back.

"What on earth are you talking about, child?" Alex murmured, moving serenely past him to the sink to run water into their little vase and stand it carefully on Libby's bedside table.

"Come on, Alex," Warren began. "You know what I—"

But he was interrupted by Libby, who opened her eyes, saw them all in her room and smiled weakly. "Hi, Mac," she said, raising her bandaged face like a child for Mac's kiss. "Hi, Alex. Thank you so much for coming."

"Well, Elizabeth," Mac said cheerfully, seating himself on the other side of the bed opposite Warren and fixing her with a fierce blue gaze. "*You* certainly caused a whole lot of trouble, didn't you?"

Libby grinned faintly. "Don't make me laugh, Mac," she said. "It gives me a headache. Alex, you look so beautiful. I always just see you in your working clothes."

"She's beautiful in her working clothes, too," Mac said serenely. "Especially," he added after a moment's thought, "those tight blue jeans."

Alex chuckled and patted his arm while Libby gazed at them, her eyes widening. "Well, well," she murmured thoughtfully, smiling at Mac.

He smiled back, his eyes bluer than ever.

Warren looked on, smiling with them, enjoying the warmth and love that surrounded the group by the hospital bed. But still he felt chilled and excluded, because Libby's eyes never moved to him, never allowed him a flicker of warmth or a trace of feeling.

"Alex, I wanted to talk to you," Libby began. All at once Warren saw how tense she was, how her fingers gripped the edge of the hospital blanket, how her face tightened and turned even paler beneath her tan.

With the depths of his love he felt her pain, and his heart ached. Impulsively he reached toward her, but she kept her eyes resolutely turned away, as if he weren't even in the room.

"I know," Alex said calmly. "And I'm here to listen. Go ahead, Libby."

"I want to make a deal with you," Libby said, moving her bandaged head carefully on the pillow so that she could look directly at Alex and Mac. There was no expression on her face at all, and her changeable eyes were as gray as a winter sky.

"I'm listening," Alex said again, gripping Mac's hand tightly. "Go ahead."

"I found a site in the community pasture that's far better than the one on our land. I want your assurance that if I promise to show you where it is, you'll stop the construction."

Alex looked at the slender girl in the bed, her eyes troubled. "Libby," she began gently, "that's a big thing to ask, you know. Construction is scheduled to start immediately. Most of the tenders have gone out and several of them have been—"

"I know all that," Libby said. "But the other site is…it's fabulous, Alex. Just fabulous."

Alex looked at her steadily. "Libby…that may be your opinion, but you're not an expert, you know. Why don't you tell us where the site is and let us have a look at it? Then we can make a decision."

"No!" Libby said with sudden vehemence, and rolled her head weakly on the pillow in pain. "I can't do that," she said in a lower voice, looking at Alex again. "I can't give it away, because I'll lose my bargaining position, and I can't trust the government to deal honorably with us."

"Can't you at least describe it for us?" Alex asked.

"No," Libby said again. "If I describe it, there's a good chance you might figure out how to find it, and I don't want that. Our family's only hope is for me to keep this all to myself, so I can retain some bargaining power."

Alex shook her head, looking down at Libby with troubled gray eyes. "Libby, you *must* understand that's far too much to ask. This is a multimillion dollar development that you're asking me to scrap just on your word. Is that what you mean?''

"Yes," Libby said fiercely. "That's what I mean. All you have to go on is my word. And I'm telling you that what I've found is one of the most fabulous things anyone's ever seen on this continent, Alex. *And I don't lie.*''

In spite of herself, Libby's eyes moved to Warren's face for an instant as she spoke, and her expression was bleak with pain. But almost at once she regained control of herself and turned back to Alex, who was staring at her in an agony of indecision.

"Libby, when you call this 'another site,' do you mean that it's another set of pictographs? Is there a valid petroglyph in the complex? Libby, you *have* to realize that we can't—''

"It's going to be a few weeks before I can ride again," Libby went on in that same low, controlled voice, as if Alex hadn't spoken. "And construction is slated to start on our land right away. What I want is your promise, Alex, that you'll stop that construction. I want your assurance that it won't go ahead."

"We could delay for a few weeks, I suppose," Alex began doubtfully.

"Not ever," Libby said. "I want your promise that there'll never be any kind of development on our land without our express permission."

"Oh, Libby…" Alex began.

"And," Libby concluded, "I want it in writing. That's my deal, Alex. You give me your assurance in writing that our land won't be developed, and then as soon as I'm well enough I promise that I'll take you to the other site."

"And if I don't?" Alex asked.

"If you don't," Libby said, her voice gaining a little

strength, "then they'll go ahead with what they're doing on our property and I swear to you, Alex, that I'll never, ever, show anybody what I've found. Not ever. And if I don't," she concluded simply, looking directly at the other woman, her eyes suddenly blazing with passion, "then the world will lose something of inestimable, incredible value."

Alex looked at her in troubled silence while the two men sat tense and still, stunned by what was happening in this bare, austere hospital room. For a long, long time the two women stared at each other, their eyes locked, while Alex considered, her beautiful, mobile face reflecting the terrible pain of the decision that she was being forced to make.

Finally she sat erect, her features strained and intent. "Very well, Libby," she said. "I'll give you my written assurance. There will be no development on your land."

Warren stared at his colleague in stunned amazement, his dark eyes lighting with wonder. He opened his mouth to speak, but Alex waved him to silence.

"And," she muttered, half to herself, opening her leather case to take out a pen and paper, "God help us all if I've misjudged you, girl."

CHAPTER FIFTEEN

"LOOK AT THE WOMAN," Mac said fondly, beaming at Alex. "Rides like a cowboy. This girl of mine never ceases to amaze me."

Beside him, Alex gripped the reins and grinned cheerfully. "I had a privileged childhood," she said. "Show jumping, fox hunts—all that sort of thing."

She did ride amazingly well, Warren thought, turning to watch her small, trim figure in the saddle, her crown of silvery hair gleaming in the autumn sunlight.

Their horses falling easily into step, Alex and Mac rode side by side and held their heads close together as they laughed and chatted. Ahead of them, Warren and Libby rode in silence, not looking at each other.

Finally Warren cleared his throat and turned to her, glancing with concern at her pale face, her red hair glowing like fire in the sunlight, her intent gaze fixed on the horizon.

"Are you sure you're all right, Libby?" he asked. "No pain?"

"Just a little," she said tonelessly. "My ankle throbs a bit, but it's all right, Warren. Really," she added, looking at him briefly and then turning back to her careful scrutiny of the distant landscape.

Warren lapsed into silence and rode quietly beside her, turning once or twice to observe how their vehicles and horse trailers were already diminishing in the distance. He felt a deep worry about Libby and an ache that never left his heart.

In the weeks since her accident she had been like this almost all the time—cool and distant, polite but noncommittal, as if he were just some casual acquaintance who was expressing an untoward interest in her life. It was as if she had never kissed him, never gazed at him with eyes shining with love, never lain in his arms and shuddered at his caress.

Warren shifted again in the saddle, his powerful body tense, his face grim.

Far from discouraging or dampening his emotion, her puzzling coolness had only fired his love, filled him with overwhelming hunger and passion, made him realize with a profound clarity just how much he adored her and how painfully empty his life was going to be if he couldn't somehow overcome whatever was standing between them and win her back.

It wasn't that she was rejecting him outright, Warren thought. She just seemed to be holding him at arm's length, waiting for something, and he had no idea what it was. The only time she had shown any animation at all was a few days earlier when she had astounded him on one of his visits to the ranch by telling him that she had decided not to return to work…that she intended to quit her job, go back to school and get training in archaeology.

"I realized when I was lying out there in that pasture," she had said, "that life's too short not to do what you really want to do."

And yet even then she had treated him not as a lover, but as a counselor, someone she was turning to for impartial professional advice about a career decision.

"Libby," Alex was saying behind them, "this place is so huge. Are you sure you know where you're taking us?"

"Absolutely," Libby said quietly.

"I'm so curious," Alex said, spurring her horse forward briefly to rein in beside Libby. "How did you find this site of yours in the first place? How did you know where to look?"

Libby hesitated while the other three looked at her with interest, and Alex burst out laughing. "Come on, Lib," she said at last. "We're actually here, you know. We're on our way to your fabled discovery, and you have my written promise that your land is safe. Don't you think that *now* you can relax just a little and quit playing your cards quite so close to your chest?"

Libby grinned back at the other woman with a trace of her old spirit. "I guess you're right," she said. "It's just that secrecy has become such a habit with me that it's hard to break."

She was silent for a moment, riding her faithful bay horse along in the warmth of the autumn sun, and then she turned to Alex. "It was a difference in perception," she said. "You and Warren—and everybody else, I assume—you all looked on the petroglyph designs as symbols, stories in picture form, you know?"

Alex nodded intently.

"Well, I started looking on it as a map, and that made all the difference. Then I could see trails, actual landmarks, creek beds, all sorts of things."

Alex's eyes kindled with interest, but Libby went on before she could speak.

"The most important thing, though," she said, "was the triangles."

"See, Warren?" Alex said. "Didn't I tell you? I *knew* there was something about those figures." She turned eagerly to Libby. "How did you interpret them, Libby? What did you see?"

"Compass readings," Libby said promptly. "They show the position of a landform relative to the sun at noon. For instance, we're approaching that sheer cliff up there and we're supposed to climb to the top of it, then sight so that the sun would fall over our shoulder in the pattern shown in the triangle, and then we'll be looking directly at the next landmark."

Alex and Warren stared at each other, stunned and speechless.

"My God," Warren muttered. "It's so obvious, Alex. Why couldn't we ever...?"

"Because you were both too well trained," Libby said quietly. "You knew too much about what you were looking at. I didn't know anything, so it was easier for me to put myself into the minds of the people who designed those symbols."

Subdued and thoughtful, Alex fell back behind them again and rode with Mac, talking to him in low tones. The miles slipped by beneath their horses' hooves while Libby led them relentlessly onward across the rugged terrain, up hills and through brush-filled valleys, heading into the horizon.

Finally, hours later, she reined in at the base of a rough, rocky outcropping. "Well," she said, gesturing at the hilltop above them, her voice husky and uneven, "I guess we're here."

Warren leaped from his horse and hurried over to help Libby as she dismounted and grimaced a little in pain. He turned to say something to Alex, but she was already scrambling up the cliff with Mac close behind her.

"Don't you want to join them?" Libby asked.

"I'll stay with you," he said quietly. "Whatever it is, I can see it soon enough." His dark eyes rested on her face, moving over her lovely, still features with a hungry, haunted expression, but she gazed steadily at the outcropping of rock and made no move toward him.

Almost at once Alex came running back down the hillside, her fine-drawn features blazing with excitement. "Warren, she's right. It's fabulous! Warren, there are two faces, one rock split to form two faces, absolutely smooth and covered with symbols."

Alex paused for breath as Mac came slowly up beside her, slipping an arm around her shoulders, and all of them looked at Libby.

She was staring into the distance, not looking at anybody, her eyes once more shadowed with that strange, remote expression, like someone gazing on unseen things, things fearful and wondrous beyond description.

"Libby?" Warren asked anxiously, taking her arm. "Libby, are you—"

"That's not all," Libby said abruptly, turning to Alex.

"Pardon?" Alex asked, staring at her. "What are you talking about, Libby?"

"The petroglyphs up there," Libby said, waving her hand at the hilltop. "They're just part of it. Warren," she said turning to him, "don't you remember showing me that spiral figure on the other rock face?"

"Yes," he said in surprise. "I remember, Libby. Why?"

"Well, you must know what a spiral figure means in

Stone Age carvings. I learned it in just one day, reading reference books at the library.''

Warren and Alex stared at her, stunned, unable to respond.

"But, Libby," Warren began finally, "those figures— the spiral figures you're talking about—have all been found on European petroglyphs but never in the western hemisphere. This is…it's sandy soil, Libby. And it's been heavily glaciated.''

"This," Libby said quietly, gesturing at the rough outcropping behind them, "is solid rock, Warren.''

Alex moved over close to them, her face white and tense, while Mac looked on in puzzled silence.

"Libby," Alex whispered, "are you saying that there's a—''

"Right over here," Libby said, her voice breaking a little. "It's quite easy to get to, really, but we should probably stay close together.''

Without another word she took a big flashlight from her saddlebag and limped over to the rock face with the other three close behind. Then she dropped to her knees, pulled back a tangle of overhanging branches and exposed a cave mouth in the wall of rock.

"Libby," Warren said huskily from behind her. "Libby, are you sure this is safe?''

"I've been here before," she said over her shoulder, and then moved forward into the darkness.

Following each other closely, they edged in breathless silence down a long, black slanted tunnel that was sometimes high enough to allow them to walk erect, sometimes so low that they had to drop onto all fours, almost crawling on their stomachs in places.

But gradually the tunnel widened and deepened and

began to grow strangely bright, as if light was filtering down from somewhere above, shining mysteriously through solid rock. One by one they emerged into a dry, lofty chamber deep within the cliff that was starred and crossed by warm bands of sunlight shining through natural openings high on the cliff face.

Alex came into the chamber, brushing off her knees, her eyes wide and dazzled.

"Oh, my God," she whispered, gazing in awe and childlike wonder at the sunlit walls that soared as high as a cathedral's. "Oh, my God, look at this. Warren, look at this."

But Warren didn't even hear her. He stood beside Libby, his arm clamped around her slender body, his dark face rapt and luminous with joy.

All around them was a spectacle that took their breath away, a dazzling, incredible display of primitive art that covered the high, smooth walls of the chamber. There were animals, many of them now extinct, drawn with exquisite detail. There were human figures in all sorts of poses, heavenly bodies in various alignments, geometric figures of all description. And the colors were as fresh and bright as if they had been applied the day before, all the umbers and ochers and tans, the brilliant crimsons and deep, dramatic yellows, the smoky charcoals....

"Oh, God," Alex whispered again, shuddering and collapsing weakly into Mac's strong embrace, her voice echoing softly in the hollowness of the big, empty chamber. "Nobody has ever looked on such a sight. Nobody in all the world."

Warren dashed at the tears that glittered suddenly in his dark, brilliant eyes. Beside him Libby stood quietly, her face tense and pale, her expression unfathomable.

"Mac," she said finally, "do you think you could...I need to talk to Warren for a minute."

With instant understanding Mac bent to Alex. "Sweetheart," he murmured, "let's go out and get the camera and the notebooks and give these two a minute by themselves, all right?"

Alex nodded without speaking and turned back into the tunnel, her movements still dazed and awkward. Mac gave Libby a gentle, encouraging smile over his shoulder and then bent to follow Alex.

Alone with him in the great chamber, Libby turned to Warren, her face taut with emotion.

"Warren," she began, "there's something I've needed to say to you for a long time ever since my accident, but I wanted to wait until we were here, in this place, because this is—"

Her voice broke a little, and she waved her hand at the soaring, patterned walls, so exquisitely beautiful, so incredibly ancient, that seemed to be looking down on them, quietly watching them.

"This is the most sacred place I've ever been in," Libby went on. "Nobody could tell a lie in a place like this. And I wanted to wait until we were here, Warren, to tell you again that I wasn't lying that last night on the hilltop."

He gazed down at her, his dark, glowing eyes still dazzled by the wonders all around him. "What do you mean, Libby? What are you saying?"

"I told you I'd decided on my own that I couldn't damage the stone," Libby said, "and you said you didn't know if you believed me or not. I know what you thought of me that night, Warren, and I can't bear the idea of you wondering for the rest of our lives if I was lying or not, if I really would have been capable of destroying something so wonderful just to suit my own purposes.''

He made a move toward her, his face softening with emotion, but she turned aside and went on speaking.

"So I wanted to wait until we were here in this sacred place,'' Libby said again, "before I told you absolutely that it was true. I was driven to a kind of insanity by my concern over my family's property, but even before you got up to the hilltop that night, I had already decided it was wrong, that I couldn't destroy the rock.'' She stopped speaking and gazed up at him, her face passionate with feeling, her eyes blazing.

He looked back at her and his dark features twisted with pain. "Oh, Libby,'' he whispered. "Oh, my darling…''

"Tell me you believe me,'' she said.

"Libby, I believe you. God, how could I ever have doubted you? You're the most incredible, wonderful—'' His voice broke, and he looked down at her with sudden intensity. "Libby,'' he murmured.

"Yes?''

"That last night, when you came to see me in my tent, you told me something else, too. Was that the truth, Libby?''

"What…what was that?'' she asked hesitantly, gazing up at him.

"You told me that you loved me, Libby. Do you? In front of all these witnesses,'' he went on, waving his hand at the ancient figures etched into the walls of the sunlit chamber, "tell me here in this place. Libby Lyndon, do you love me?''

"Oh, Warren,'' she said, her face glowing, her eyes suddenly wet with tears. "Oh, I love you so much. Here in this place, in front of these witnesses, I'm telling you, Warren McIntyre, that I love you with all my heart.''

''And will you marry me, Libby?'' he asked softly. ''And will you love me forever?''

She was too overwhelmed to answer him, but her shining eyes told Warren all that he wanted to know.

He laughed softly and drew her into his arms, holding her close as the strange, filtered sunlight played over them and the ancient, timeless artwork looked down on them.

Slowly from the depths of the cavern a soft, gentle music began, gradually swelling in volume, singing through the rocks with an ancient, mystic rhythm, rising and swirling all around the man and woman who stood locked in each other's arms in the center of the vast chamber.

Harlequin Romance®

Delightful

Affectionate

Romantic

Emotional

Tender

Original

Daring

Riveting

Enchanting

Adventurous

Moving

Harlequin Romance—the
series that has it all!

HROM-G

HARLEQUIN PRESENTS®

HARLEQUIN PRESENTS
men you won't be able to resist
falling in love with...

HARLEQUIN PRESENTS
women who have feelings
just like your own...

HARLEQUIN PRESENTS
powerful passion in
exotic international settings...

HARLEQUIN PRESENTS
intense, dramatic stories that will keep you
turning to the very last page...

HARLEQUIN PRESENTS
The world's bestselling romance series!

Harlequin® Historical

From rugged lawmen and
valiant knights to defiant heiresses
and spirited frontierswomen,
Harlequin Historicals will
capture your imagination with
their dramatic scope, passion
and adventure.

Harlequin Historicals...
they're too good to miss!

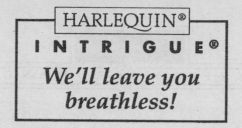

HARLEQUIN SUPERROMANCE®

...there's more to the story!

Superromance. A *big* satisfying read about unforgettable characters. Each month we offer *four* very different stories that range from family drama to adventure and mystery, from highly emotional stories to romantic comedies—and much more! Stories about people you'll believe in and care about. Stories too compelling to put down....

Our authors are among today's *best* romance writers. You'll find familiar names and talented newcomers. Many of them are award winners—and you'll see why!

If you want the biggest and best in romance fiction, you'll get it from Superromance!

Available wherever Harlequin books are sold.

 HARLEQUIN®

Not The Same Old Story!

 HARLEQUIN PRESENTS®
Exciting, glamorous romance stories that take readers around the world.

Harlequin Romance®
Sparkling, fresh and tender love stories that bring you pure romance.

HARLEQUIN® *Temptation*
Bold and adventurous— Temptation is strong women, bad boys, great sex!

HARLEQUIN SUPERROMANCE®
Provocative and realistic stories that celebrate life and love.

 HARLEQUIN® AMERICAN ROMANCE®
Contemporary fairy tales—where anything is possible and where dreams come true.

HARLEQUIN® INTRIGUE®
Heart-stopping, suspenseful adventures that combine the best of romance and mystery.

 LOVE & LAUGHTER™
Humorous and romantic stories that capture the lighter side of love.

Look us up on-line at: http://www.romance.net   HGENERIC